THE NEW
ADVENTURES

ANOTHER GIRL, ANOTHER PLANET

Martin Day and Lén Beech

D1600731

First published in Great Britain in 1998 by
Virgin Publishing Ltd
Thames Wharf Studios
Rainville Road
London W6 9HT

Bernice Summerfield was originally created by Paul Cornell

Cover illustration by Fred Gambino

ISBN 0 426 20528 6

Typeset by Galleon Typesetting, Ipswich
Printed and bound in Great Britain by
Mackays of Chatham PLC

My thanks and gratitude to Martin Day for introducing me to Benny and suggesting the project. Thanks also to my long-time friend Laurence Sumeray for co-ordination skills, his bag of goodies and a love of guanacos and related camelids; to Sue Baddiley, Dave Brawn, Barry and Heather B. and to John Little for info and SW tazo 24; to Ben Leech, Phillipa Stephens (don't call me babe!), and especially to Steve Bowkett, whose intelligent and lively contribution made this book half possible.

Dedicated to Jon Pertwee, whose hand I was proud to shake just two weeks before he moved higher up and farther in.

LB

Thanks to (random order) Trina, Elsa, Ben, Audra, Mark, Felicia, Paul, Dave, Gary G., Jac, Keith, Gary R., Helen, Andy, Lisa, Judi and Steve, for a party I won't forget in a hurry, and to everyone at or behind the scenes of Gallifrey Nine; to Helen, for bravely letting me go (without whom, etc.); to Mum and Dad, Pete W., Sarah (and Phil), Marianne (and Colin), for practical and material help; to Paul and Keith (X-treme patience (groan)); to *Time Team* for making 'research' such fun; to Roland Barthes, Julian Cope, The Lover Speaks and the Only Ones; and to Steve Bowkett, John McLaughlin and Simon Winstone.

Dedicated to Lisa Gaunt, Felicia O'Sullivan and Audra McHugh. You know why.

MD

The statue of embracing lovers was the colour of a burning sunset, marbled with filigree shadows of burnished gold. Deep blue water cascaded over entwined hands, urgently pressed lips, eyelids closed in adoration.

Visitors circled the square, seemingly ignorant of the fountain at the centre. Only Assan sat at the feet of the lovers, familiar and comfortable with their passion, staring into their abandoned faces as flecks of cooling water ran down his neck. He revelled in the honesty of the carving – the almost touchable texture of the skin, the hinted-at muscle and bone beneath, the florid flush that seemed to grip the couple's cheeks and torsos – and the timid embarrassment it engendered in those who averted their eyes and quickly passed by.

For Assan, his weekly supplication at the feet of the statue was something to be enjoyed, a brief release from the constraints and demands of the project. The obsession of his colleagues knew no bounds, bar the ultimate sacrifice, the final step into the unknown that scared them all. In every other regard the negotiators had so lost a sense of self, of individuality, that Assan thought they were in danger of ceasing to exist, of becoming mere machines.

1

Only Assan, and his beloved Kaygish, held on to life in all its fullness.

It was beneath the statue that Assan felt truly alive, truly at one with his emotions and passions and fears. Here he was able to watch the sun glinting on the fountain water and the shattered rainbows that danced over the faces of the people that passed. To them, he was an anonymous young man, enjoying the fine weather and the hubbub of the city. No one would recognize him as a negotiator or would have guessed the vital nature of the work he did. Even Kaygish, the project's leader and public face, was able to achieve a degree of anonymity in the shadows of the embracing lovers.

Assan was fully alive, and the teasing excitement, the nervous anticipation, was part of the pleasure.

But not today. Something was wrong.

He closed his eyes for a moment, striving to analyse his thoughts. There had been nothing in Kaygish's behaviour recently to indicate that her feelings for him had cooled, although it was difficult to be certain, as they spent most of their time together in formal meetings with their cold, emotionless colleagues. And Assan was sure his own behaviour – and certainly his incandescent passions and desires – were unchanged. What, then, was the source of the depression that had gripped him this morning?

It was irrational paranoia, the natural insecurity of a lover, heightened by his fears for the project and its implications for his entire world.

It had to be. He *prayed* that it was.

Kaygish came towards him through a crowd of fevered traders, a self-conscious grin of apology on her face. And how beautiful she was, her blonde hair cut short to frame her features, her eyes bright with impish grace. Every time Assan saw Kaygish it was as if he was seeing her for the first time.

She did not relax into his embrace, her features softening. Instead, she held him tightly, awkwardly. And in that moment, Assan knew that he was right.

'We need to talk,' she murmured.

They walked in silence from the square. Kaygish allowed Assan to hold her hand, lightly, as if a last concession to the past.

They found a seat by the river. Assan's senses were heightened by his hurt, the wood and stone beneath his legs feeling alive with the sun's warmth. He watched the waterfowl dancing and diving on the choppy surface of the water, blissfully ignorant of events on the bank. Ignorant of the fact that Assan was already dead, and that only an outer shell remained.

Assan wanted to be somewhere else. Anywhere else. *Anywhere.*

'This can't go on,' Kaygish said simply.

'But . . .' Assan paused. But what? How could he tell her that his life had no meaning without her? If she didn't realize *that* then their entire relationship had been a tired sham, a fiction of Assan's own invention.

Kaygish reached for the small knapsack. She always brought it with her, and it was usually crammed full of bits of old bread and animal fat bought at the market. Assan let his fingertips brush against the bag, as if he could touch her through it.

Kaygish sat and fed the birds, looking anywhere but into Assan's eyes. If she had shed tears over her decision, it had been some time ago. Cold logic enveloped her now.

'What have I done wrong?' Assan wanted to know.

'You've done nothing wrong,' she said, a hint of anger in her voice. Perhaps she was angry at herself, for allowing it to end like this.

'I can't believe this is happening.'

Kaygish shrugged. 'I'm sorry . . . But it is important that we clear up these matters. There is still much work to be done.'

'Damn the work!'

Kaygish sighed, ignoring Assan's outburst. 'The project still needs you.'

'No,' said Assan, with spiteful finality. 'Don't you understand? It was you I fell in love with. Not the project.'

'But you have put so much time – so much of yourself – into our negotiations. To pull back now, to work elsewhere, would be to deny yourself. To deny your people!'

Assan stared with unfettered contempt at the men and women who passed. How could they even begin to guess that their futures, their fate, lay in the hands of the lovers arguing on the bench overlooking the river?

'Damn them all,' he said. 'The decisions *we* have taken have been *yours*. I've merely given your ideas substance. I have merely *obeyed*.'

'It wasn't like that.'

'No? Well, there's only one course of action open to me now.'

'You cannot . . . You should not be the first.'

'A sign of trust between our peoples. They said they needed a volunteer.'

'But the unknown . . .'

'The unknown no longer scares me,' he said. And he was right. Even death, in that irrational instant, seemed preferable to the half-life that he was about to return to.

Kaygish seemed almost shocked by the absence of fear in Assan's eyes. Perhaps alone of his race, he was prepared, in that instant, to stare into the pit of the unknown and not flinch.

'I had better go,' she said, getting to her feet. 'There is much to do.'

'Indeed there is,' Assan replied with stiff formality.

4

Kaygish reached out to hold Assan one last time. And he knew nothing but tears.

Minutes turned to hours. Assan found himself back at the lovers' fountain, feeling alone in the teeming, happy city. The shadows stretched and branched as the light of the sun gave way to the glow of the twin moons, and the lovers were transformed. The male figure was now forcing himself upon the woman, choking her cries for help into silence with his own lips. Her fingernails, deep in her lover's palm, were tiny daggers. Her arched back was an expression of disgust, not ecstasy.

The faces of the people walking past the fountain were alive with expectation, with a sense of carnival. But the foolish innocents, fed whatever scraps Kaygish felt were appropriate, knew only that they were not alone in the cosmos, and that the future was bright.

No one even stopped to enquire why the young man, who had seemed so happy earlier in the day, was now sobbing beneath the statue.

Assan watched the shadows lengthen across the square.

Assan volunteered before he could change his mind. The outsiders were delighted that a member of the negotiating body would be the first to leave their world behind – the first to escape from its gravitational pull, and be able to hold his hand over the entire disc of the planet, blotting everything out.

Yes, he was looking forward to that moment. To annihilate the world: his work, the city, his past life.

Her.

There was nothing to do but wait. Assan could not bear to see Kaygish again, so he walked through the empty shell of his life in enforced patience. He stared at the walls. He stared at the people making romantic gestures in the cafés.

He stared at the shape of the river, and watched the arcing trails of bats in the glittering twilight.

A hundred years seemed to pass, a hundred years of emptiness. And then, at last, it was time for him to leave.

Assan saw Kaygish's face everywhere as he walked through the crowds for the last time. A glance, a murmured phrase, a glimpse of golden hair or the sound of laughter. It was almost too much to bear.

Finally he came to the antiseptic room that marked the divide between his old life and the new and unknowable one. The outsiders welcomed him warmly, and promised him much.

Assan didn't care. He wanted only release.

He sat in numb silence as the vessel prepared for departure. They had just started their ascent when other craft appeared. Through the window they resembled a swarm of black flies alighting on a fresh corpse.

Assan's world was a shining gem in the ebony sky by the time the screaming started.

CODED MESSAGES, POISON LETTERS

Letter from Lizbeth Fugard to Bernice Summerfield (Private)

Hi, Benny. Thanks for the latest note/complaint/dissertation, complete with attachments. My screen nearly died trying to get to grips with it all. So much for my state-of-the-art equipment.

Ha! State-of-the-art! You should see what I've got access to at the dig. A full range of sonic and resistance plotters, the latest digger drones, and more processing power than you could shake a corpse pole at. The 'troops' have even got new brushes and shovels!

It's going OK, thank you for asking (sarcasm). We're making good progress on one of the main mines; less so a processing plant some five kilometres further south. The underlying rock is very unstable there. One false move and the whole lot will come tumbling down. You should see the strata, though – it looks like a Gut Bar.

(Which reminds me, I'm starving. I must get some chocleine when I finish this.)

I tell you, it's weird doing something where I'm not

thinking about funding the whole time. I've got all the equipment I could wish for, and more volunteers than I know what to do with. I'm not entirely sure how willing they all are, but I've weeded out the clumsiest, and am keeping faith with those who can tell their silicrete fragments from their elbows.

Oh, I'm looking forward to all that 'post-split' music you've promised. I'm listening to nothing but Pachar opera at the moment, and it's driving me crazy.

Bye.

Letter ends

Bernice awoke to the sound of driving rain, which was normal, and great and loud movement about the college, which was not. Feet splashed through endless Dellahan puddles beyond her window, and voices cried out in a bewildering array of accents and inflections.

Odd. It was dark enough to be the middle of the night.

'Rector!'

The artificial voice drilled into her mind like a spiteful dentist. Was it Bernice's imagination, or did Joseph, her porter, sound almost shocked? Surely he – it – had no business disturbing her yet?

'Rector!'

With Herculean effort, Bernice pulled her face from the pillow. Immediately she squinted against the light that flooded into her eyes. 'Uwwww,' she groaned. 'Wattimeissit?'

'Two thirty p.m.,' announced Joseph.

Now that her eyes were becoming used to the brightness, Bernice realized that the darkness had been that of the pillow into which she had collapsed, face down. She stared at the floral material, dumbfounded. It maintained the canyon-like imprint of her slumbering head, complete with meandering river of saliva that had crept from her open, and doubtless snoring, mouth.

Bernice wiped her chin. Goodness but sleep could be a messy business.

The small white sphere darted around the room with obvious agitation. 'You appear to have "dropped off". If you remember, you told me not to disturb you while you "digested the wisdom of the greats".' Joseph paused before delivering the hammer-blow with impeccable timing. 'I trust you dined well, Rector.'

'Oh ha-bloody-ha,' grumbled Bernice. Truth be told, she felt worse now than she had before her nap. That was the problem with sleeping during the day: to a tired body it seemed to offer much, but it delivered little bar a pounding headache and a complete sense of bewilderment.

Bernice bent down to retrieve the book she had been reading. It had fallen into a knotted pile of tights on the floor. Bernice struggled to recollect what had happened: she had started the book in the comfortable chair near the window, and then made her way towards the bed. She'd held the bulky volume over her face at first, so that if she dozed it would bring her back to consciousness with a rap on the nose; then – and this was the point of no return – she'd rolled over on to her side. She began skipping over paragraphs of text, her mind drifting, and ended up struggling to re-read an entire section on the limitations of the technology that underpinned the rise and fall of geophysical archaeology. Her eyelids kept sliding shut like security shutters over shop windows.

She remembered nothing more until Joseph had buzzed into her bedroom, an indignant and disapproving worker bee striving to wake its queen.

Bernice struggled to her feet, trying desperately to smooth away the creases from her crumpled clothing. Her skin felt rather lived-in as well.

I'm turning into something very baggy and uncared for, like a despised jumper, thought Bernice. *Turning into?* queried a mocking voice.

Damn. Even her inner insecurity was starting to sound like Joseph.

'I need to get out more,' she announced loudly.

'Rector?'

'Metaphorically speaking.' Bernice paused. 'No, literally, too.' She reached out for the little round porter, but it spun backwards, wary of physical contact, especially from Bernice. And anyway, you couldn't very easily put a *Please be honest with me* arm around a spherical drone. 'Joseph,' she asked with a weary sigh, 'am I getting older, or are my pupils getting younger?'

'Your eyes, Rector?'

'My students, Joseph. I used to thrive on late nights,' she said, walking over to the window. People were running past, in the direction of Goodyear College, their capes flying against the steady drizzle.

'I ought to remind you that you have a tutorial in twenty minutes, Rector,' stated Joseph.

'I know.' Bernice stared through the window until the water droplets on the glass and the image beyond became an unfocused blur.

'And I have compiled the music you wished to send to Ms Fugard.'

'No compression?'

'I followed your instructions to the letter. Although I still maintain the improved capacity of digital compression more than compensates for the five per cent aural degradation . . .'

'Five per cent? Joseph, you are a philistine. Have you ever listened to Relik in real-time? Compression would ruin the haunting simplicity of their work.'

'Indeed,' said Joseph, although he sounded less than convinced.

'And you put it all down in the order I asked for?'

'But of course,' said Joseph, sounding hurt. But Bernice

knew better. Once she'd wanted all her favourite, most miserable pieces of music on a single storage bead for ease of access, and Joseph had *insisted* on ordering the songs chronologically. Now, where was the fun in that?

'I still maintain that the Pachelbel is a somewhat hack-neyed choice –'

'Joseph,' interrupted Bernice, a stern note of warning in her voice.

'And I could only find the song you requested by the Verve on one of your bootleg Digital Audio Tapes from the early 2000s. I can't say I approve of the language, either.'

'*Joseph.*'

'And as for your selections from *Outta My Way Monkey-Boy* and *The Greytest Hips of Johnny Chess* . . .'

'Joseph!' snapped Bernice, sending the little drone scurrying for cover. 'That's enough. I just want to know that you've done it.'

'But of course, Rector. You can send it with your next message to Ms Fugard. I believe a transmission arrived from Dimetos this morning.'

Bernice had started corresponding with Lizbeth Fugard some months previously. It hadn't been difficult to recognize a kindred spirit: young female academics specializing in archaeology weren't exactly thick on the ground. Having said that, Bernice wasn't sure *she* counted as 'young' any more. Fugard, on the other hand, was still in her mid-twenties. And drop-dead beautiful. Thankfully, Bernice was mature enough not to give in to jealousy.

Not very often, anyway.

She strolled towards the screen in the main room. 'Have you been looking at my mail again, Joseph?' she queried.

'Only with your best interests at heart, Rector,' said the drone, with what passed for an obsequious bow. 'You seemed . . . "Somewhat the worse for wear" when you awoke this morning.'

'You try getting through one of Dr Follett's intimate soirées without the aid of alcohol or mind-numbing drugs. Or a gas mask, for that matter.'

Bernice ran through the expected Dellahan downpour, a scarf at her throat to keep her warm and a plastic body suit held over her head to ward off the worst of the rain. Even as she did so, she shook her head against stern mental admonitions to *Wrap up warm or you'll catch something* and *Make sure you don't get a chill on your chest, dear*. It seemed that centuries of matriarchal worry had now seeped into the average *Homo sapiens* at the genetic level.

She dodged students and porters trying to escape the rain – as if this wasn't how it was almost every single sodding (or sodden) day on Dellah. Bernice pined for unobscured sunsets, and snow, and fog, preferably all at the same time. But whenever she went off-world, sampling a bedazzling variety of climatic and meteorological conditions, she often found herself feeling homesick for the drizzle of Dellah.

Homesick? Dellah is *not* your home, she scolded herself firmly. You *have* no home.

A rounded portal, not unlike the entrance to an Inuit igloo, offered sanctuary from the rain. Bernice paused, brushing droplets of water from her sweater. She risked a glance at her watch. Ten minutes late.

The door opened inwards with a resigned murmur, and Bernice jogged down the corridor. She concentrated on the comparative archaeological papers that would be most appropriate to the subject at hand, and wondered if there was an excuse she could offer that would seem at least partly convincing.

She stopped outside the tutorial room.

'Sorry I'm late,' she said, strolling in with feigned coolness. 'I got held up by –'

The chamber was empty, though the haphazard jumble of

chairs around the central table spoke of recent occupancy. Someone had left a message on the screen. Bernice triggered playback with an impatient stab of her thumb.

'Benny? We've decanted to the bar. Maybe we'll do the tutorial there. OK?' The voice cut off with a low click.

'Bugger,' said Bernice, with feeling.

The man was surrounded by so much smoke that it was difficult to tell where the tobacco smoke ended and his long coat, the colour of a cold grey puddle, began.

The hand-rolled cigarette of 'sub smouldered in a green ceramic ashtray on the table in front of him; it seemed to have been there for some time. His hands were a steeple in front of his face, which floated in the black pool of shadow cast by a shapeless hat and the turned-up collar of his coat.

He looked up the moment Bernice walked into the room, glancing away only when she held his gaze and stared back. The faintest flicker of a smile twisted his lips; he reached down for his cigarette, and sucked in a great lungful of smoke.

Bernice turned to the young man behind the bar. 'You're late for your tutorial,' he said, sounding only slightly less stern than Bernice's head of department would have done.

'Bloody hell,' said Bernice, taken aback that her failings were such public knowledge. 'How'd you know?'

'Word travels fast,' said the man. 'Especially in a bar. Your group is over there, waiting for you.' He pointed; the students were clustered around a small table, laughing furiously. One of them saw Bernice at the bar, and waved enthusiastically. A tiny triangular maintenance drone, fiddling with a broken glo-bulb over the table, was forced to take evasive manoeuvres.

Bernice ordered a drink. And then a second.

'I heard you were at Dr Follett's party last night,' said the man.

Bernice grunted. 'Is there anything you *don't* know about me?'

'Oh, plenty. But it goes without saying you're one of the most talked-about lecturers on campus.'

'Thanks,' said Bernice, downing the whisky in one. 'I think.' She glanced back towards the table where the students sat, although she soon became distracted by the drone overhead. With a loud crackle the glo-bulb started working again, and the tiny pyramid dropped into the purple cocktail of a first-year student. There was a loud hiss and what sounded like gargling, drowned out by the cheers of the drinkers.

'I need to get out more,' she announced loudly, and then remembered that she'd only been back on Dellah for six weeks.

'Sorry?' said the man behind the bar, distracted by the drone's attempts to extricate itself from the glass.

'It doesn't matter,' said Bernice, picking up her remaining drink and walking across the ale-stained floor of the Witch and Whirlwind.

'But isn't there intrinsic value – and beauty – in any one particular retelling of a myth?' one of her students wanted to know.

'Of course,' said Bernice. 'But that's not the point I'm making. All I'm saying is that if your interest is the truth, then your approach has to be comparative. It's the difference between history and art.' She paused. The stranger in the shadowy corner of the bar was getting to his feet and moving towards the door. 'For example,' Bernice continued, 'if you wanted to build up a clear impression of an accident involving two vehicles and three pedestrians, you'd get statements from everyone you possibly could. But you wouldn't expect all the stories to be the same, would you? Some would blame the driver, others would place the blame elsewhere. You might not even get agreement on the actual, physical facts. But sift all the reports, and somewhere at the bottom is the truth.'

'So,' said one of the others, 'you're saying that when myths purport to have a basis in historical actuality, the contradictions between various retellings of the myth can be as instructive as the areas of agreement?'

'In a nutshell,' said Bernice. 'Look at the legends of Robin Hood. Two entirely different origin tales, with the hero hailing from wildly different social strata. The reworking of legend can be a political activity.'

'*Propaganda and Myth*,' stated the first student. 'You're quoting from your own paper.'

'But of course,' said Bernice. 'That's my point again. If something's worth saying once, it's probably worth saying again, but differently.'

There were groans from around the table.

'So,' said Bernice brightly. 'Whose round is it anyway?'

When Bernice stepped out of the bar a man was waiting for her. 'Dimetos,' he said, without introduction. 'Unusual place for a holiday.'

Bernice's eyes narrowed. It was the shadowy man from the bar. His face looked indeterminately vague, even up close. 'I'm not planning on going there.' Bernice paused, her hands on her hips in what she hoped would be a defiant pose. 'Look, who are you?'

The stranger seemed not to hear her question. Instead, he lit a cigarette with great deliberation, and watched as the smoke drifted up to the brick-coloured ceiling. 'Still, I'm told the air is getting better all the time.'

'And how do you know I'm even remotely interested in Dimetos?' queried Bernice, her usual tiredness turning into a blunt irritation.

'You will be,' said the man, turning away without another word.

Bernice swept into her room, swearing under her breath. Joseph's sensors picked up every nuance of her irritation, and he shrank back as if fearing her wrath. 'Rector?' he enquired meekly.

'I'm not going to Dimetos, am I?' she asked – though in truth, she made it sound more like a statement than a query.

'Well . . .' began Joseph, almost ducking behind a tatty chaise longue.

'I mean, you've not booked me a holiday or anything without telling me, have you, Joseph?'

'Of course not, Rector.'

Bernice threw herself on to the couch with a great expelled sigh of triumph. 'Well, there you go, then! What was that bloke on about?'

'Bloke, Rector?' Joseph made a little clicking noise as he ascended. He hadn't been quite himself recently.

'Oh, it doesn't matter,' said Bernice, but then she decided that it did, and that she may as well tell Joseph. 'Someone mentioned Dimetos to me earlier this afternoon. It's as if he knew that I'm in touch with someone there.'

'And the "bloke" in question is . . .?'

'I don't know,' said Bernice. 'I've never seen him before.'

'Well,' stated the Porter, 'I said you weren't planning a holiday to Dimetos, and I spoke truthfully, but very precisely in the present tense. I fear your thoughts may change.'

'But it's a dump, Joseph! If I'm going to take a break, that'll be the last place –'

Joseph ascended imperiously. 'There has been an emergency communication, Rector. From Ms Fugard.' He came to rest close to the screen. 'I believe your presence is required,' he announced.

**Letter from Lizbeth Fugard to Bernice Summerfield
(Private and Encrypted – successfully decoded)**

Benny. Can you come and visit? I know it's a long way. And
short notice, too. You see, I'm being stalked. I'm sure of it
now. I'm very, very frightened, and I need a friend.

Please help me.

Letter ends

FRAGMENTS FROM A LOVER'S DISCOURSE

Extract from the diary of Bernice Summerfield

I should be used to this by now, right? I mean, I've been all over, through time and space. And yet I still don't think of myself as a good traveller. Better to journey hopefully than to arrive? Not for me, it isn't.

I'm writing this in the hope that at least it will stop me fidgeting.

It's only now, as I sit on the ship an hour or two into the flight, that I can even begin to relax. It's not that the length of the trip bothers me – plenty of time for reading and writing and sleeping – or that I'm one of those poor loonies who spends the entire flight thinking about what would happen if the outer hull were breached and we'd all be sucked out to explode in the vacuum of space like so much overripe fruit (change the subject, though, eh?). I suppose a lot of the feelings that are rushing around my head come down to the fact that I've been thinking about nothing else for weeks: once I know I'm going somewhere, that's all I can think of, and I can't see past it. It's a black hole that pulls in light and prevents me from seeing beyond, to the future. When I left, one of my students said 'See you in a couple of weeks', to which I replied 'Hopefully'.

What on earth am I expecting to happen on Dimetos?

Nothing, is the answer. It's a lump of a world – my research when I first got to know Lizbeth tells me that much. The stranger was right about one thing – it's no place for a holiday.

So why am I going? To help a friend? True, but I hardly know her. We might loathe each other. Perhaps that's part of the niggling unease I feel. It's too late now – I've applied for the leave, been granted it, and am now on the ship that'll take me there. But what do I know about this woman who I'll be staying with? We share similar interests – but then hell isn't just other people, it's being trapped in a room with your best friends. If her letters are any sign, she seems to have an ability to grab life by the scruff of the neck, and shake what she wants from it. (This is how people view me, but I'm not sure they're right. Only you, dear diary, see the real me. Or something close, at least.)

Facts: Lizbeth Fugard has better (or at least more legitimate) qualifications than I do. A while ago she changed her area of specialization from ancient ruling powers to recent industry. Now, that's weird – they're pretty much at opposite ends of the spectrum. So what's going on there?

Then there's her personal life: steady boyfriend for years. (Am I jealous? Discuss in not more than 2000 words, with reference to . . . Oh, change the subject, Benny.) Married in all but name. (I find myself wondering: what happened to her youth? Is she familiar with one-night stands and eternal parties and waking up in a pool of ale; or was it always 'Alex will be waiting at home with the meat and two veg, the pipe and slippers'? I need to know. Really.)

Then they suddenly split up. She's not given a reason – and that's fine, we hardly know each other – but it puzzles me. What makes a person change? Or – switching things around – what makes them put up with the same old routine for years. When do you begin to want out?

Routine . . . You could hardly say my time on Dellah – or away from it, even – has been routine. Until her message about the stalker, I was getting tired of Dellah, resentful of the grinding routine of seminars and tutorials, of the fresh faces that seem so eager to learn but can be just as closed as the books in front of them. And yet during the last few days, as I've been preparing to leave, I suddenly found myself looking at the buildings as if for the last time, thinking of the people I'll miss, the Witch and Whirlwind, Joseph. Even the interminable rain.

And I have to ask myself again, what am I expecting to happen on Dimetos? Not much. Maybe even a few scrapes. But nothing out of the ordinary.

I notice I've started fidgeting again. So much for the diary.

Extract ends

Post-It note over the above entry

Nice, relaxing trip. No problems. Not much to say.

Dimetos unfurled for the descending passenger craft like petals from behind shrivelled leaves. As the ship came down through the broiling clouds the barren grey rock gradually gave way to pockets of terraformed soil and sprawling buildings. Both had battled valiantly against the elements. The city's numerous spires and towers of silicrete tore holes in the prevalent mist, allowing the sun to shine.

Bernice was surprised. The capital – imaginatively called Dimetos City – wasn't the shanty town she had imagined. It was a tiny jewel, held in a cracked old hand of rock. Only the lowest streets, far below her and in perpetual shadow, hinted at the filth and poverty that she had expected. Elsewhere, the sky was criss-crossed with walkways, on which stood tidy-looking booths where neatly costumed men sold their wares. The most luxurious apartments and shops towered overhead, emporia and boudoirs of champagne-coloured metal and endless, fluted sheets of glass.

Despite her expectations, the sky over Dimetos seemed reasonably free of pollution. The days of thoughtless mineral extraction were long gone; the authorities here were concerned with other things now.

Beyond the city, it was as if the planet's surface was formed from enormous slabs of rock gently pushing against each other. Plate tectonic movement had forced up enormous and precarious peaks of stone, and mountains seemed to simmer with volcanic power.

There was a sonorous roar – not the rocks moving, but the sound of the ship's landing rockets kicking in. The craft came down through a gap in the buildings like a free-falling elevator. Bernice forced herself to look through the window – she'd feel worse if she didn't – and saw a couple of sporty one-person hover cars streak past.

It took her a moment to work out what was wrong with the vehicles – they were flying upside down, with the protective canopies drawn back. Their drivers were hanging downwards like children at a funfair. The hover cars spun around each other like amorous flies, narrowly avoiding a lumbering air tanker that was shifting position – its indignant horn was audible even over the sound of the retros on Bernice's ship. Then the smaller craft darted upwards almost vertically.

Moments later a black-and-white-striped vehicle emerged from its hiding place on the side of a building, and set off after them, siren wailing.

'Kids,' came a voice from Bernice's side.

'Sorry?' Bernice turned. The woman next to her was middle-aged, her expression pinched into something that might have been mild disapproval or sly admiration. She'd been engrossed in a game of virtual Mah Jong for the entire journey, and hadn't spoken before.

'More money than brain cells,' said the woman, with a half-hearted smile.

She was built like a walrus, but Bernice was determined not to hold that against her. Bernice indicated the city. 'I wasn't expecting such affluence.'

'Affluence. Decadence. You'll find it all on Dimetos.' The woman wore enough jewellery for Bernice to know that she was talking from personal experience. 'We're not as backward as off-worlders might think.'

Ah, thought Bernice. A local. 'I've not been to Dimetos before,' she offered tentatively. 'I just mean that it's not quite what I expected.'

'You don't have to dig too deep in Dimetos City to find *exactly* what you expect,' commented the woman. She gave another equivocal smile, and returned to the conclusion of her game.

Bernice stared out of the window again. They'd slowed to a vertical crawl, and the interior of the tube-like structure down which they were travelling was covered with adverts for Gut Bars – 'Stop your tummy rumbling with a Gut' (charming) – and nicotine substitute (bafflingly, now with added nicotine).

Moments later they landed. The pilot told the passengers that it was a beautiful day in Dimetos City, apologized for the slight delay while in geo-stationary orbit, and advised that all belongings be taken off the craft.

By the time Bernice looked up, having stuffed the books and journals back into her rucksack, the ship was almost empty.

Bernice saw Lizbeth Fugard standing close to the arrivals gate, nervously surveying the flow of people into the launchport proper. Bernice recognized Lizbeth instantly from a picture she'd sent as part of a recent communication – it pained Bernice to admit it, but it hadn't done her justice.

Startling blonde hair fell around the face of a mischievous angel; her eyes were as wide and blue as those of a child playing hide and seek. She wore torn denim trousers and scuffed boots, as if she'd just come from the dig, and a thigh-length black coat over a cropped vest the colour of over-washed smalls. A couple of gold rings pierced her navel: one carrying a small red gem in the shape of a heart, the other an ivory-pale skull.

Bernice extended her hand and her broadest grin. 'Hi,' she said, dropping her rucksack on to a service drone that had obediently trundled up beside her. 'Thanks for meeting me at the port.'

'Bernice,' said Lizbeth. Her smile seemed both relieved and genuine. 'Thanks so much for coming. I'm very grateful. I expect you could do with a drink.'

'Actually, a bite to eat would be nice,' said Bernice. 'I didn't like the look of the last couple of meals on the flight.'

Lizbeth nodded, and led the way towards a café at the far end of the launchport that offered an excellent view of one of the city's most thriving commercial sectors. A great blister-shaped window extended overhead and underfoot; they found a small table right at the end. It was like floating on air. The drone dumped down Bernice's rucksack, and scurried back towards the arrivals lounge.

Below them a walkway-cum-road stretched between two great bulbous buildings whose pinnacles were invisible in the haze that just diminished the glare of the sun. On one side of the walkway was an apartment store, its opulent frontage all frosted marble and burnished gold. Bulky simian creatures, roughly stuffed into archaic uniforms, watched as well-dressed humanoids strolled through the doorways. One of the doormen was arguing with a scruffy young man; Bernice could make out what they were saying even from where she was sitting, and it wasn't pleasant.

Across the street, the row of much smaller, specialized shops were less choosy about the attire of their clientele. The succession of humans and brightly plumed aliens that streamed into the arcade of delicatessens and palmtop supply outlets were more ready-to-wear than haute couture.

'I was saying to a *charming* woman I met on the trip over,' said Bernice with brutal emphasis, 'that Dimetos City isn't quite what I was expecting.'

'This is the bit the government wants people like you to see,' observed Lizbeth with a smile. 'Even so, it's difficult to establish a new reputation for a place. Especially when for centuries Dimetos really was a pimple on the backside of the galaxy.'

'But I get the impression that you quite like the place,' suggested Bernice.

'Oh, I do,' said Lizbeth. '*Quite*. It has its good side and – though it's very shallow of me to think in those terms – most of our sites are in those more affluent areas. You'll see what I mean tomorrow. Anyway, it makes staying here that little bit more enjoyable.'

A spider-faced creature in an immaculate black suit glided towards their table. He held a discreet voice-recording palmtop in one hand – appendage – and a cavernous mouth broke into what passed for a welcoming smile.

'Good evening. Are you ready to order?'

Bernice plumped for a sushi starter made from Alphan rice pods, followed by a Cardellen curry in the New Caledonian style. 'And lashings of lager.' Lizbeth chose a large Dimetan dish whose chief ingredients Bernice recognized as fried, diced sausage and mashed potato.

'Tell me about the man who's stalking you,' said Bernice once the waiter had departed. There didn't seem to be any point avoiding the issue.

24

For a moment, Bernice wasn't sure that the younger woman had heard her. Lizbeth prodded at the menu, as if having second thoughts about what she had ordered. It was only when she finally started speaking that Bernice realized that she had tilted the reflective surface of the palmtop so that she could see who was seated behind her.

'He's difficult to describe. I've never got a really good look at him. He passes me in the street, and sometimes I don't even know he's there until he's gone. This is going to sound so paranoid, but I just *know* when he's around. And he watches me, with these strange, sad eyes . . .'

'When did you first notice him?'

'Round about the time that Alex and I . . . split up.' The final words, so light and inoffensive in their non-verbal communications, sounded like a death sentence now.

'You think there's a connection?' probed Bernice gently.

Lizbeth shrugged. 'Possibly. We fell out, said a few stupid things. But, ultimately, I thought we'd parted on good terms. Best mates, you know? But I suppose he is prone to jealousy. A while ago, there was one guy he thought was staring at my breasts – smacked him in the face. Broke his nose and two or three teeth.' Bernice tried to keep her face neutral, but Lizbeth saw her shock and surprise. 'Oh no,' added Lizbeth hurriedly. 'Alex was never violent towards me. It's just . . . Well, I suppose he might have hired a Pink or someone to keep tabs on me. Just to see if there's someone else in my life.'

Bernice glanced up as their starters arrived. 'Why did you split up? I've meant to ask you before, of course, but bounced relay link is such a clumsy and impersonal way of communicating . . .'

Lizbeth's nervous fingers started pulling at a loose button on her coat. 'It's difficult to say,' she whispered, avoiding eye contact. 'Sometimes things happen that make you reassess your life. Where you're going – or not, as the case may be. With us – me – it was my miscarriage.'

Bernice, fiddling with her chopsticks, almost dropped them to the table. 'I'm sorry,' she said. 'I had no idea –'

'It was a while ago now,' interjected Lizbeth. 'Time heals most things, don't they say? I suppose I'm over it now. I wasn't very far gone – a few months, that's all. It didn't hurt much – physically, I mean.' She looked up, and the vulnerability of her startling blue eyes was almost shocking. 'It's quite common for women to lose their first . . . child. Does it count as a child? I don't know. Anyway, when my mother heard, she was very sympathetic. Said it had happened to her.' With a tug the button she had been fiddling with came free, nestling in Lizbeth's hand like a jewel. 'All these years, and she'd never told me.'

'I know what you mean,' said Bernice. 'At least, in terms of those big events. I was married once, you know. It all went . . . pear-shaped.'

'I didn't know that,' said Lizbeth. 'I suppose there's a lot we don't know about each other yet.' She paused, glancing down at the floor. 'I hope it doesn't bother you – me talking about my miscarriage, when I hardly know you.'

'Not at all,' said Bernice. 'We need to be honest with each other. Ah, look, our starters have arrived,' she added brightly.

As the two women talked and ate their food, many people passed by. Few glanced in their direction, their focus instead on departure times or tax exempt shopping or the imminent arrival of relatives from off-world.

Only one man regarded the table where the women sat with anything more than idle curiosity. He stood in the shadows of one of the launchport's main structural columns, hands deep in pockets, eyes unblinking. His gaze spoke of madness and terror and love.

Their meal completed, the two women got to their feet,

and made their way towards the exit. Not once did they glance behind and see the dark man who was following them.

Bernice and Lizbeth took a taxi back to Lizbeth's apartment. The hover car that pulled up outside the launchport seemed brand-new, the leatherite fabric recently cleaned, although Bernice noticed that one small window towards the back had been shattered.

A flat-screen drone hovered around in the back compartment, showing constantly updated information on the distance travelled, the current estimated time of arrival, and, most importantly, their fare. Lizbeth explained that a law had been passed recently which meant that the passenger should always be aware of the likely charge, thus making it more difficult for unscrupulous drivers and operators to rip off their customers. That was fine, thought Bernice, but the drone had an annoying habit of getting in the way, especially when she wanted to look out of the window. It was as if the little robot had been over-programmed to constantly present the information. The end effect was of a child striving for attention.

Bernice shooed the thing away from the transpex just as the hover car plunged down into a darker area.

'Scenic route,' explained the driver, his voice crackling over the intercom. 'Everybody should get at least one good look at Chinatown.'

'Heard that one before,' muttered Bernice under her breath. It seemed that the drivers had worked out other ways of extracting extra money from unwary tourists.

Bernice glanced across at Lizbeth, but she seemed unaware of the sudden alteration in their route. Her eyes were distant, focusing not on the gaudy adverts and shop windows that formed a kaleidoscope of splashed colours behind the window, but on something within herself.

Only a few days ago Bernice had noticed a student in her tutorial whose eyes were inward-looking and empty. There was a big grin permanently stitched across the bottom of his face, and for a few minutes Bernice wondered if he was high on something. Then she noticed that the student's hand – as if unbidden – was scribbling intricate floral triangles across his notepad. The young man was from Tivo, where geometrical shapes had the same cultural resonance as cartoon hearts did on Earth.

The boy was in love, and he couldn't help but trip on it.

Lizbeth Fugard, on the other hand, was reaping the dark side of the process: the pain behind the eyes that follows separation, the constant cold accusation of an empty bed and an emptier soul. Not for the first time, Bernice wondered why there wasn't a way of enjoying the first state of mind without the inevitable come-down of the second. In that way, love was very like an addiction, and if you were unlucky the cold turkey would kill you. But then, what was the alternative? Bernice had met people who refused to give anything of themselves to their relationships, and they were as cold and as depressing as the Dellahan rain.

And then she thought of Jason, and it was like fingering an old operation scar, a daily ritual until the white line of stitches finally fades from view. According to Terran symbolism, the jagged arc should be somewhere between her breasts, signifying the seat of her affections, but long ago – and even during the good times they'd shared together – she'd realized that all this affection and hatred and self-loathing made itself known far lower. Love is a pain in the guts.

She massaged her stomach. Either that, or the sushi was disagreeing with her.

'So, what have you discovered at the digs?' she asked suddenly, her voice splitting the silence like ice thrown into water.

Lizbeth jerked away from the window, as if someone had electrified the seat. 'Sorry,' she babbled, clearly embarrassed. 'I was miles away. Not being a good host, am I? Um.' She paused marshalling her thoughts. 'The digs. Right. Well, most of what we have found has confirmed a lot of recent work, rather than launching us out into some new direction. For instance, Kupple's position on EB's wholesale assimilation of local architectural techniques has been supported by a lot of the fragments we've found. Obviously, metallic infrastructure sections have survived a good deal better than the other materials, but I think the case is proven.' She paused. 'You know, I get asked this sort of thing a lot at social functions. It's so nice to be able to share this without the other person's eyes glazing over.'

Bernice smiled. She hoped her own weren't about to do just that.

'It's a shame, but industrial archaeology really isn't very exciting for the lay person,' continued Lizbeth. 'Let me give you an example. My favourite find so far has been a wooden shower handle, which would have been used in the miners' communal area. Now, I think something like that is just fantastic – a little bit of real life. Thousands of grubby digits would have pulled on this bit of tree.' She sniggered. 'Plus, you can't help but be intrigued by the thought of all these butch and hairy-arsed men getting into the shower together. I wonder if they were aware of the homoerotic flix that purported to come from such factory planets.'

Bernice thought this most unlikely, but she'd drink to the suggestion, anyway.

'Now, I tell that to your average little madam on the government, and she's almost reaching for the smelling salts.'

'Good job you haven't found the latrine trench yet,' observed Bernice.

'Well, funny you should mention that,' said Lizbeth, 'but only the other day we –'

'You mentioned Eurogen Butler,' interjected Bernice. 'Why are the government so keen for you to investigate their activities on Dimetos? I'd have assumed that they would rather make a clean break with the past.'

'Well,' said Lizbeth. 'Let's just say that the government subscribes to the idea that all publicity is good publicity, even archaeological expeditions to discover more about the EB Corporation. As grotesque as it may sound, Eurogen Butler is the closest thing this planet has to a cultural heritage.'

'Blimey.'

'I know. It's terrible, isn't it? EB, despite the grotesque things they did, still has a mighty reputation in these parts. Some folk hanker after the good old days of Eurogen Butler, when at least there were jobs and you knew who was in charge.'

'And the Dimetan government are hoping that some of that fascist machismo will rub off on them?'

'I guess so,' said Lizbeth. 'To be honest, I try to have as little to do with the government as possible.'

'Any chance they could be responsible for this man who's tailing you?'

'I wouldn't have thought so,' said Lizbeth. 'I'm here at their request, so –'

'But perhaps they're trying to hurry you along or something.'

'Funny way of doing it,' said Lizbeth.

'Or perhaps it's just a bit of gentle pressure. Make sure you only find out exactly what *they* want you to find out.'

'Maybe so,' said Lizbeth, 'but I have no idea what they're trying to hide. I've found nothing of any political interest at all.'

'Do you think your sponsors expect you to?'

'No. Or I don't think I'd have been invited. This place is democratic – up to a point. Look, I'm under no illusions. I'm just one cog in a machine that maintains Dimetos's high profile with the neighbours and with potential investors.'

'Never forget the potential investors,' said Bernice.

'That reminds me . . .' Lizbeth scrabbled around in her jacket for a gilt-edged square of card. 'I've been invited to a dinner-dance-type thing the night after next. Lots of posh nobs who don't mind us digging in their gardens, plus sundry folk who are happy to bankroll the government, and a minister or two. Fancy coming?'

'It's not really me,' began Bernice. 'But then, I have brought my best party frock . . .'

Lizbeth Fugard's apartment was high in a tower block at the centre of a leafy square framed on two sides by buildings that dated back to the area's industrial past. Huge metal pipes hissed steam through fractured valves as they plunged below the planet's surface, seeking out the thermal energy needed to warm the area. The façades of long-closed shops, now converted into studio flats, were studded with pillars of metal that carried fibre optic, Hv and 'plain vanilla' electricity cables. Unblemished stems of metal sprouted from the concrete sidewalks, bearing exotic glass fruit holding inert gases. But the light thus produced did not penetrate far. And, even when it was dry, the splash and drip of water could be heard from somewhere.

Away from the gloom of the older buildings, the apartment block was airy and expansive. Fugard's rooms were high up in the tower, with split level floors and windows the size of walls making the best of the light. Fans in the ceiling circulated filtered air.

Bernice smiled. 'I'm impressed.' She ran a hand over an exquisite set of kneeling chairs, seemingly hand-carved in traditional Mulo style. She turned her head to fully appreciate the stark simplicity, the almost oriental mini-malism, of the apartment. 'I guarantee I'd make this place look like a complete tip in less than a week.'

Lizbeth smiled. 'Well, I have two confessions to make. Firstly, they send a cleaning drone in every other day. And secondly . . .' She walked over to a door of ink-tinted glass, and pushed it open. Beyond was a small boxroom, stuffed to the rafters with stale clothing, old computer equipment, soft toys and still unpacked personal effects. 'This is my junk room. You'll be sleeping here. Is that OK?'

Bernice grinned. 'Just like home,' she said.

Bernice decided to go to bed almost immediately. The long journey had caught up with her, and the gathering shadows beyond the windows told her that the Dimetan night wasn't too far off. She changed into an enormous T-shirt covered with cartoon characters and the legend 'Oh my God . . . He killed Kenny!' which she had found in a cupboard on Dellah while packing. She was sure she'd never even seen it before.

The bathroom was outrageously bright, a whole row of glo-bulbs set into the ceiling. The mirror behind the sink was enormous and crystal-clear, showing every blemish, every imperfection, of Bernice's face and neck with unflinching and brutal honesty. A small spot had developed just to the side of her nose; in here, it looked like Mount Vesuvius, ready to explode.

Bernice clamped her eyes shut, and got on with the job of brushing her teeth. Anything else could wait until morning.

When she emerged from the bathroom, Lizbeth was curled up in the middle of an enormous white sofa-pillow, her hair a blonde halo around her face. She was snoring lightly.

A screen – showing an interminable discussion of Dimetan politics, which, Bernice supposed, was enough to send anyone to sleep – had detected Lizbeth's slowed breathing and had dimmed the image and reduced the volume.

Bernice rooted around for a blanket, and finally found one in a cupboard near the kitchen area. She pulled this over Lizbeth, who murmured something, but otherwise did not stir. Then Bernice padded back to her temporary bed in the junk room.

And proceeded to spend the next two and a half hours scribbling random notes and impressions in her diary, and trying to fix a broken hairdryer she'd found on the floor.

No More 'I Love You's

Extract from Dimetan Infobase (Public), as requested by Professor Bernice S. Summerfield

Eurogen Butler came to Dimetos in 2142. They found a barren rock of a world, and transformed it into something almost as hideous. With precious little wildlife or other ecological considerations to trouble them, the EB Corporation set about plundering the mineral wealth of the planet. Although much of Dimetos is geologically unstable, which made open cast mining possible in only a few areas, the deposits of jebusk and argonite were rich enough to make other forms of extraction profitable. Dimetos was one of the first of EB's infamous 'factory planets'.

Contemporary accounts speak of the squalid conditions in which the human and humanoid miners lived and worked; of the perpetual grey clouds that blocked out the light of the sun. Eurogen Butler's activities were unregulated: their only objective was profit through round-the-clock mineral extraction. In 2147, when a pit shaft at the third site on the southern continent collapsed, killing between a hundred and two hundred and fifty miners (reports vary), the entire area was made safe with polystene. The dead were left where they fell; work carried on unhindered around the site of the tragedy.

Interviewed at the time, an anonymous EB official spoke of 'sadness but no regret' at the tragedy. It is believed that such insensitivity caused a riot and general strike in 2149, which was ruthlessly quelled, but all records from this period are lost or unreliable.

The EB Corporation left Dimetos in 2151. A colony of miners and other officials – it is not clear whether they were sacked or whether they voluntarily left the employ of EB – remained behind, attempting to make a new life for themselves. Given the parlous state of the planet's atmosphere, and the inherent danger of earthquake and massive subsidence, it is a miracle that any of them succeeded.

Extract ends

When Bernice trudged into the living room the next day Lizbeth was already dressed and working at the screen. It looked as if she had been up for hours, the blanket and the sofa-pillow having been tidied away. The door to Lizbeth's room was closed, so Bernice couldn't tell if she'd slept in the lounge all night or had later awoken and sought out the comfort of her own bed.

Bernice grunted something – she was just plain *crap* at mornings – and Lizbeth turned with a smile.

No one deserved to look that good early in the morning. 'Hi, Benny,' she said. 'Sleep well? I was just about to wake you. We ought to be off to the dig soon.'

'Give me twenty minutes in the bathroom,' said Bernice. 'If I'm not out by then, send in a search party armed with caffeine syringes.'

'Fine,' said Lizbeth. 'I'm just catching up with my mail.'

Bernice shambled towards the bathroom, pushing the door open with her head. 'Oh, and I mended that hairdryer you had in bits on the floor.'

35

'Thanks,' said Lizbeth automatically. 'Er . . . why'd you do that?'

'I couldn't sleep. And when I did, I had the most bizarre dreams you can imagine. One minute I was attacking Jason with electrical flex and a blunt screwdriver, the next he was attacking *me* with yoghurt and the biggest erection you've seen this side of . . .' She switched on the light, squinting against its brightness, and pushed the door closed. She leant against the sink, like a drunk grateful for support. 'No,' she said to herself. 'Let's leave that image right where it was.'

She grimaced at the mirror, then stuck out her tongue. It looked normal enough, but she felt dreadful. Perhaps she should have had a night cap before retiring, just to –

There was a muffled cry from the living room. Even from where she stood, Bernice could hear the shock in Lizbeth's voice.

Bernice pushed open the door. 'What's the matter?' she asked.

Lizbeth tried to affect a smile, but she looked lost and wounded. 'I've just had a very . . . interesting . . . message.'

Bernice walked across the room. 'Interesting, as in . . .' She paused, reading the communication on the screen. 'As in downright nasty.'

Lizbeth sniffed back the tears and walked into the kitchen area. Bernice read the message again.

Ms Fugard. A warning from a friend: tread carefully. I'm told archaeological digs can be quite dangerous. All those tools lying around, all that earth waiting to collapse . . . But then, I'm sure you're conversant with safety regulations. You know how to stay out of trouble.

Bernice turned. Lizbeth was emerging from the kitchen with a glass of water, which she sipped, gingerly. 'I don't know

36

what to think,' she said, in a tiny voice. 'I've never had a message like that before.'

'I'm glad to hear it,' said Bernice. She ran her fingers over the touch-sensitive screen, but there was no way of establishing where the communication had originated. The transmission protocols had been fooled by a source ID that was valid just long enough for transmission, but had collapsed in on itself shortly afterwards. 'And they've covered their tracks pretty well, though I suppose we could try an intuitive stealth algorithm . . .'

'You just made that up,' said Lizbeth.

'I know.' Bernice rechecked the message relay details, knowing that she was well out of her depth. There was a world of difference between hairdryers and integrated communication packages. She sighed, then turned back to Lizbeth. 'Any ideas who this is from?'

'No.'

The response was so automatic that Bernice distrusted it in a moment. 'Oh, come on,' she said. 'We're into serious "You'll take a walk with the fishes" territory here, and you can't think of a single reason why?'

'Everything is political on Dimetos,' said Lizbeth after a moment's thought. 'I've already told you that I'm only here for PR reasons –'

'So who wants you *not* to discover something?'

'There's nothing *not* to discover,' said Lizbeth. 'It's all bog-standard industrial archaeology. Dimetos City isn't the Valley of the Kings!'

Bernice persisted. 'Yes, but this is recent archaeology, so the descendants of the original miners and EB personnel are still around . . . Doesn't that mean it's *more* likely you'll find out something that you shouldn't?'

A flicker of emotion – it could almost have been pain – crossed Lizbeth's face. Bernice could tell that Lizbeth was trying hard to keep a lid on her emotions, but she wasn't that good an actress. 'I suppose you're right,' she said, although she did not sound convinced.

'What else could this message be about?'

'It must be from Alex,' said Lizbeth suddenly.

'He'd do something like that?' queried Bernice. 'Something so spiteful?'

Lizbeth paused. Bernice noticed for the first time that there was a framed photograph standing on a table to one side of the screen. It showed Lizbeth – looking even younger – and a handsome, well-muscled black man. They were holding each other, laughing and pulling faces for the camera, streamers covering their heads. Blurred partygoers jostled in the background; only the two figures, locked in the amber of a carefree moment, were in focus.

Lizbeth was staring at the photograph, as if searching for a trace of aggression in the features of her former partner. 'No,' she said at last. 'He wouldn't do anything like that.' She reached towards the screen, and deleted the document with an impatient stab of the thumb.

And didn't mention the message again until they were far beyond the apartment.

The cab was late, and the clouds were turning increasingly dark. Lizbeth and Bernice stood in the lobby, waiting for the right hover car to appear. Conversation was coming out of them like drips of rain.

'I'll take you to the office later,' said Lizbeth. 'Show you the data.'

'Ah, good,' said Bernice. And she meant it, but somehow it came out like strangulated sarcasm. Not that Lizbeth seemed to have noticed. She wore a permanent, girlish grin like a mask that concealed any deeper feelings.

'One thing I've been meaning to ask you,' said Bernice, tired of watching the service drones sweeping the streets. 'You're an industrial archaeologist, right? Means studying things, what, a few hundred years old at most?'

'Something like that. The definition is rather complex, and of course depends on the society –'

'Of course,' said Bernice. 'It's just that I recently came across a paper of yours that dealt exclusively with the ancient civilization on Sekka.'

Lizbeth looked almost embarrassed. 'Yes . . .'

Bernice shrugged. 'Why the change of emphasis?'

'It's still archaeology, isn't it?' said Lizbeth, somewhat defensively.

'Well, I suppose so,' said Bernice. 'Though I must admit, if it's not at least a thousand years old, I tend not to be interested.'

'But whether you're investigating a two-hundred-year-old industrial complex, or searching for the tombs of kings from previous millennia, there are always gaps in our knowledge. And filling those gaps is what archaeology is all about.'

'I'm sure you're right,' said Bernice. 'I'm just a bit more interested if the society we're looking at was very different from our own. It's escapism, I suppose.'

'Oh, believe me, you'll find some real differences between Dimetos now and how it was,' said Lizbeth.

By the time the hover car arrived, it had started raining, the weather adding an extra note of gloom to the increasing darkness of Bernice's mood. Bernice and Lizbeth climbed in, operating their energy harnesses just as the craft rose into the air. Almost immediately the vehicle pitched to one side to avoid an enormous cargolugger that slid past, horns blaring.

The rest of the journey was uneventful. Bernice fidgeted like a caged animal, suddenly wanting nothing more than to stop the vehicle, go back to the apartment and pack her bags, and then hop on the first flight back to Dellah – or anywhere else, come to think of it. Even as Lizbeth made some chatty remark about how much better she felt with Bernice around, Bernice was wondering if this was all one big mistake.

'I suppose the companionship counts for a lot,' Lizbeth was saying. 'You know, having someone you can trust, to talk things through with. A friendly shoulder.' Lizbeth gave a grateful smile and the sour knot in Bernice's stomach tightened a fraction further.

The hover car slipped swiftly through the low cloud above the suburbs of Dimetos City. A three-dimensional simulation, rendered in real-time with seamless fluidity of movement, played across hi-plasma panels set into the sides of the vehicle in place of windows. It conveyed an impression of the terrain and buildings below: Italianate towers and low-pitched roofs; piazzas and water gardens; generous lawns and clumps of designer shrubbery to break up the symmetry of the layout and delight the eye. The image on the screens could be manipulated to sweep low over the landscape, or stop at any location to look around at the easy opulence enjoyed by the rich elite of Dimetos. The ever-helpful comfort drone informed Bernice and Lizbeth that in some cases you could actually take a virtual tour through some of the apartments.

The real world by contrast – just visible towards the front of the vehicle – was dismal and grey. Rain spat at the transpex canopy of the hover car, the drops tadpoling quickly around the smooth curvature of plastic and out of Bernice's line of sight. She pointedly turned away from Lizbeth, not out of pique, but simply to try to pin down the source of her emotions.

It was deep. That much became clear as soon as Bernice allowed her thoughts to turn inwards. It was something to do with Lizbeth, and an inner resilience that Bernice detected in the other woman. Bernice was beginning to wonder why Lizbeth had asked her here at all. Despite the younger woman's show of gratitude, Bernice was sure that Lizbeth was actually one pretty tough woman who could look after herself in almost any situation. Such capability, so attractively packaged, could disconcert anyone, and Bernice wondered for the first time if Lizbeth was being entirely straight with her.

'ETA at our destination is four minutes, ladies,' the drone informed them in sickly PR tones. 'And might I add at this point what a pleasure it has been to travel with you.' Bernice thought that perhaps the Dimetan government was taking its image cultivation programmes just a little too far.

'The dig is sheltered,' Lizbeth said, stirring herself to check her rucksack. 'No need for weatherproofs.'

'Glad to hear it. Is that the site?' Bernice pointed to the display sim woven in delicate light, watching its perspectives change as the vehicle dropped down through the misty undercroft of cloud.

Lizbeth nodded. 'Luckily some of it lies on government-owned commonland. Private individuals charge the earth for us to excavate on their property.'

' "Charge the earth".' Bernice chuckled mirthlessly.

Lizbeth's friendly smile shrank fractionally. She turned back to the haversack, searching for her palmtop, allowing Bernice to complete her introspective assessment.

Maybe at the heart of her unease was the similarity between them. The thought came up from the depths quite unexpectedly. The little green-eyed-god thing was all on the surface, dwelling on whatever Lizbeth had that Bernice didn't have – youth, beauty and other trivia – but missing the point entirely. Both women shared a love of the past. Both had suffered the failure of a relationship that had meant so much. And now Lizbeth was standing on the brink of important events, as Bernice had done on many previous occasions. There was intrigue, there was danger, there was the prospect of making a difference to somebody, somewhere. Or, if one was to be brutally honest, of being wiped out and rather quickly forgotten.

But it was in this determination to face the odds and prevail that Bernice saw the essential link between them both.

The hover car arrived amid the declining harmonics of its engines powering down, then swayed gently on a stasis field as the canopy swished back and Lizbeth and Bernice stepped out to the drone's effusive goodbyes.

'It's just a short walk up the hill,' Lizbeth said, pointing through the trees. And in that moment Bernice felt the compass needle of her thoughts swing round to the positive. It is wisely said, she recalled, that when you feel animosity towards someone else, it is really some aspect of yourself that you dislike. In Lizbeth she had seen herself mirrored. The ambition and the fragility, the fear and the absolute bloody-mindedness, was Bernice, some ten years younger.

Elsewhere it would have been easier. The incredibly advanced race known only as the People would simply manipulate energy fields to peel back the turf, slicing down through topsoil and clay to the archaeologically significant material beneath – not that they showed much inclination to leave their vast Dyson sphere home. On Kaus Nunki IV the dig would be entirely unnecessary, the Kausians having kept such complete records throughout their history that it was believed that no new facts existed to be unearthed.

Here on Dimetos things were more familiar, and Bernice found herself again at the wet end of the science, despite Lizbeth's assurance of shelter.

They followed a steep track through the trees – a genetically adapted variation of copper beech, to Bernice's eye – emerging a couple of hundred metres further up the hill on a plateau, itself clear of woodland, but surrounded by further tracts of beech and a species of robust conifer that Bernice couldn't identify. The plateau had obviously been part of the mining operation originally: Lizbeth flicked open her palm-top and pressed buttons. They both watched intrigued as a miniholograph grew out of the screen, back-extrapolating the appearance of the area to the time of the EB Corporation's peak activity.

'As you see, the pithead existed just about on that spot.' Lizbeth indicated a rubble pile of huge boulders, grassed over now and half hidden by saplings. 'I've not been able to ascertain how far generations of local inhabitants have landscaped the area, but I suspect it's quite substantially. The Dimetans have always loved the wild-tamed look.' She grinned cheesily. 'Doesn't make our work any easier.'

'I'm surprised nobody's thought of building up here,' said Bernice. 'Space seems to be at such a premium on Dimetos.'

'Don't let the tranquillity fool you,' said Lizbeth. 'It's all very unstable. The trees can probably handle a couple of centimetres subsidence every year. I doubt a house would.'

'Where are you currently digging?' Bernice asked. The soft drizzle was penetrating down through the leaf canopy and Bernice was getting quietly and thoroughly soaked. Lizbeth swung her arm through thirty degrees, indicating the distance beyond where the shaft winch had stood.

'Because the impossible takes a little longer, we're leaving the really major excavations a while. The current focus is an area that we suspect used to be the miners' living quarters. Much more interesting, actually.'

'Absolutely.' Bernice remembered Lizbeth's earlier mention of the wooden handle, and was pleased to be able to agree unequivocally. It helped salve the effects of her earlier musings. 'A piece of graffito, some personal belongings, a notebook, a bit of jewellery . . .' She continued with a sudden rush of enthusiasm, 'Give me those rather than an official historical record any day!'

'Speaking of which . . .' Lizbeth hit the keypad and the miniholograph scrolled upwards, bringing a labyrinth of mineworkings into view, a three-dimensional version of the find-your-way-out-of-the-maze puzzles Bernice had enjoyed solving as a child.

'This is speculative, of course,' Lizbeth said, 'based on extant documentation and comparison with other Dimetan workings previously excavated. They did tend to follow a pattern, though with plenty of variation due to local geological conditions.'

'How far have you got with the dig?' Bernice wondered. Lizbeth made a face that summed up a whole clutch of feelings Bernice knew very well.

'Scratched the surface. You know how it is: under-resourced, overstretched. The government's image building programme only translates into so much extra cash.'

'Tell me about it,' said Bernice, thinking of the shoestring budgets of most of the digs organized by St Oscar's. And then she remembered the expensive hover car they'd come over in, and Lizbeth's earlier, gleeful messages. 'Hang on, I thought you said you had more money than you knew what to do with.'

'That was a while ago. Our funding's been cut, at least on site. Most of our "volunteers" have found other, more diverting, occupations. We've still got half a dozen digger drones, two with AI capability in a master-slave relationship with the other four. That gives us a self-sufficient work-force, able to continue round the clock, though the slave drones require a couple of hours off-shift each cycle to recharge themselves.'

Bernice acknowledged with little businesslike nods as

they continued through the clearing. The set-up would have been standard on a thousand worlds. She wondered if the cut in funding was significant, but decided not to pursue it. 'And I take it the drones conform to a dominant/subordinate hierarchy, to keep initiative programs within reasonable parameters?'

'Yes. The alpha-drone will always stop the excavations and report directly to me if there's a glitch, or if it sees something it fails to recognize.'

'Then it looks like something's buggered up the works, to use a technical term . . .'

Bernice had been gazing ahead as Lizbeth studied the palmtop and talked. Now, coming around the slate-dark bulk of a house-sized boulder, both women stopped dead.

Ahead of them the opalescent material of the cellathene canopy sheltering the dig was in tatters, banners of the stuff hanging from branches and the skewed and toppled support poles that covered the trench. There was no sign of the diggerdrones, though one of the master machines – the subordinate, Bernice reckoned – lay smashed by the wayside, a mangled mess of fragments that still sparked here and there with residual charge.

Bernice waved a hand back and forth across its visual sensors, noting the lack of reaction.

'There's a blackbox recorder,' Lizbeth said heavily, stepping among the remains.

'Maybe it'll give us some data on this.'

'Maybe.' Bernice looked around, cautiously but not fearfully. Instinct was telling her that the damage had been done. The perpetrators had come in fast, completed their work, and cleared off with minimum delay. It might, however, be worth scanning for explosives.

Just as Bernice considered this, Lizbeth gave a groan from some metres away. The kind of groan that said *Well, it's back to bloody square one again, isn't it?*

'What's wrong?' Bernice left the drone and moved towards the excavation trench, where Lizbeth was leaning on one of the buckled support poles.

The little drone work party had been busy and very efficient. Over the past few weeks they had cut a trench some twenty metres long by three wide, while uncovering, logging, describing and noting hundreds or thousands of artefacts and related items before downloading the data in a constant stream back to Lizbeth's office.

It was the kind of efficiency and effort that one took entirely for granted, unless something went awry, as it had done now. For apart from the fact that there was no trace of the other five drones, Bernice saw that the trench they had created had been neatly and infuriatingly filled in with supertough, flash-dry polystene.

Homam Matar Sadalbari made a clicking sound with his tongue and shook his head with the same kind of weary resignation that Bernice, in sympathy with Lizbeth and her endeavours, felt inside.

'To be precise, it's a derivative of polystene called buck-minsterfullerite. Lighter than aluminium, more durable and less brittle than mylar.'

'Bit of a sod to shift, then.' Bernice had heard about this stuff before, though this was the first time she'd seen it in use.

Homam looked up from the trench and treated Bernice to one of his more winning smiles. He was sapien-Arabic/ Denebolan hybrid, an eminently workable genetic combination, but one that made his mouth disconcertingly wide. Folk tales around St Oscar's perpetuated the myth that people like Homam could put both fists in their mouth at once; that they possessed retractable stabbing fangs and were able to dislocate their lower jaws at will. Bernice wondered fleetingly what kind of a snog Homam would be able to offer, and then wondered whether the idea disgusted or excited her.

'Correct, Ms Summerfield –'

'Benny. It's just Benny.'

'Benny,' Homam echoed, stretching the smile a fraction wider.

Bernice decided it was excitement.

'So, how *do* we remove the polystene?'

'Carefully. You see, this looks like nothing more than a delaying tactic. The drones should be able to dig it out inside a week.'

'Well that's no good!' Lizbeth's voice sounded high and brittle, the immediate shock of the discovery having worked itself round to a gathering rage. 'One of the drones has been trashed, and the digging team is nowhere to be found. You know that, Homam!'

Bernice watched Homam's reaction to this outburst. From all accounts, he had worked with Lizbeth ever since her arrival on Dimetos, so he might well be used to these moments when her usual brightness became single-minded intensity. He perhaps also knew something of the stalking and the threats, and the consequent pressure she was under.

Homam rubbed his chin, as if considering his response. Then, with sudden and catlike grace, he leapt lightly out of the trench, his robes billowing about him. He stepped over to Lizbeth and put a comforting arm around her shoulders. Bernice, standing just a couple of metres away, breathed in the scent of cassia bark, the natural odour of Homam's breed.

'Listen,' he whispered reasonably. 'It doesn't make sense that the digger drones were removed just to be destroyed. They'd have been smashed like the other one and left lying, wouldn't they?'

'I suppose so.'

'They're hidden, then. Therefore we can find them.'

Homam beamed startlingly, though it was a second or two before Lizbeth understood and fumbled in her haversack for the palmtop.

'A locator signal,' Homam explained helpfully to Bernice, as Lizbeth keyed in the sequence. 'All drones have them, each with an individual signature of course. Or you can program a team-trace. Best try that first, Lizbeth –'

The sine tone beeped from the palmtop even as he said it, followed by a complicated spiralling of flatscreen pixels as the tracer software reconfigured. A detailed plan of the excavation and locale popped up a moment later.

Bernice's mouth dropped open. 'We're standing on them!'

Homam pointed a lean finger towards the rippled surface of the polystene infill.

'Ingenious. Except whoever buried the digger drones has seriously underestimated their capabilities. They were originally developed for deepspace asteroid mining, with von Neumann replicating driveware – breeding programs, to you and me. So, a hundred machines can become two hundred, then four hundred, then eight hundred. With that kind of strategy you can dismantle a rock the size of a continent in under a year.'

'Is this relevant?' Bernice wanted to know. Homam shrugged in a way that clued Bernice in to the fact that his musculature must be significantly different from her own.

'The point is that the basic constructional patterns of our drones are similar to those of their ancestors. They're built to last, and a hundred or so tonnes of buckminsterfullerite aren't going to stop them. So don't worry. Lizbeth, if you'll allow me, I can rig up a self-recovery strategy. Perhaps we could set half the team to dig themselves out, while the other half continue with the excavation: working under the polystene won't be a hindrance. It just means that it'll be some days before you start getting artefacts again – though the data will stay on-stream throughout.'

'Sounds fine.' Lizbeth handed over the palmtop without argument, and as Homam got down to machine code level, Lizbeth took Bernice to one side. 'Whoever did this must be pretty stupid, then,' she said.

Bernice's expression begged the obvious question.

'Well, I mean, from what Homam has said, our work schedule has hardly been interrupted,' continued Lizbeth. 'Surely that wasn't the idea . . .'

'There is of course the matter of the smashed subordinate.' Bernice glanced over to the shattered carapace and scattering of jewel-like innards. 'Whoever did that used some force. And how convenient that the drone was left just where we'd stumble across it.'

'As a warning?'

'Well, what do you think?' said Bernice.

Extract from the diary of Bernice Summerfield

Of all the bars in all the towns in all the worlds, I had to end up in this one in this one on this one. The trouble with being helpful in circumstances like these, of course, is that it does impinge on one's social life.

What am I saying? *What* social life? It's been pretty quiet back on Dellah recently, and I guess I had no naïve expectations about what I'd find on Dimetos. Lizbeth didn't really drag me out here for a girlie weekend around the shops. She's into something that's making waves, maybe big time – and I hereby revise any earlier ideas I might have had that her fears are the result of hysterical overreaction. Homam's a good friend of hers, it seems; something of an adviser and confidant (why the hell couldn't she have contacted him instead of me at the outset?), and he was of the view that the delaying of the dig required some considerable resource. It isn't that easy to transport a hundred tonnes of liquid polystene into the hills. Similarly, there isn't any lo-tech way of destroying a digger drone so efficiently that you can virtually strain the results with a sieve. Something very powerful came up to the site and did its work without leaving any identifiable clues. And the more I think about it, the more I reckon the subordinate drone was smashed and left above ground as a definite warning about what could happen to us.

I kind of mentioned this to Lizbeth, without turning it into a scare story, which she may have interpreted as being *my* hysterical overreaction to events. I decided not to discuss this with Homam. It's not fair that he should in any way be put at risk. Hell, all he was asked to do was offer his technical advice on spinning the dig up to speed. Job done, and I expect he'll be back in a week to check on progress and oversee the emergence of the digging team, and review the results of their ongoing work.

Meantime, I have to nurse my worries and – would you believe it? – Lizbeth's attempt at reconciliation with her ex, Alex Mphahlele.

At least that's what I'm assuming it is. Homam mentioned to me how intense Lizbeth is in all aspects of her life – all important aspects, anyway. But the payback is emotional turmoil when things go wrong. She has a brittle brilliance about her. When she said she wanted to meet with Alex again, and indeed had gone ahead and arranged it, who was I to put common sense in her way? If it had been me, I'd have let him whistle in the wind. Actually, I'd never have hooked up with him in the first place. Who needs a high-explosive lovebomb rigged to a trigger that sensitive?

Mind you, if looks were everything he'd be pretty hard to ditch. But I'm jumping ahead.

Cold logic forced Lizbeth to concede that there was nothing useful she could do up at the dig for the next few days. The drones would take as long as they needed to fulfil their modified programming. Therefore, time would be better spent consolidating the data they'd previously produced; liaising with the appropriate government department for a little extra funding to replace the smashed unit; and maybe making some tentative enquiries about why the event had happened, and how it was linked, or if it was linked, with Lizbeth's stalker.

A stalker, I couldn't help but notice, who neither of us had seen since my arrival. Anyway, Lizbeth said yes, yes and yes to my plan. But she also insisted on seeing Mphahlele again, despite any concerns that we might have had that he was somehow connected to the threatening stranger. Men can get utterly warped by jealousy, and when the object of their desire is as beautiful as Lizbeth, perhaps extreme reactions would be the result. Maybe Lizbeth was far more familiar with these violent games than she was letting on.

I didn't even know at the start of the evening if Lizbeth was going to broach that subject with him. I told her to be careful, of course, and she said she would, but that she would feel that extra bit safer with me there, observing Alex Mphahlele from a distance with a neutral's detachment. And ready to intervene if necessary.

What could I do? We took a cab across town to the rendezvous, though alighted a full block away and approached from separate directions. Pretty cloak and dagger, eh? But the cloak was useful since it was raining again (causing an unexpectedly powerful pang of quasi-homesickness just when I didn't need it).

The exterior of the Neon Night restaurant was as tacky as its name suggested, a tall, drab brownstone decked out in bright lights and a gaudy canopied entrance. The Dimetans are such a strange lot: fanatically Terran in their cultural accoutrements, a Californian/Tokyo neo-cyber-retro 1930s amalgam that seems to blend the very worst qualities of them all. The planet is fundamentally a mined-out nest of workings, geologically wobbly, archaeologically tedious, virtually bankrupt – and yet with a prosperous elite who fart money and will go to any lengths to preserve what they regard to be their admirable self-image of dignified nobility. But check this out, they've created a façade of downtown squalor in *uptown* areas, where they can drink overpriced cocktails and indulge their fashion fantasies in safety.

The Neon Night was in one such zone, a kind of Capone-esque theme park which was part of the wealthy enclave of Dimetos City, fenced off from the real, crappy poverty.

I watched Lizbeth breeze past the doorman with a gleaming smile which, if it was feigned, was still effective. Luckily I wore a sleek black Chanel-style dress and an air of fresh-faced innocence (one hundred per cent totally feigned); I'm not sure if I looked like a virginal angel or a devilish tart (probably both), but it got me by.

Inside, the restaurant was opulent and surprisingly tasteful, though achieving it through a minimalist approach to furniture and decor that could easily have been misjudged. Lizbeth had booked a table for herself and Mphahlele, a private nook tucked away among the soft-lit shadows to the right of the dais where a combo was playing lazy-as-molasses blues with effortless ease. Beyond them and the tables in close proximity, a huge panoramic window showed the glittering cityscape, while above it through a speckling of raindrops on the glass I could see the coloured tag-lights of many ships moving slowly across. It was truly magnificent, for all my cynicism about Dimetos.

I sat at the bar and worked on my non-verbals: a posture which said *I'm waiting for someone and spoken for*, and a facial expression reflecting appreciation of the music, slight impatience that my hypothetical date was late, underpinned by a sense of weariness that someone of my calibre should have to be here at all.

It worked for the first fifteen minutes, anyway, during

which time Alex Mphahlele entered the room and walked with an athlete's grace to his seat opposite Lizbeth, ordered drinks, and then some delicate hors d'oeuvres, which they nibbled while I debated whether to eat or simply observe and be ready for action.

Talking of body language, for all I've said about Lizbeth's highly strung nature, she seemed pretty relaxed. It's never easy chatting to your ex, as I know only too well.

Before I continue, let me sketch for future reference my impressions of Alex Mphahlele.

Wow! Cor! and all that. He can't be more than a thumbnail-width short of two metres tall, broad-shouldered and slim-waisted. His skin looks flawless, and if that seems a strange thing to say about a man, well so be it; in Alex's case the black's just short of blue-black, and indeed it took me a while to notice the subtlety of the rich brown sheen when he moved – so – and the cast of light across his cheekbone and jaw. And his smile is every bit as powerful as Lizbeth's, creating a charisma born of sheer beauty.

I spent a good ten minutes just – how do they say it in the pulp paperbacks? – just drinking in the sight of him. He was gorgeous, setting off in me a negative feedback loop of self-pity and stirring up such memories and feelings it took all my force of will to keep them down.

But at least I succeeded in that. Lizbeth failed.

A waiter came along to take away the little china hors d'oeuvre plates and the empty cocktail glasses. That left a gleaming white table cloth and a slim-necked vase between the couple, a vase containing a single perfect black rose. Call me old-fashioned, but it was the most romantic thing I'd ever seen. The rose petals were so striking that I could feel their velvet and was tantalized by the scent that must have been as exotic as the appearance of the bloom itself. Alex Mphahlele's hands as they reached across the snowy cloth were complemented by the flower. He was saying something softly to Lizbeth, and there was such pleading in his eyes that I felt my own start to prickle with emotion.

Lizbeth did not accept the offer of his hands, and I thought she shook her head ever so slightly.

I was so wrapped up in being the gooseberry that I only felt the hand on my knee when it moved, sweeping slowly and suggestively up towards my thigh. I nearly jumped off my stool, but managed to compose myself as I looked witheringly to my right.

'Hi. Tell me, what's a nice girl like you doing in a joint like this?' He was Dimetan, a businessman I guessed, mid-fifties and oozing lustful intentions even more freely than the oily sweat on his brow. I cursed my ill luck and his timing.

'Give me a break,' I said.

'Can't get a table? I can help you out there, doll face.'

He smiled, showing teeth like old ivory dotted with embedded gems: diamonds, emeralds, starstones. I learnt later this was the way the Dimetans who had wealth showed it off.

I told my unwanted companion to engineer a voyage into his own Swarchzchild singularity, or words to that effect; and felt immensely relieved when he shrugged, taking no offence, and moved along to the next countertop lush who, I noted with a small burst of amusement, responded with an overblown display of coy flattery and a rather obvious heaving of cleavage.

A change of tempo from the band brought me back to myself and the task at hand. Alex was still talking to Lizbeth, perhaps a little more intensely now, and she continued to answer him with denial on her face; an oddly inappropriate response, I thought, in light of the trouble *she'd* taken to set up the evening.

But there was something else niggling at me, something that didn't obviously or immediately impinge upon my consciousness.

Like I said, for all its air of sleaziness externally, the Neon Night was a professionally run establishment; the dark nooks and low uplighting and the massaging seductiveness of the music were cleverly integrated to produce the required effect. You could imagine deals being done, promises made and broken, loves gained and lost amid the thin, smoky veil of unadulterated tobacco, the quietly efficient coming and going of waiters, the bright glassy busyness of the bar . . . Essentially it was a friendly and welcoming place with a certain streak of childlike innocence about it.

And that's what had changed.

I concluded this reluctantly as my eyes were drawn towards one of the darker corners of the room, where shadows were overlaid with shadows.

A small table, bare save for the obligatory white cloth and a cocktail glass filled with a clear reddish liquid. There was a man – I assumed it was a man – sitting there watching, not me, thank God, but Lizbeth and Mphahlele as they talked. It was odd that I had not noticed him before; odder that he produced this chill in me now, this fearfulness of an evil in him which was entirely speculation on my part. There was nothing I knew to connect him with Lizbeth or me or the incident at the dig . . . Maybe he was an incurable old romantic like I was, warming his heart by the heat of Alex's obvious passion for Lizbeth . . .

Who was I kidding? He was cold and dark and his manner possessed the latent viciousness of a switchblade. He leant forward to pick up his drink, moving fractionally into the penumbral shadows cast across the cloth.

His gaze swung round to take me in, and I never noticed any details of his face, but only of his eyes, the cruellest, most beautiful, most frightening eyes I had ever seen. They were the eyes of the most passionate lover, the coldest killer – it was a gaze that encompassed and understood *everything*.

Take it easy, Bernice, he knows nothing about you – not your name, not your business, not anything!

My little mind-voice sang its calming song as I looked away from him to sip some mineral water, determined not to be terrified. But I knew deep down in myself that I was in danger of becoming entwined in his web.

I glanced back at him. And *was* terrified.

Extract ends

AN ARCHAEOLOGIST IN THE HOUSE OF LOVE

Bernice watched Alex Mphahlele and Lizbeth Fugard eat their meal. Her own stomach felt dry and nauseous now; even her glass of sweet wine tasted bitter. The man in the corner had retreated back into the shadows. Only his hand, unmoving, was visible on the table top. But Bernice could imagine his eyes, staring in blank fascination at Lizbeth. Bernice's head moved back and forth, not sure now who she should be watching.

When their meal was finished, Mphahlele and Lizbeth spoke briefly before leaving separately. Bernice glanced over to the shadows, and was shocked to see that the mysterious onlooker had already departed, although she hadn't noticed him leave. One moment he was there, the next he had gone.

Bernice wondered what to do next. She supposed that it was just possible that Mphahlele, rejected once more by Lizbeth, would head straight for his private detective-cum-stalker, if that's who the shadowy man was. If Bernice was quick, she might just catch Mphahlele and the stranger together.

She followed Mphahlele from the restaurant. The streets were busy with people, but it was easy to spot Mphahlele, a full head taller than most of the people around him. He forged a path through a group milling outside a total immersion flick joint, his striding gait appearing unhurried but actually pushing him forward at great speed.

He turned a corner sharply, and Bernice hurried after him. Just for a moment she thought she'd lost him in the shadows and crates of refuse at the back of a department store. Then she saw the old-fashioned headphones he was wearing on the back of his head, glinting in the light cast by a pair of drones who were struggling with the refuse. 'Mind your backs!' one trilled when Bernice brushed against it.

Mphahlele, some distance in front, seemed not to hear. He strolled into an even smaller alley.

Bernice ran to the intersection, and stood there, hands on hips. The alleyway was absolutely empty, terminating in a wall of crumbling brick. There were some windows high overhead, but, unless Alex Mphahlele had a secret super-heroic identity, there was no way he could have shinned all the way up there.

She'd lost him. Bollocking buggers, that wasn't supposed to happen.

She exhaled slowly, letting the tension drain from her. She'd best head back to Lizbeth's apartment.

There was a tap on her shoulder. Bernice fought to suppress a startled whelp of surprise.

'You lookin' for me?' said a deep voice, half an inch from her ear.

Bernice turned slowly, giving herself as long as possible to affect a certain composure and think of something witty to say. In the end, the best she could manage was a croaky-sounding 'Hi'.

'You followed me out of that restaurant, right?' said

Mphahlele. He looked really big up close. Drop-dead gorgeous – his jaw was square, and his eyes sparkled with humour – but, still, *really big*. Hadn't Lizbeth said something about him beating up people who took an unhealthy interest in his woman? A man prone to anger. He probably didn't like being followed much, either.

'Yes,' said Bernice, with a grin. 'I'll cut the crap, shall I?'

'That would be cool.'

'I'm a friend of Lizbeth's. I just wanted a chat.'

Mphahlele chuckled, his head swinging back. His laughter sounded like a minor god trying his hand at thunder. Then his face snapped towards hers, his eyes unblinking. 'We've just had a fine time. What is it that she couldn't ask me then?'

'Someone's following her. And been sending her threatening messages. We had to make sure it wasn't you.' The last sentence came out before Bernice had really thought it through, and she flinched inside, but Mphahlele seemed only to pick up on the violence implied against Lizbeth.

'Following her?'

'Yeah. I think I caught a glimpse of him tonight. He was watching the two of you. Didn't you notice?'

'I saw no one.'

'Well, he was there all right.'

'And he's been sending messages to Lizbeth?'

'Well, it could be him. Lizbeth received one this morning. Real Mafia stuff. "You know what we want, so stay out of trouble." That sort of thing.'

'It's to do with the dig, right?'

'Well, probably,' said Bernice. 'There's been some . . . interference.' She glanced back at the drones which were still sorting and grading the refuse. 'Anyway, why do you ask?'

'I still care for her,' said Alex Mphahlele. 'Don't let anyone tell you different. And, in the diplomatic circles in which I move, I hear things. And I'm *very* good at hearing things where Lizbeth is concerned.'

'You know something about what's been going on?'

'Only that the government are probably more interested in the dig than they – or Lizbeth – make out.'

'I guessed as much. Lizbeth is really cagey when I ask her about it, though. She's happy to talk about the archaeology, but says she has no idea why she's being followed.'

'You're an archaeologist, too?'

'Yeah.' Bernice suddenly realized she hadn't introduced herself. 'Bernice Summerfield. Benny to my friends, Professor to my students.' She extended her hand.

Mphahlele shook it. Firmly. It was like placing your palm and fingers in a great big vice and tightening the jaws just for the fun of it. Bernice became acutely aware of every bone in her hand. And how fragile they seemed.

'Does archaeology and beauty always go hand-in-hand?' said Mphahlele with a charming smile. 'Forgive my rudeness,' he continued, before Bernice could respond, 'only I don't like being followed, and I don't like strangers. But, if you're a friend of Lizbeth's, then I suppose I'll make an exception – for the moment, at least.' He smiled broadly, but the threat in his voice was unmistakable. *I am entrusting the woman I still love to you. Don't neglect that trust.*

'I was sorry to hear that the two of you had split up,' ventured Bernice, wondering how much to say. 'To be honest, I only got to know Lizbeth recently. But it's obvious she's still very fond of you.'

Mphahlele glanced up at the sky. 'It all seems a long time ago now.'

Abruptly he turned to walk back to the brightly lit streets. As Bernice followed she saw that his eyes had become hard again.

'You believe I'm innocent now?' he asked.

'I think so,' said Bernice, though, in truth, she had no real evidence on which to base any sort of conclusion. 'But perhaps you care about her *too* much.'

'Damn right,' he said. 'Tell me about the guy you saw tonight.'

'Creepy-looking. Sad, too – apart from his eyes. They were beautiful. The deepest blue you'll ever see.'

'When did he start following Lizbeth?'

'Quite some time ago,' said Bernice. 'You see, I'm here more as a friend than as an archaeologist. For some reason, Lizbeth thought I could help her track this man down. Sort the problem out.'

'She should have come to *me*,' said Mphahlele in a plaintive voice.

Yeah, thought Bernice, and we all know how *you'd* like to sort the problem out. 'She couldn't,' said Bernice. 'She wasn't sure –'

'She really thinks I'd stoop low enough to get someone to tail her?' said Mphahlele. 'Her life is her own.' They were back on one of the brightly lit streets now, not too far from the restaurant where the evening had begun. He turned to face Bernice, his eyes shining in the bright light of the street's glo-bulbs. 'Anyway, if I *was* tailing Lizbeth . . . I'd make sure *she* never realized.'

Bernice made her way back to the apartment. Lizbeth was already there, fixing herself a night-cap in the kitchen. 'Want one?' she asked brightly.

Bernice nodded. 'Yeah. It's been a funny old evening.'

'Where did you go?' asked Lizbeth. 'I waited for you, but I couldn't see you anywhere.'

'Went after lover boy,' said Bernice, more brutally than she intended. 'You saw the man who was watching you both from the corner?'

Lizbeth shook her head. 'I was rather preoccupied.'

'Well, anyway, I was wondering if Alex had arranged a meeting with this man – who may or may not be your stalker. It appears he hadn't, incidentally.' Bernice sat down on a couch, tugging off her shoes. 'Funny, Alex seemed not to have seen the man in the corner of the restaurant either.'

Lizbeth glared at Bernice. 'You told him?'

'Do you still not trust him?' Bernice countered. She remembered Lizbeth's apparent rejection of Mphahlele in the restaurant, and began to understand her niggling resentment. Some naïve, hopelessly optimistic, part of herself had hoped they *would* get back together, because then it would mean that love could rekindle itself. Instead, she'd watched as the norms of romantic fiction had been replaced with the grim finality of everyday life: when it's over, it really is over.

Lizbeth struggled with Bernice's question. 'I don't know,' she said. 'In all honesty, not at the moment, no. Trust needs strength, and I feel too fragile for anything like that now.'

'Then why the meal?' Bernice asked gently. She realized it was unfair to see her own aspirations and insecurities played out through the actions of Lizbeth and Alex Mphahlele. Perhaps the only thing that she would learn from them was that people are unique and frustrating and wonderful and crass; that the only generalization is that there should be no generalizations.

'I just wanted to see him again,' said Lizbeth in a weak voice, seemingly on the verge of tears. 'That's not so terrible, is it?'

'No,' said Bernice. 'No, of course not.'

Lizbeth bent down to pull a wine bottle from a rack, and the conversation effectively ended. Lizbeth's introverted preoccupation was such that she didn't even ask about the stranger who Bernice had observed spying on them; and for her part Bernice wanted to hear nothing more about Lizbeth's meal with Alex Mphahlele.

They watched the screen in near silence for a few minutes, and then Bernice went to bed.

She woke some hours later, her stomach grumbling and complaining of its emptiness. It was only then that she remembered that she had not eaten earlier at the Neon Night, and that she'd only had a biscuit and a glass or two of wine on her return to Lizbeth's apartment.

Bernice lay in the darkness, alternatively trying to guess the time and ignore the low murmurs of her hunger. When she became bored of counting the lights that flashed past the curtained window, she decided to get up and make herself a sandwich.

She padded into the kitchen, flicking on a couple of dim lights to guide her way. She discovered half a loaf in a large earthenware pot, and, with the most vicious-looking knife she had ever seen, she began to carve herself doorstops of bread.

As Bernice began spreading the butter, she found herself replaying the conversation with Alex Mphahlele in her mind. Could he be trusted? He was charismatic, for sure, but, as he himself had implied, he probably had the contacts and experience necessary to tail Lizbeth properly. Any diplomat, after all, is at best one step removed from being a spy.

In Bernice's mind, that led to the worrying possibility that Lizbeth's stalker was just that: not a hired detective or a Pinkerton at all, but a *stalker*, a plain and simple, everyday loony with some sort of crush on Lizbeth. Lizbeth had mentioned the helpers who had been on site in the early days: perhaps it was worth investigating the archaeological volunteers, to see if any of them had a history of mental illness or a past conviction for date-rape or stalking.

And then Bernice remembered the eyes of the man in the

restaurant: how deep they had been, and yet how beyond comprehension.

Bernice suppressed a shiver, and reached for a pot of honey.

It was then that she saw the spider.

It had just approached the edge of the circle of light cast by the glo-bulb over her head, as if attracted by Bernice's movement. Its legs drummed faintly on the work surface, most of its body still in shadow. Bernice could just glimpse some of its compound eyes, flashing like polished diamonds in the gloom. Its bristled head came forward slightly, its jointed mandibles twitching.

Without moving the rest of her body, Bernice slowly reached for the carving knife. It wasn't that she had a particular fear of spiders, but she had no idea if Dimetan fauna tended to be poisonous or not. And in any case, she told herself, there is a world of difference between a tiny little creature that builds webs to hold the early morning dew, and this fist-sized slab of arachnid grotesquery.

She grasped the imitation bone handle of the knife just as the spider jumped. Its huge rear legs snapped straight, powering the creature forward like a cricket.

Bernice whipped the knife upwards instinctively, just clipping the thing as it arced through the air. It tumbled to the polished floor, where it rested on its back, its legs twitching. Bernice didn't know whether it had aimed its jump at her, or towards the darkness beyond, but she wasn't prepared to give it a chance.

She slammed the bread-bin lid down on to the spider. The disc of pottery shattered over the creature's concentrated bulk, sending orange-coloured shards into the air.

Before it could move again, Bernice thumped the blunt end of the knife against the creature's carapace. It was like hitting something made of stone. However, one side of its body had split open, and a couple of legs had fallen away.

But no blood flowed from the jagged gash; as it twitched again, globules of silver fluid dripped on to the kitchen floor.

Bernice reached for the bread bin, placing its bulk squarely on top of the spider, and then ground and twisted with all her strength. There were bits of the creature left when she'd finished, but nothing big enough to frighten anyone.

She slumped to the floor just as Lizbeth appeared, pulling on a dressing gown.

'Looks like someone's been spying on us,' Bernice said, poking at the remains of the arachnid with the bread knife.

Lizbeth flicked on all the lights, and walked over to the kitchen area. She could scarcely believe it. 'A spider?' she said, dropping down to her hands and knees to look at the creature.

Its body was made out of some sort of black-green plastic, supported by an internal musculature of silver alloy. The bristles that covered its head were tiny metal aerials, some not much thicker than a human hair.

And behind the eyes, themselves no more than a few millimetres across, trailed strands of almost invisible fibre-optic cable.

'Which all raises the question,' said Bernice, calm despite the adrenaline rush that still gripped her body, 'why? Either the sicko who's pursuing you fancied some intimate shots of you getting into the shower, or there's something else going on here . . .'

'I don't like the sound of either explanation,' said Lizbeth.

'Perhaps Alex could tell us what this thing is.'

Lizbeth shook her head. 'No,' she said firmly.

Bernice could see her point. It was impossible to establish how long the spider had been in the flat, but it had certainly appeared just after both of them had come into contact with Mphahlele. Although he did not strike Bernice as being a man driven by jealousy, he, perhaps more than most, would have access to equipment like this.

And she remembered what she had told herself earlier: *Any diplomat is at best one step removed from being a spy.*

Extract from the diary of Bernice Summerfield

We went back to bed soon after that. Well, once you've squashed the life out of a robotic spider, there's not really much more to be said.

I barely saw Lizbeth the next day. She told me she had a number of important meetings with her sponsors in the Dimetan government; I said that was fine, as I suddenly felt very tired. It all catches up with you, in the end. She also said that she wanted to see what Homam made of the arachnid.

I'm not sure I even emerged from my bed properly until midday, but when I did, the gooey, glittering mess in the kitchen had all gone. Once awake and decent, I contented myself with reading and catching up with correspondence. It was only really as I looked back on that day that I saw it as a turning point: not because of anything that happened (although plenty did), but because of what *didn't*. It would be quite some time until I saw much of Lizbeth again.

My afternoon was interrupted only by a call from Alex, with reference to the party that night, which Lizbeth had mentioned soon after my arrival: he would be going; would I care to accompany him? I wasn't sure what to say, given the events of the previous night, but avoiding him wasn't going to answer any of our questions. So I said 'Yes'.

That usually works for me.

Extract ends

Once, on the holiday planet of Alnasl, Bernice had been swimming in a shallow sea the exact purple-blue colour of lapis lazuli. Looking down through the perfect transparency of the water, she had seen a golden shadow of herself hanging between the surface and the sugarsand bed. Her companion at the time, a young woman named Zavijava Akubens, had explained that this delightful phenomenon was caused by the presence of Midan zooplankton in the water, gathering beneath their bodies for shelter. Bernice recalled her total enchantment at the sight – and her subsequent fear as the twinkling shadow-phantom flew apart in a billion struggling pixels.

For a second she was confused, before detecting for herself the vibrations of the approaching craft through the water. Bernice broke surface and lifted her head, in time to have it almost taken off by the waterskeet as it flashed past virtually in silence, at unguessable speed. Then came the slipstream; a terror of bubbles and spray and a tangled surging of currents that disoriented her totally.

Bernice squeezed her eyes closed in the here-and-now and actually held her breath, immersed as she was in the power of her memory.

The 'skeet was a common watercraft on Alnasl; very popular with tourists because of its simplicity and power. There were of course strict standards regulating its use. But maybe on this occasion Bernice and Zavijava had drifted too far out beyond the swimming zone, or perhaps the driver of the 'skeet was not paying attention, or had been careless or stupid, or perhaps . . .

The two girls had wrapped their arms around each other until they were over the shock. Bernice noticed a cut below Zavi's left eye as she cried, and the blood drops plipping into the water and twisting down, down, unravelling and fading . . . And how the Midan particles had clamoured to feast on this unexpected nourishment from above.

And ever since that day, Bernice had never allowed herself to be beguiled by the illusion of beauty, nor would she ever relax completely, no matter how peaceful or apparently safe was the setting.

'Unusual, Benny. Yes?'

Alex Mphahlele's voice, as rich as his skin tone and as seductive as his smile, cut through Bernice's reminiscence and caused her to shudder. The symbolism of her memory had dropped like a jigsaw puzzle piece with uncanny precision into the current events of her life. Ahead of them, above the grandiose mansion which was their destination, a million swirling molecules of light were gathering and breaking, swirling and separating in the starry sky. Now a thin veil of silvery smoke, then a perfect Mandelbrot Set unfolding with fractal complexity; now a twisting galaxy, becoming a fountain of red and golden fire spouting above the trees. The display was utterly breathtaking – as Bernice felt her muscles tightening, her instincts warning of possible danger beyond.

'Microbots,' Mphahlele explained. 'Or "nanocules" as they're popularly called. Programmed for entertainment. Look at one under a microscope and you'll see it's mainly self-fluorescing glass operating through a piezo crystal effect caused by the friction of the bot's body with the air . . .'

'Fascinating.' Bernice smiled, but did not permit herself to be carried away on the slipstream of Mphahlele's attractiveness and charm. She frowned fractionally. 'But how do they all know what they're doing? I mean, this display is coordinated.' She glanced briefly through the hoverlimo's passenger window again – into the pulsing multicoloured heart of a nebula – before turning back for an answer.

'Morphic field technology. It's something the Jauza race have developed; highly secret; profound implications for the military; probably limitless applications in a thousand other areas of research –'

'And they're expressing this technology as a load of pretty lights!'

'Catches your attention though, doesn't it?' Mphahlele grinned. 'And you can bet your eye teeth that if the Jauzans are releasing this much, they already have the jump on just about everyone else researching in the field. It's a PR exercise, of course. Roll up, roll up! Look at our cute little microbots, then learn how you can use the principles for psychosocial engineering, or simply to wipe out your enemy. Word on the street is that the Bantu Cooperative are acting as intermediaries for the Jauzans. You might be interested to hear that Cooperative representatives will be here tonight, at the express request of the Dimetan government. Wheels within wheels.'

'Within wheels,' Bernice agreed. 'But why don't the Jauzans come here to peddle the goods themselves?'

'Perhaps they have.' Alex's smile grew mischievous and Bernice wondered then if he was teasing. 'Thing is, using MorphTech they can also make themselves invisible.'

'I see,' Bernice said as the limo tilted slightly in the sky and began its smooth approach to the landing area. 'Or rather, I don't.'

The hoverlimo came down on an immaculate lawn of clipped, perfect grass. It was one of a score of such vehicles coming in like slowly falling leaves to deposit their passengers and rise again with a sigh.

Bernice found her anxious caution being tempered by the glitter of the whole occasion, by Alex Mphahlele's suave attention, and – though it pained her to admit it – by the ease with which she had been admitted into the higher echelons of Dimetan society.

'Tell me,' she said, inclining her head in the direction of Mphahlele as they walked into the great house, 'why am I here with you? And why is Lizbeth coming – presumably – on her own?'

Alex answered readily enough, though at the same time Bernice wondered if he was keeping things back, leaving her intrigued and infuriated.

'Lizbeth and I are not . . . reconciled,' he said, his muscles bunching and rippling under his perfectly tailored tuxedo. 'It would be inappropriate for us to arrive together. Etiquette allows us to converse during the evening, however.' Bernice couldn't help but notice that Alex had a diction for every occasion. She supposed it went with the territory.

'Etiquette?' she queried.

Alex nodded. 'And common sense. On the other hand, it is perfectly legitimate for me to chaperone you, Benny. Whether you realize it or not, you are a Dellahan representative, an ambassador for your world just by being here . . .'

'I must try not to dribble mayonnaise down my dress. OK, I'll buy that.' Bernice struggled to make her voice heard above the many voices and languages. 'The Dimetans are consummate self-salesmen. They are keeping this planet from bankruptcy by wooing the governments of a hundred different worlds. They're living on credit and need to keep cultivating relationships. Dellah, I dunno, Dellah might be interested in dealing one day. But I have no connection with that at all.'

'Look around,' Mphahlele said smoothly. 'This is one big advertisement for Dimetos. You came, you saw, you reported back favourably.'

'Well . . .'

'That's the idea, anyway. Besides, if I may say without being accused of false flattery, the name Bernice Summerfield is not entirely unknown on this world. Your articles and monographs are well thought of among the historical fraternity on Dimetos.'

'Why thank you, kind sir –'

'I'm serious.' Mphahlele guided Bernice towards the lights and soft music and relaxed bustle of the balconied patio. 'You will perhaps already have realized that the Dimetans' drive to promote themselves has led to an outrageous over-inflation of the collective ego. This manifests itself in part as an intense enthusiasm for all things academic. It's a kind of intellectual snobbery, disdained on many other planets in Dimetos' area of influence –'

'You mean, they like my work because it helps them show off!'

Mphahlele laughed richly. They were reaching the fringes of the crowds now, and Mphahlele's conversation with Bernice had become punctuated by little nods and acknowledgements, subsidiary smiles and small social hand movements directed at a number of other people. Bernice realized that he was operating on two levels; the personal with her, and working the social dynamic among his friends, acquaintances and contacts.

'You misunderstand.' Mphahlele held up his hand to forestall any upset. Bernice noticed that the palm was creamy-coffee-coloured and looked surprisingly smooth. 'Your own achievements are undoubted, and deeply appreciated among many researchers on Dimetos, Lizbeth included, of course. She has a profound respect for your work – as has our old friend Homam Matar . . .'

'You know Homam?'

'Homam has many flexible fingers in any number of pies. Industrial archaeology is just one of them. That boyish enthusiasm for his job conceals a shrewd mind and a business sense sharp as a scalpel – which he uses with surgical precision on many occasions, I can tell you. We may even see him around here this evening . . .' Mphahlele scanned the distance, looking tall and strong, like some magnificent antelope gazing over the plains.

Bernice nudged him in the side. 'Anyway, you were lavishing praise on my work.'

'Ah, yes.' Alex looked directly at Bernice, his seductive

eyes the colour of teak. 'The point I make is that you are welcome here for many reasons. So please don't think we are simply being polite or courteous. Certainly there are some individuals who are probably already wishing you had never arrived – whoever poured polystene in the trench at the excavation site, for instance.'

Bernice questioned him with a glance.

'Oh, I spoke to Homam earlier today. He is most forth-coming where Lizbeth is concerned.' Mphahlele paused, and just for a moment his unflappable veneer faded. 'As I said yesterday, I still worry about Lizbeth and would never want to see her harmed. So on a personal note, Benny, I too am glad that you're here.'

Mphahlele took Bernice's hand and raised it to his lips and gently brushed her knuckles; not so much a kiss as a sampling of the scent and texture of her skin. In that moment, he was no longer a king antelope, but one of the predatory big cats.

Bernice stopped herself from blushing. Just. Alex led her over to one of the long tables of food and drink, allowing himself the luxury of surveying the magnificent array of delicacies spread before them. His attention swung away from Bernice while he picked at a morsel of food, and Bernice felt a subtle kind of release, a freedom to be out of his spotlight. Alex Mphahlele was a powerful man: wonder-fully self-assured, supremely capable at getting what he wanted – except Lizbeth Fugard, whom Bernice noticed some distance away inside the drawing room adjacent to the patio. She was wearing a simple dark blue dress; she was absolutely stunning, and she knew it. Bernice guessed that Lizbeth had seen her, or at least had seen Mphahlele and concluded that Bernice was there by association, but she seemed intent on pretending that they weren't there. Instead, she was chatting animatedly to a young man Bernice did not recognize, sparkling in front of him, laughing at his jokes.

'Jeeerahh?' Mphahlele was holding out a small plate containing four wafer-thin slices of a dark pinkish fruit that resembled smoked salmon.

'I don't know it. What's the attraction?' Bernice asked.

'It's gustatorily hallucinogenic,' Mphahlele said with a grin. 'It tastes of whatever you like, just as you think of it.'

'Wow.'

He leant closer. 'Living cells, genetically altered so that they can create a psychobiological feedback loop between your own mind and the fruit itself. You have to eat it fresh. And you have to eat it now: Jeeerahh's very rare, very expensive, much sought after. I only got this nibble because I'm bigger than the other guy who was reaching for it.'

Bernice chuckled at his mischief, then wondered at its dark undertones. She picked up a slice and studied it closely, as though expecting it to start wriggling.

'Go on,' Mphahlele dared. 'Give your taste buds an orgasm.'

Bernice popped the whole slice on to her tongue. It began to dissolve, giving off bursts of absinthe, apples, peaches, elderberries, vanilla, cherries, carrots and juniper as Bernice's mind jumped from one flavour to another.

'Yes,' she said. 'Oh yes!'

But by then Mphahlele was talking to someone else, a tall willowy redhead (literally a red head, as she was from Mirach), gallantly offering her a slice of the Jeeerahh fruit as well.

The final tastes became bland and were lost as Bernice's mood swung downwards. She brightened only as Lizbeth and her companion approached, having apparently only just noticed Bernice and Mphahlele.

Lizbeth's companion was certainly striking. His skin had a discernible opalescent sheen which Bernice found intriguing, so much so that she had to make an effort of will to avoid staring at him rudely.

Lizbeth introduced Bernice and Mphahlele before indicating her companion. 'This is Karl Csokor. Karl comes from the Thuban Zone and is here on business.'

'But you aren't here as a Thuban representative?' Mphahlele pitched it as a question, just.

Csokor's chromium-tinted eyes indicated the negative. 'I'm here for myself. But then as you know, all business is selfish.'

'Gosh, that's heavy.' Bernice smiled broadly, endeavouring to lighten up the conversation. A tension had developed, emerging like the universe itself out of nothingness. Suddenly she felt uncomfortable without knowing why, and was a little frustrated that her instincts had nothing to say on the matter. But Lizbeth was obviously captivated by Csokor and was unashamedly hanging on to his every gesture and remark. Maybe it was a ploy to punish Alex, Bernice thought; surely she couldn't have shifted the focus of her affections so quickly?

'So what business are you in, Mr Csokor?' Mphahlele wondered, testing for reaction, just as you might prod with a stick at some unknown and potentially dangerous animal.

'Import-export. Is there any other sort?'

'Well, possibly not. But it would be bound to be selfish nevertheless.'

'Quite,' Csokor said with a humourless flash of teeth, pointedly turning away to refresh his glass.

Bernice spent a few panicky seconds considering how this whole encounter might be salvaged, though was spared further effort when Mphahlele suggested he introduce her to a number of people he'd just spotted.

'Delegates from the Bantu Cooperative,' he explained as they took their leave of Lizbeth and Csokor. 'They specialize in defence systems. But since the best form of defence is attack, I guess the Cooperative boil down to plain old-fashioned arms dealers in the end.'

Bernice wished profoundly that being part of the social undercurrent of Dimetan high society wasn't such damned hard work. Mphahlele signalled his intention of joining the Bantu delegation with a wave and a high keening cry that, it later transpired, was one of the galaxy's countless variations of hello. The reddish-skinned delegates responded enthusiastically in kind, briefly drowning out all other noises in the room.

Bernice glanced back. Lizbeth appeared hardly to have noticed. She was gazing up into Csokor's eyes, reading them intently as she might a complex multi-layered book. He seemed to be doing most of the talking, to Lizbeth and one or two others who had joined them; yet his face was barely animated, contrasting unusually with the hot mercury of his eyes and with the taut anger he had displayed at Mphahlele's mildly provocative questioning. He accompanied one particular comment with a brisk stabbing movement of an index finger into the air at eye level. Fugard and the other listeners laughed loudly. Csokor grinned his barracuda grin.

'Benny, allow me to introduce you to Mas-ta-ba-gal-gal-al-kharatani of the Bantu Cooperative . . .' Mphahlele's large hand was in the small of Bernice's back, guiding her round to meet the Bantu delegation. Before struggling to remember the first tonsil-knotting name, she had time to reflect on how happy Lizbeth looked, how captivated she seemed in Csokor's company . . . Except, she reminded herself, the trouble with captivity is that you place your freedom into someone else's hands.

Extract from the diary of Bernice Summerfield

Mas-ta-ba-gal-gal-al-kharatani. There, no problem. Incredibly, this was the shortest and simplest of the names among the delegates. They were an OK bunch, I suppose, given that they had devised some of the most astonishingly efficient and destructive weaponry in the known universe, as far as I can judge – capable of wiping out the known universe over the course of a long sunny summer afternoon, if Mas-ta-ba-whatsisname's post-prandial tales were not entirely apocryphal.

Alex handled them brilliantly, of course, with a respect and diplomacy which endeared the Cooperative to him, and which also, coincidentally, laid the groundwork for what was shaping up to be a rather significant deal between the Bantu delegation and the Dimetan government. Something to do with using morphic field technology to retrodevelop the unstable areas of Dimetos. I asked Alex about it during a brief lull in discussions, and it seems that retrodevelopment is a cutting edge version of ancient alchemy, transmuting mined-out wasteland and the like into prime, fertile, real estate within the span of a human lifetime. Add a pinch of nanotechnix, eye of bat and ear of toad, and Bob's your mother's brother. It sounded pretty scary to me: Alex was getting rather excited at the prospect.

I kind of tagged along for the ride, trying not to drift into slipstream mode. I did not want to be Alex Mphahlele's shadow, even less his ornamental bimbo in front of the rich and pissed of a dozen worlds. To be fair, he never once treated me as such, and even steered the conversation round to archaeology (bless him), and to a couple of my ongoing pet projects. The Cooperative showed polite interest, and one of them – Shad-la-wa-na-na-na . . . oh, I forget – extended an open invitation for me to visit the Cooperative's primeworld and excavate a couple of sites of military importance. Whatever that meant. I could just see myself crouched over some bloody great ancient bomb, debating with myself: cut the green wire, Benny – no! it's the red wire; no, it's the green wire, you fool!

Apart from the invitation, Shad also offered me a hatal nut, which was supposed to be a powerful aphrodisiac. Apart from having no one to share its effects with, I didn't like the look of it. The shell was yellowish and translucent, showing something inside which had many legs and was stirring slightly. It reminded me a little of the robotic spider from the night before.

Shad explained that I would need to crack the shell with my back teeth, and then quickly swallow the nut without chewing – presumably releasing the creature live into the stomach? Well, what a turn-off.

I thanked Shad politely and declined. He ate the hatal nut himself, grew rather flushed, and went off in search of relief.

From that point the evening opened out into a daze of conversation and laughter. I talked archaeology and had them listening attentively. Mas-ta-ba-gal-gal-al-kharatani repeated the invitation for me to visit, and this time, after five or six cocktails, it sounded more attractive.

All in all I conducted myself rather well, I thought, except for dribbling mayonnaise on my dress towards the end of the evening.

It was no big deal. The Cooperative didn't notice, and Alex pretended he hadn't. I reached into my hip bag for a tissue, and discovered instead a plastic business card; a card I'd seen nobody place there, though during the past hour or so someone clearly had. For a second or two it was perfectly blank, then sprouted a gold embossed address and a brief message – *I know* – together with a date and time.

I lifted my thumb from the datapad built into the card. It was programmable, naturally, and was probably hooked up to a computer network elsewhere on Dimetos. Micro-optics might even, at that moment, be transmitting an image of my face to some distant terminal, together perhaps with goodness knows what other data drawn from my skin.

77

I wondered what to do about the card. Slip it back in my hip bag, show Alex, chuck the thing away?

And while I was wondering, a spark cracked across its surface, spread into a wave of blue liquid flame, and caused it to disintegrate on its way from my fingers to the floor.

Extract ends

The early morning sun glinted on the startling green water of the marina, encircled as it was by a 'u' of silicrete and rose-coloured metal. Bernice wondered if high levels of copper or some other mining effluent had changed the colour of the sea.

The strong tang of ozone blocked out any other smell that might also indicate the legacy of Dimetos's industrial past. Although, from what Bernice had seen in Lizbeth's apartment, it seemed quite possible that the air had been filtered in any case. There was, after all, more money in the marina area than most of the people who stayed there knew what to do with.

Like those of a child pressed against the glass of a toy shop, Bernice's eyes grew wide as she looked at the craft that rose and fell to the slow heartbeat of the water. There were dart-shaped ultraboats, with their powerful chemical engines, jostling with sedate yachts, complete with sails and masts and all the trimmings. There was a cluster of anti-grav ships out above the deeper water, motionless some metres above the gentle waves.

'Luxury.' The drone pilot whistled as the taxi made its way slowly past the marina. 'You've gotta be absolutely loaded to keep your boat here.' Its head clicked slightly to one side. 'Actually, you've gotta be loaded to have a boat in the first place.'

'Do you know who any of them belong to?' asked Bernice as they passed a gleaming jet yacht about the size of a small village.

The drone turned its head away from Bernice. A shutter slid up to reveal a simple screen set into the back of its skull. A different voice emanated from the pilot as it moved swiftly into one of its tourist programs. 'The marina is the home, especially in summer, of many of the richest and most powerful men on Dimetos.'

Bernice's eyebrows arched. It seemed whoever had programmed the drone had introduced a subroutine for sexism, which Bernice thought was taking old Earth realism a little too far. What next? *You won't believe who I had in the back of the cab the other day. Yeah, and them darkies are lowering the tone of this area, know what I mean? And as for the government . . .*

The drone continued in its soulless monotone. 'Many of the businessmen have their main offices within their luxury yachts. These days, the busy executive rarely needs to venture into town.'

Of course, thought Bernice, if most of the rich folk who lived here *were* male, it would explain a lot about the excessive size and power of many of the boats. Penis substitutes, and no mistake.

'We are now passing a yacht owned by KK-Vert Industries, as you can tell by the use of the corporate colour scheme. As chief executive Marc Duk commented when the boat was commissioned –' the voice clicked into an audio sample taken from a news broadcast '– "you can't lose any opportunity to promote yourself, no matter what the scale." '

The vast craft resembled a purple and silver blancmange, its masts festooned with info-feeds. 'I can live without the adverts,' snapped Bernice irritably. 'Are we there yet?'

The drone changed modes again, the screen sliding shut. 'Almost there, darling. I tell you, not all the drivers would come out this far, but, when you said the government was paying, well, I thought to myself –'

Bernice pressed a muting button set in the back of the drone's neck, and revelled in the silence.

They drew up alongside a typical yacht, typical only in that it was as extraordinary as its neighbours. Children – at least, they looked like children – in dirty clothes ascended masts the height of a small tower block; more smartly dressed men and women were busy scrubbing the decks.

Bernice checked behind her. Mphahlele's own hover car was still following at a discreet distance. Lizbeth had offered to come too, but Bernice could tell that she'd rather be checking the latest data from the site. While Bernice still wasn't entirely sure she could trust Mphahlele, the only alternative was going alone to the address on the card, and so she decided to give him the benefit of the doubt.

Bernice authorized the drone to take the fare from her account, and watched the car rise swiftly into the air, before darting off towards the mountains that sat between the city and the bay area. Within moments it was a dot in the sky, almost indistinguishable from the black gulls and pale skuas that wheeled overhead.

As Bernice turned towards the yacht she noticed a young man, not in uniform, making his way purposefully towards her. He stepped on to the mock-wood walkway between the boats, a big grin etched on to his face. The arrogance of rich youth seeped from every well-maintained centimetre of his body, and the obtuse message on the business card suddenly made sense to Bernice. If Mphahlele was at least acquainted with espionage, then here was a boy playing at being a spy.

'Hi,' he said. 'Glad you could come. Saw you at the party last night. Terrific, wasn't it?' He paused just long enough to suck in half a lungful of air. 'Thought you looked gorgeous, too. If I can say that. You're not married, are you?'

He seemed not much more than eighteen years old. Bernice finally managed to get a word in. 'And you are?' she asked.

'Oh, gosh, yes, sorry. Afraid I can't tell you. This is all hush-hush.'

'Bit of a public place for a meeting,' said Bernice, glancing around. Mphahlele had parked the hover somewhere, and was talking to a man just inside the doorway of a small shop a few hundred metres away. Probably discussing fishing, or something.

'Oh no, there's no one else here, apart from the servants, and they're very discreet. Father's away, you see. On business.'

'And Father is?'

The young man paused. 'In the government. I'll say no more.'

'Your message said that "you know". Know what?'

'Your friend. The archaeologist. I know what she's discovered.'

'And that is?'

The young man began to walk away from the yacht, casting an anxious glance over his shoulder. None of the uniformed individuals cleaning the ship seemed to be paying him the slightest attention, but Bernice could understand the man's caution. People who indulged in intimidation and vandalism probably weren't averse to spying on kith and kin either.

'The original EB Corporation maps are inaccurate,' the man said in a whisper.

Bernice couldn't help but laugh. 'You're joking,' she spluttered. 'Is that all?'

'It means a lot.'

Bernice had read a number of papers on the political significance of maps – that to be in a position to disseminate maps and control their content was to be in a position of great power – but she couldn't see why this would interest the political rulers of Dimetos. She said as much to the young man.

'Think back to where we were last night,' he continued. 'The landscaped gardens, the imposing buildings. Imagine what would happen if you told people that their homes were built over an unmarked nuclear reactor.'

'What?'

'When the original dwellings were built – and you've probably noticed that good quality land is very scarce on Dimetos – the area was investigated and passed as fit. But, in truth, when the government checked, they didn't do much more than just glance at the old EB maps to make sure there was nothing untoward buried underground.'

'But there is, because the maps are wrong.'

The young man nodded. 'Like I say, in this particular case, it's an old nuclear reactor. Who knows what's under the rest of the city.'

'So the government want to suppress this information?'

'Yes. Panic and fear – especially among the upper classes – is not good for trade. Now, I'm not entirely sure your friend fully understands what's going on. She might not even understand the evidence her own work is revealing. But there are people on Dimetos who leave nothing to chance.'

Bernice nodded. In an instant, the young man seemed to have offered an explanation for the stalker, the spider, the threatening message, and the destruction at the site. She just couldn't believe it was that simple.

They stood at the end of the walkway, in front of most of the ships, the artificial harbour walls stretching away behind them. A gull alighted on a mooring post and watched them quizzically, its dark eyes as soulless as computer screens.

'You know all this from your father,' said Bernice.

'I'm in a very good position to hear all sorts of interesting titbits. I found out who you were at the party last night, paid one of the butlers to slip the card into your bag. Probably thought I wanted to chat you up or something.' He smiled nervously, staring down into the slowly lapping waters. 'I mean, I don't suppose you'd be interested in someone like me . . .'

'No.' Bernice hadn't meant it to sound so curt and final, but she'd blurted the word out without thinking.

The young man seemed to take it in his stride. In fact, he looked almost relieved, and carried on talking. 'I thought you'd be worth contacting. An outsider. Not mired in Dimetan politics.'

'What else do you know?'

'That's about it, really. Obviously, I see things, but I rarely get close to actual physical proof.'

'Why are you doing this? Won't your father be annoyed if he finds out?'

The boy turned back towards the yacht. 'He won't find out. He mustn't.' There was just the faintest quiver in his voice as he pointed to the luxurious boats that surrounded them. 'All my life I've been really lucky. Lots of money, lots of opportunities, the finest education money can buy.'

'I gather that your father isn't interested in politics as a way of serving the populace, then,' commented Bernice, although the young man seemed not to hear.

'Some might say that I was educated *too* well; that despite my father's hopes, I developed a sense of morality.' He sighed. 'Others would just say that I'm a spoilt brat who hates my father's guts. Everything I do is a payback for all the privileges I've been blessed with.' The contempt in his voice was obvious.

'So I'm not the first person you've contacted with a bit of governmental gossip?'

'No,' said the young man. He approached the smaller walkway that led up on to the deck of his father's yacht. 'I'd better be going.'

'You've been very helpful.'

'Thank you. Though I warn you, if you ever come back

here, I'll deny all knowledge.' His voice picked up a notch as a group of children dressed in ragged sailor suits climbed down from the rigging behind him. 'Really was most splendid of you to come and see me. Perhaps we'll meet again at another bash before too long.'

'Let's hope so,' said Bernice, beginning the walk to where Mphahlele would be waiting. When she glanced back at the yacht, the young man had already slipped from sight.

On the way back to the city, Mphahlele turned to Bernice. 'So, what did the guy say?'

Bernice scratched the back of her head absently. 'He indicated that the government are behind the attack on the dig, and the threatening message. Lizbeth has discovered – or is about to discover – that the original EB maps are not to be trusted, and I guess they're hoping that she won't go public with the revelation.'

Mphahlele nodded, concentrating for a moment on ascending the mountains between Dimetos City and the ocean.

'You see, a lot of buildings have been constructed on sites that aren't as safe as they appear,' continued Bernice.

'I see,' said Mphahlele. 'And did our friend say who he was?'

'Son of a minister. High-ranking, I guess, given what he knows.'

'Do you trust him?'

'Yes,' Bernice answered automatically. 'Well, I think so,' she continued. 'He seems harmless enough.'

'Perhaps that's what *they* wanted you to think.'

'It's possible,' admitted Bernice.

'Do we tell Lizbeth what we know?'

'If what the boy said is to be believed, it could be her ignorance that's kept her alive this long. Whenever I ask her about what's going on, she genuinely doesn't seem to know.'

'Either that, or she's too frightened to tell us what she knows.'

'Maybe.'

The city lay below them, a pale square of construction in a turbulent, broiling landscape. A passenger ship, not unlike the one Bernice had come in, was just coming down through the churning clouds. Following it was a smaller vessel, its filigree wings extending to catch the thermals.

'A driftop,' commented Mphahlele. 'I'd kill for one of those.'

The butterfly-like craft spun lower. Bernice could see now that it was a two-seater, the transparent cockpit rising to twin points like eyes. The rest of the vessel was a black protective carapace adorned with the circles-and-triangle logo of the Bantu Cooperative. 'Corporate hospitality,' breathed Bernice. 'Say you're interested in the latest percussive crater bombs, and they'll take you for a ride.'

'In every sense of the word,' agreed Mphahlele, plunging the hover car downwards without a word of warning.

Bernice clutched at her stomach, letting out a groan of discomfort.

'I like you, Benny,' said Mphahlele. 'If that was Lizbeth, she'd pretend she didn't mind my driving.' As if to accentuate the point, he flipped the craft over.

Bernice felt herself hanging downwards in the soft enveloping arms of the protective energy harness. 'You mean she's more cool than I am? Thanks.'

But Mphahlele seemed not to hear. He was too busy chuckling to himself. 'The latest craze is to fly upside down with the canopy open,' he said, flipping the hover car back over again.

'Yes,' said Bernice, through gritted teeth. 'I remember from my arrival. The police seemed to be taking a keen interest.'

'Saves them looking too hard into the real issues,' said Mphahlele. 'Forgive my cynicism.'

They were on a level with the tallest buildings now, the horizon cut through with communication arrays and slabs of penthouse.

'Talking of which,' continued Mphahlele, 'did this guy give you any proof?'

Bernice shook her head. 'No. And he said that if we contacted him again, then he'll deny that we even had the conversation.'

'Then that's what we'll do,' said Mphahlele with a smile of satisfaction.

As Mphahlele's hover car zigzagged above the streets towards Lizbeth Fugard's apartment, a similar-sized vehicle slotted into an uncomplicated tracking pattern just behind. It was a military vehicle, somewhat resembling a squid, its interlocking panels of rust-coloured metal disguising state-of-the-art scrambling and surveillance equipment. It was entirely invisible to the hover car in front: only if one of the occupants happened to glance behind would the vehicle be seen, tracking them exactly. And then it would be easy to change course, until the moment passed.

Like the earlier driftop, it bore the logo of the Bantu Cooperative. But this time the mark was smaller and more discreet. This craft had seen action.

Inside its armour-plated cockpit, real-time and recorded information flowed along a number of virtual head-up display screens. A pair of suited men concentrated on the audio tracks relayed through cochleal implants.

. . . I'm in a very good position to hear all sorts of interesting things. I found out who you were at the party last night, paid one of the butlers to slip the card into your bag . . .

A well-manicured finger advanced the playback impatiently.

. . . And he said that if we contacted him again, then he'll deny that we even had the conversation.

Then that's what we'll do.

You sure?

Hell, yes. The dude'll be even more forthcoming if we threaten to blow his cover . . .

The two suited men nodded to each other approvingly.

The squid-like craft left the hover car in peace, accelerating away towards the mountains.

LOVE IS: 'I GAVE YOU EVERYTHING!'

**Extract from Dimetan Infobase (Level Two), as
requested by Professor Bernice S. Summerfield**

. . . The current political situation on Dimetos is stable,
albeit with a simmering undercurrent of 'subversive'
activity. The incumbent government is democratically
elected, but rumoured to be strengthening its links with the
military in case of future electoral opposition. It swept to
power on a platform of austerity measures and anti-
inflationism; its relative popularity has declined ever since.
Its failure to deal with the problems of unemployment and
poverty – problems so long-standing as to have been
prevalent ever since Dimetos gained its de facto independence – have prompted a groundswell of antagonism and
cynicism. Cita Rul wrote in *The Zette* that 'were it not for
the bewildering array of fringe and splinter groups in
Dimetan politics, it is unlikely that the KYO party would
ever have come to power. The leadership is nothing if not
skilled at exploiting weaknesses beyond its own power
structures.'

Recently, the Dimetan government has turned its attention to its neighbouring worlds. It has an enviable – if

somewhat puzzling – reputation in its sector as being a safe place to do business. The government believes in good publicity above all else, and is desperate for continuing and increasing external investment. It is even said that +

Download encrypted from here until conclusion

Bernice spent the rest of the day with Alex Mphahlele. Lizbeth was again busy with work – or so she said – which gave Bernice plenty of time to do some overdue shopping. Mphahlele followed obediently, the long-suffering boyfriend-dragged-through-malls look etched on his face. But he remained cheery, even as the bags he carried multiplied in size and number. He offered the occasional comment on Bernice's proposed purchases, although they tended to be along the lines of 'it makes you look like a tart' or 'that would look nice, if it was a curtain'.

The only time his eyes really lit up was when Bernice had stepped into the discreet lingerie section of one of the bigger stores. He found it hard to conceal his disappointment when Bernice had ordered him to stay put ('preferably with your eyes closed').

Mphahlele dropped Bernice back at Lizbeth's apartment, and Bernice settled down to wait for her to return. She suddenly felt very maudlin indeed. Perhaps it was the result of seeing Alex's sadness, as obvious and painful as a tattoo gained after combat. He'd be talking about nothing in particular, and then a sudden look – it was the crushed puppy-dog look, Bernice recognized it of old – flooded his features. He'd stare into the air, as if watching a memory play across the front of his eyes. It all made that big, butch man look faintly soppy.

She'd seen the hurt of their split from both sides now, and neither looked especially cheerful about the situation. And to think she'd trivialized the whole thing by compiling a collection of sad and happy songs to cheer Lizbeth up. It seemed so crass in retrospect.

And Bernice, of all people, should have known better.

Bernice activated the screen, but could find nothing of interest: the news was uninteresting, the interactive immersion progs were old-hat, and the aniprogs were strictly for the children.

She deliberately took a chair to one of the big windows, and sat there, looking at the street and the cars and people that crossed it. She felt very, very alone, in a big city where almost no one knew her.

She remembered a time when she and Jason had made love, a week or two after their wedding. She couldn't recall the exact location, but the feelings came flooding back, as fresh as an oozing wound. Unfettered intimacy had given way to plain, uninvolving humping. Lying there, Jason banging away, seemingly in his own little world, she experienced a crushing sense of loneliness. The only communion she felt was with anyone else who was out there in the dark, being made love to but feeling unloved, uncherished and worthless.

It was very dark now. Shutters were drawing across windows; lights were switching on.

In bars and strip joints, restaurants and apartments, people lived out their vacuum-sealed lives, far beyond Bernice, ignorant of her thoughts, looking only for affirmation and love.

Soon Bernice was asleep.

Lizbeth shook Bernice's shoulders. 'Come on,' she said, 'it's not bedtime yet.'

'Sorry,' said Bernice, waking at last with an enormous yawn. 'I'm making a habit of this . . .' She rubbed her eyes, sitting up straight on the couch. It was nine o'clock. The sky through the enormous windows was the colour of gently smoothed velvet. 'Busy day sightseeing.'

'I've got something to show you,' said Lizbeth, walking towards the screen. 'An update on the excavation from Homam. Mainly technical stuff about the drones themselves, though there is some puzzling data from the expanded trench.' She pointed to a particular schematic on the screen. 'Looks like there are anomalies in the holomaps the digger drones were using to continue their work beneath the polystene.'

Bernice stretched. 'I suppose . . .' She paused, as if waiting for her brain to warm up. 'I suppose the drones' circuits could have been trashed during the attack . . .'

Lizbeth nodded. 'Yeah, that's what I thought at first. But Homam indicates they're running acceptably. If they are fine, then they're simply coming across passageways and the remains of walls where there shouldn't be any. Oh, and the background rad readings and other indicators are way off predicted levels.'

'*That* could be frazzling the drones.'

Lizbeth shrugged. 'I suppose so. I'm no expert.'

She played through Homam's entire communication again for Bernice's benefit. The women watched it together, Homam's typically excited exposition presented with split-screen scroll-downs of relevant facts and figures.

'So.' Bernice leant back in her seat when Homam was done and pushed her fingers through her hair. 'Could it be that pouring polystene into the transect has caused the plot to thicken?'

It was a bad pun which Lizbeth thought Bernice was using to avoid making any meaningful comment. 'But why would the government sponsor the dig and then try to sabotage it?' she asked.

'You tell me,' said Bernice. 'You met your bosses today.'

'Nothing happened that gave me any insight into all this.'

Bernice sighed. 'Well, perhaps you're doing your work *too* well.' She regarded Lizbeth frankly. 'Could it be that the image-sensitive government wanted only to be seen to be magnanimous in preserving their "cultural heritage"? In short, they wanted window dressing. Here you are, Lizbeth: young, pretty, with a dynamic approach to your work. The perfect advertisement –'

'I'm not sure I like that.'

'I'm not saying you aren't competent, but maybe the government didn't give you the credit you deserve. Perhaps they thought you'd pull a few pots out of the ground and never bother about the underlying motives that generated the project.'

Lizbeth's temper was up despite Bernice's assurances. And even as she snapped back at her guest, Lizbeth knew her anger was down to the way Mphahlele had looked at Bernice at the party the previous night, and the way Bernice had responded to his attentions. 'That's crazy,' she said. 'The polystene incident has drawn attention to the dig. Why would the Government do that if they wanted a low profile on the job?'

'The story never hit the headlines, Lizbeth,' Bernice said. 'We've already speculated that its purpose might be to warn us away, just like the scare over your stalker, and possibly even the spider that was spying on us. Apart from me, Alex and Homam, to how many other people have you dared to confide your suspicions?'

'Karl Csokor, actually,' Lizbeth wanted to say. But she shut up instead as Bernice continued with a quiet passion.

'Point is, we're vulnerable in these circumstances. We have potentially damaging evidence of some kind of cover-up – metaphorical as well as literal – and only a handful of us know. Our safest course of action would either be to back off entirely, or to go public and blow the lid off the whole can of worms.'

'We could end up looking like fools.'

'Better than ending up looking like corpses, Lizbeth.'

'Being wrong could ruin our careers –'

'So could being right.'

'So what the hell do we do?' Lizbeth knew that she sounded like a hysterical child, and was ashamed of herself; ashamed of doubting Bernice's good intentions, ashamed of her petulant and ungenerous behaviour towards Alex Mphahlele. And ashamed, more subtly, of the new thoughts she was having about Karl Csokor.

New thoughts, but underneath bubbled deep and ancient emotions.

Extract from the diary of Bernice Summerfield

I was too tired to argue: I didn't even know what we were arguing about. I didn't know what to say, what not to say.

We shuffled off in our different directions, to bed.

When I awoke, Lizbeth was already up. Apart from when I saw her crashed out that first night, I'd seen little evidence that she ever slept. Well, whatever it is she does at night, she looks good on it. Sort of radiant, like an advert for a body spray or something.

And yet that morning there was something at the back of her eyes, like a hangover that even the most invigorating of pummelshowers can't shake off. She looked at me, just for a moment – then she was all sweetness and light – but I spent the rest of the day turning that gaze over in my mind. Was it embarrassment, contempt, anger, cynicism, distrust? It was only later in the day that I realized that it was all of these feelings, rolled into one.

Extract ends

'Sorry I woke you last night,' said Lizbeth.

'S'OK,' said Bernice, reaching across the table for a jug of juice. 'I was interested to see what Homam had to say.'

'I meant to ask you, did you find anything at the address on the card? Any link to the man who was following me?'

Bernice shook her head. 'No one there. Just another person playing games with us,' she lied. She felt another section of a wall of deceit slide between them.

'You said the man who *was* following you,' she continued.

'I've not seen him since before that evening in the restaurant,' said Lizbeth, with a smile of relief that was clearly genuine. 'If that *was* him that you saw then it was the first and last time he really came out of the shadows. Since then . . . I just *feel* that he's gone. I can't really explain it.'

'And having a new man on your arm probably helps,' Bernice blurted out. And then winced. What little subtlety she had refused to surface before midday. At the earliest.

'Karl has been really sweet,' said Lizbeth, ignoring or not noticing any potential malice in Bernice's words. 'He's helped me to see one or two things a bit more clearly.'

'I'm glad, Lizbeth, really I am.'

'Good,' said Lizbeth, getting to her feet and activating the screen.

'No threatening messages today?' asked Bernice, sprinkling caff-sub drops into her orange juice.

'No,' said Lizbeth. 'I've copied across the latest energy flux readings from the office.' She pointed to a three-dimensional schematic of a number of buildings, overlaid with the contemporary landscape. 'Along with some of the other information that was getting Homam so excited.'

'Seeing all that work done without lifting a sodding sod,' said Bernice, 'just makes me want to get out a spade and start shovelling.'

Lizbeth smiled. 'I've never been as hands-on as you, Benny. Still, I'm thinking of going over to the dig some time this morning. You want to come?'

'Alex has kindly offered to show me around,' said Bernice. The truth was that Mphahlele had suggested that they return to the marina and try to talk to the politician's son again. 'Maybe I'll join you at the office this afternoon. We can have a look at the results we saw last night.'

'Fine,' said Lizbeth. There wasn't any trace of bitterness in her voice. Which either meant that she was good at concealing her jealousy, or she genuinely didn't care about Mphahlele any more. Bernice didn't know whether she felt relieved or disappointed.

Extract from the diary of Bernice Summerfield

What do I feel about Alex? I just don't know. There's an animal attraction there, to be sure, but surely I'm too old and spinsterish for all this biological messing around.

Anyway, Lizbeth left soon after, and I stared into my juice, thinking.

Extract ends

Note in right margin (pencil, very scrawled handwriting)

Don't dance around the issue. You know what they say about bla–

Rest of note unreadable

Alex Mphahlele expertly brought the hover car down to street level, parking it between an executive flyer and a rusty-looking Trudger that hadn't moved since Bernice's arrival. Hyperdraulic pistons opened the passenger door for Bernice, but Mphahlele stood and helped Bernice in, like a well-trained chauffeur. Bernice wondered if he was going to play the gentleman all day, but it didn't last long.

'Is madam wearing her new panties today?' he asked with a lascivious grin moments after take-off.

'What makes you think she's wearing *any*?' replied Bernice in an instant.

Tart, she scolded herself.

Mphahlele chuckled, and placed a pair of dark sunglasses over his eyes. He asked politely about Lizbeth, but Bernice was unsure how best to describe the woman's new-found confidence and happiness (seeing as how that seemed to be in the arms of one Karl Csokor), and so instead mentioned what Lizbeth had said about the sudden disappearance of the stranger. 'I suppose I may as well go home,' said Bernice, playfully. 'I mean, *that's* the only reason I'm here.'

'But you *like* adventures and mysteries,' said Mphahlele. 'I saw that in your eyes when we first met. At the very least, you want to uncover why it is that Lizbeth is unpopular with the government.'

'What you saw in my eyes,' said Bernice, remembering the encounter in the alleyway, 'was "Oh bugger, he's found me. I hope he doesn't beat me to a pulp."'

Mphahlele laughed. 'I've not beaten anyone to a pulp for at least a week,' he admitted. 'In fact, you could say I'm a reformed character.' They were far from the city now, and Mphahlele brought the car down into a deep valley, a chasm of purple and red stone. Where the rock had split, silver-coloured strata were visible, ruler-straight marks stretching as far as the eye could see. Deeper still in the ravine, where the early morning sun had barely penetrated, huge clouds of white smoke jostled for position like sheep in a pen. Mphahlele skidded the car just along the top of the super-heated water. The plumes of steam seemed solid enough to touch. Bernice imagined getting out and walking from here to the marina.

Then the car plunged deeper, right into the clouds, and the temperature rose immediately. Water rained on to the transpex screen, sounding like pebbles thrown by children. The entire craft bucked and jumped in protest at the gases assailing it.

Mphahlele grinned and pulled the vehicle upwards and back into the relative coolness of the valley's shadow. 'I thought we'd take the scenic route today,' he explained.

Bernice smiled. 'If I was a geologist, I might just live here,' she observed. 'Dellah seems so old and set in its ways compared to this world.'

'But you must travel a lot,' Mphahlele said. 'See different places, different planets.'

'My job is very academic,' said Bernice. 'Lots of teaching, lots of books and journals and commenting on other people's fieldwork. Perhaps too little of my own.'

'Time for a change?'

'Maybe. You can never rule out change, can you? The moment you think you're in comfortable pipe-and-slippers territory is just when you can guarantee something will come along and knock you base over apex.'

'I think you're missing your home.'

'I'm missing something,' said Bernice, and then realized how that probably sounded. 'Oh good,' she said brightly, as the marina came finally into view, 'there it is.'

'Let's go and have another look,' said Mphahlele.

The same opalescence that distinguished Karl Csokor's skin was also present in his fingernails, giving them the tint and delicate lustre of abalone. Lizbeth found herself intrigued by the satiny slide of light off the nails as Csokor reached forward and plucked a morsel of food from the cool tray. He paused with the titbit to his lips, glancing sidelong at Lizbeth before looking at her fully with a smile.

'Oh – I'm sorry.' Lizbeth grew flustered and reached for her cup, fumbled it and spilt the sadallberry juice on the blanket between them. She might have lost it completely then, collapsing into a welter of emotions she didn't understand, but instead grew very quiet and slowed her breathing, letting it settle her. Her blushing subsided.

'You must have thought me very rude, Karl. I didn't mean to stare . . .'

'But of course you did.' There was no criticism in his tone, and his smile widened as if to reaffirm that. 'You have never seen anyone quite like me before; at the very least I'm a curiosity, and at best – well, perhaps you'd like to know more.'

Lizbeth read his eyes for arrogance and failed to find it in their liquid metal depths. Karl's eyes were even more impressive than his complexion. They changed minute by minute like a coastal sky: now watery and fathomless, now silvery grey and semi-opaque, revealing nothing. She wondered what caused them to move through their spectrum of shades and hues. His moods? Atmospheric conditions? Or was the phenomenon partly or entirely under his conscious control? In which case, what was their significance? The eyes being the windows of the soul was an adage far older than any artefact Lizbeth had ever uncovered. She realized it was true also for whatever eyes failed to reveal.

'I would never regard you as a curiosity,' she told him honestly. 'That is so patronizing I can't believe you thought it of me!' The brief flare of anger was good, clearing away the confusion, setting her on an even keel. 'You interest me, Karl, I'll admit it.' She smiled coyly and was pleased to see him react. 'Why else would I invite you out here today?'

He shrugged beneath his robes. ' "You interest me." What a beautiful euphemism that is. How wonderfully ambiguous. On many worlds you will come across the invitation to "have an interesting day". I have always found that to be as much of an insult and a warning as it is an expression of friendliness . . .'

'Well, if you'd rather leave –' A pulse of hot spite came to the surface and Lizbeth tried to swat it from her mind like an irritating mosquito. Csokor had the knack of stirring her – in a number of ways – bringing out feelings unexpectedly, so that she had found herself steering erratically through a suddenly complicated emotional landscape. Or maybe now she was reading too much into things: maybe he was just an uncaring bastard like several men she'd known, failing to recognize or care about her sensitive state. Since she'd finished with Alex – since the life they had tried to create between them had failed – she had projected a thin gloss of coping and getting on with her job. But how fragile was that façade, how easily bruised and broken. She had hoped that meeting with Alex again would have helped the healing process, or at least put what they'd had into perspective. But knots like theirs were never easily untangled. And her meeting Karl – and no less significantly, Alex's seeming interest in Bernice – served simply to burden her with other worries.

Csokor had fallen silent by way of reply, and continued eating from the picnic she'd prepared. Well, his saying nothing said something, Lizbeth supposed.

Csokor poured her another measure of sadallberry juice, his face serene, his eyes full of reconciliation. He offered Lizbeth the glass and she took it, a simple little ritual that served to salvage their afternoon.

Going home, she reflected that it was all probably a rebound thing anyway. It would follow the usual course: that first kiss, the early passions, sex, seeing more of one another, more sex, the plateau of their feelings, seeing less of one another, less sex, no sex, the suggestion that they separate for a while, or perhaps the final parting. A tedious chapter in the story of an ordinary life. Ultimately knowing Karl would mean nothing and yet, Lizbeth realized with a pang of self-pity, her existence and that of countless others was entirely composed of such trivialities.

He had offered to take her back to her apartment, and Lizbeth had readily agreed. It would have been easy enough to call a cab, but Karl had insisted and Lizbeth took that to be a small compliment to her company.

He drove capably, and seemed to be enjoying himself,

taking the hover car up high above the summer sunny cloud layer and into the wide blue, so that only cirrus hung between them and the heavens.

'What is it like, where you come from?' Lizbeth asked him at one point. Csokor checked the positioning display in the dash, a grid-crossed space showing the few tiny motes of other craft. Just for an instant, a look of bewilderment crossed his face as he flicked the vehicle into autocruise. Then he smiled, surprising Lizbeth by leaning back in his leatherite seat and putting a casual arm around her shoulders.

'The Thuban Zone? Well, it's a conglomeration of many worlds and many cultures. We're an ancient race, as you may know, deriving from a number of disparate peoples. Millennia ago we evolved beyond the pure need to survive, so that our primary drive now is to flourish – but not at the expense of other beings' lives and freedoms . . .'

'In line with Petrakis's concept of the hierarchy of motives.' Lizbeth was familiar with the idea from her undergrad studies. But it was a pure idea no longer, for here was a living example of a primary drive very different from her own – and yet, how similar she and Karl Csokor now seemed.

He nodded. 'Beyond the need to survive is the need to be. Ruchbah also predicted it a thousand years ago in her Theory of the Development of Galactic Consciousness.'

Lizbeth mirrored his gesture, though back in her student days Alhena Ruchbah's work had been several levels of complexity beyond her understanding.

The hover car made a slight adjustment to its course, compensating for the flight path of another craft still beyond visible range. The world far below tilted slightly upwards to the right; Lizbeth took advantage of the shift to nestle a little more closely into Csokor's arm. She was getting bored with talk of grand abstracts.

100

'The Thubans' greatest achievement has been the large-scale engineering of our stellar system: basic terraforming of inner worlds, the partial dismantling of several gas giants for raw materials, and the establishment of three gravity sinks from interstellar dust reserves to help soak up detritus and maintain the stability of the system's cloud of cometary debris.'

'I heard your people actually towed a planet out of a nearby system and into Thuban space.'

Csokor's eyes changed the depth of their colour, becoming a lighter shade of pewter grey. Suddenly Lizbeth could see her own convex reflection, smiling back at herself wistfully.

'Well,' Csokor said with a little laugh. 'Yes, we brought a world home. And many times I've watched the archive footage as Giausar settled into place among our retinue of natural planets. Speed-framing the process, compressing a decade into a few seconds, makes the whole thing look like a well-placed shot in a pool game! But, you know, the most magnificent sight is of the Hummingbird Nebula in which our system is embedded. Imagine that whole sky, Lizbeth, on a dark and clear night, overarched by veils and streamers of mist, green, red, pale blue, sprinkled with stars themselves richly coloured in golds and emeralds – and one, Vindemiatrix, just three light-years distant, the colour of caramel . . .'

Csokor illustrated this with sweeps of his hand, drawing Lizbeth with a gentle mesmerism into the wonder and romance of his vision. And then his hand moved towards her, cupping her chin and tilting her face upwards, urging her closer.

Lizbeth closed her eyes and allowed the moment to happen. The Hummingbird Nebula was a delicious dream in her head, and Karl's lips were cool and moist on hers. But still one sane and wide-awake part of her was minutely disappointed that the predictable path of their love had now started its sad and inevitable course.

Lizbeth saw the flash of fast-moving metal and plastic as Csokor walked her across an esplanade in the direction of her apartment. The early morning overcast had largely disappeared now: the sun was out and the air beginning to vibrate with an afternoon heat.

Even as the thing swooped towards them and she started to flinch, Csokor was grabbing her hand and swinging her out of harm's way.

But the tiny device stopped a few metres short and unfolded itself into a glittering read-me screen displaying Homam Matar's mischievously grinning face – though Lizbeth did notice the slight frown of unease there as well.

'It's a memodrone,' she told Csokor, who looked furious. 'A bit juvenile I admit, but it keeps messages private. Are you voice-checking?' she asked the device.

'Voice and retinal patterning, ma'am. Identity confirmed. Lizbeth Fugard. Communication from Mr Homam Matar Sadalbari follows –'

Homam's face became animated and he spoke briskly. 'Lizbeth. I've just double-checked the message I transmitted to you last night. All the information about the anomalies discovered by the digger drones is present and correct, but my preliminary report about the robot spider was entirely deleted. I'm trying to find out how this happened. I'll re-send the details, but, suffice it to say, your friend Benny was right. It's a miniaturized spy drone, capable of the instantaneous transmission of any information it uncovers. Its primary capability is to download computer information – one of the "fangs" is a data probe, able to physically penetrate just about any information system to extract the information required.'

Lizbeth glanced at Csokor, but his face showed little discernible emotion.

Homam's message continued. 'Oh, and one other thing you should know. The other needle in the arachnid's head had a much simpler function. It was a micro-syringe loaded with fast-acting poison.' He gave a cheerily inappropriate wave, terminating the recording.

The memodrone tucked itself back into a more compact and aerodynamically suitable shape, spun round with a slight cellophane crackling of power fields, and shot vertically upwards.

Mphahlele brought the hover car down, leaving it some distance beyond the marina complex itself. He said he was damned if he was going to pay over the odds for a parking space. Mphahlele and Bernice played the happy tourist couple, just out for a stroll to see the ocean and the expensive boats. Mphahlele took her arm in his, and Bernice, after some consideration, relaxed against him.

'It's amazing,' he said, 'that people still want to travel the seas in boats. Seeing as you can zip across them in mere minutes in fliers and hover cars.'

'I'm glad that they do,' said Bernice. 'It shows that . . . I don't know, some spark of romanticism, of the spirit of adventure, hasn't entirely been crushed by civilization.'

'It speaks to me,' said Mphahlele, 'of a lot of very rich men showing off. But I take your point. They could be spending their money on something really disgusting. Like guns.'

Bernice nodded, remembering the weapons dealers they'd seen at the ball, and the Bantu craft they'd spotted the previous day. She hadn't really given them much thought, but, from Mphahlele's fixed expression, it seemed quite possible they'd had quite an effect on him. 'You're thinking about the Cooperative, aren't you?' asked Bernice.

Mphahlele nodded. 'We all want investment in Dimetos. But why does it always have to be like that? It seems to me we've exchanged one bunch of fascists for another.'

He lapsed into brooding silence then, staring out to sea as they walked. Bernice wasn't sure if she was just picking up Mphahlele's own unease and disquiet, or if something about the marina itself had altered. There were less people milling about than there had been, but then this place was somewhat off the beaten track. The sun was shining again, the water lapped and sucked against the boats . . . What had changed?

She realized what it was when the berth they were looking for came into sight. The yacht had gone. Nothing surprising in that, of course, but somehow it felt wrong. That yacht didn't look the sort to go anywhere without an awful lot of fuss and hard work. 'Oh well,' said Bernice brightly. 'That door seems to have been closed on us.'

Mphahlele said nothing, looking into the glittering expanse of water as if a clue rested there. A dark slick of oil lay where the yacht had been, but Bernice didn't read too much into that. For all their apparent retrogressive charm, most of these yachts had back-up engines and turbines, and that meant lubricants and fuel and God knows what else.

Bernice turned to watch a single seagull land somewhat clumsily in the middle of a knot of birds at the bottom of the walkway. The others abandoned their quarrel over discarded food, and flew off with a series of cackling cries, leaving the solitary individual behind to patrol the area.

'Don't look now,' said Mphahlele, 'but I think we're being watched.'

'What?' It wasn't entirely clear where Mphahlele was looking, his eyes unfathomable behind his shades, but with a nudge of his hand he indicated what he meant. Bernice looked back towards a little row of shops and saw a sedan-hover of such shining darkness that it wouldn't have called more attention to itself if it had been sky-blue pink.

'It's just arrived,' whispered Mphahlele. 'And I don't like the look of it.'

A door flicked upwards like a gull's wing, and two suited individuals stepped out. They tried very hard not to look over towards Bernice and Mphahlele, but subtlety was not their forte.

Bernice stared back, and the men ambled along the harbour side, as if they had nothing better to do and were just out for a stroll. One was as tall as a blo-ball player, but built like a silicrete shit-house. The other was tiny and skinny, and he seemed to do little but talk. The brains of the outfit, no doubt.

'They look like Laurel and Hardy,' breathed Bernice.

'Who?'

'Doesn't matter. I suppose we'd better be going.'

Mphahlele nodded curtly. 'Good call.' He took Bernice's arm, and steered her back up the walkway.

Bernice risked a glimpse over her shoulder when they were part way across the marina complex. The two men got back into their sedan, which rose a foot or two above the ground, its powerful engines just audible over the noise of the gulls overhead. Then it began to move forwards, slowly, after the couple.

'Poo,' said Bernice. 'I think they're coming after us.'

With a whine the hover car picked up speed, its blunt nose still pointing towards them.

TRACK 6

LA FOLIE

Extract from the diary of Bernice Summerfield

Stupid thoughts and images ran through my mind. Not quite
a whole-life-before-your-eyes jobby, but rather a heightened
version of the clutter that fills your head all the time. Or
maybe it's just me. I've never asked. The way you suddenly
think about your parents in the middle of a lecture, or
remember a bag of fish and chips in Blackpool when you're
ordering a pint in the bar. That sort of thing.

As we ran from the black sedan, I suddenly saw – as clear
as anything I saw that day – manicured fingers unwrapping
a bandaged fist. The skin being stroked, the little hairs on
the back of the hand just visible in the chiaroscuro lighting
of a cell. And then a burning cigarette stabbing down, just
behind the knuckle. A scream of pain.

And then I remembered that the scream was mine – or
had been, rather. My interrogation by a Nazi called Oskar
Steinmann.

What was my subconscious trying to tell me? That this
was the worst thing that had ever been done to me? That this
was the lowest of the lows, and that nothing else – even

running away from a hover car – would compare? Chin up, Benny, and all that?

Maybe.

It doesn't really matter, I suppose.

All that matters is that I ran.

> *A light pencil line runs through all the above, leaving only 'I ran' unmarked*
>
> *Extract ends*

Bernice risked a glance over her shoulder. The sedan, skimming a metre or so above the sea-lashed silicrete of the marina, was less than fifty metres away now. It was accelerating all the time, its blunt nose dipping like the head of a charging bull.

Blind panic took over long before Mphahlele tugged her arm, encouraging Bernice to turn her half-casual trot into hell-for-leather sprinting. Their own hover car was tucked out of sight down a back street; if they could only reach the next turning they might be able to lose their attackers in the criss-cross of narrow lanes behind the waterside shops.

The engine noise – a mild, dissonant throbbing, well within stringent noise pollution parameters – grew stronger all the time. Bernice resisted the temptation to look behind, concentrating instead on forcing every last surge of forward motion from her legs. Her throat felt cold and raw, sucking in undignified gulps of air with feverish intensity. She was aware of a hammering noise from somewhere, and assumed it was her heart, pounding away like a percussive industrial rhythm heard on someone else's WalkPerson.

A shove from Mphahlele sent her sprawling, and Bernice cried out in instinctive alarm. With a rush of warmed air the sedan flashed overhead, its motors chuckling like amused demons.

Mphahlele pulled Bernice to her feet, then ran towards the corner a few metres away, dragging her with him.

The black hover car, sunlight fracturing off it like broken glass, slowed and rose higher in the air, rotating as it did so. It seemed to be recalibrating their position.

Mphahlele and Bernice staggered around the corner. The street, bisected by shadow, was little more than the gap between the esplanade and a large residential dwelling. Underfoot the surface was cobbled with sea-smoothed pebbles and glass, which glinted in the light like a fairy-tale path to safety.

They were just approaching a criss-cross of alleyways when Mphahlele turned his head to spot their attackers. The sedan was tracking them, flying high over the buildings rather than coming down to street level. 'Looks like they're worried about scratching their paintwork,' he breathed.

He rounded a corner, slowing to a jogging speed which Bernice could match. 'Safe . . . for a . . . bit . . . then . . .' said Bernice between gasps. She couldn't help but notice that Mphahlele was barely out of breath.

'Yeah. And if we can get back to our hover we might just be able to lose them.'

The black shadow of the sedan slid over them. By the time it had passed down the length of the street and was turning again, Bernice and Mphahlele had reached their hover car and were impatiently waiting for the doors to swing open.

Mphahlele operated the motors the moment he was in his seat, the vehicle rising into the air before the canopy had closed securely. A flash of light from the uncovered sun was enough to trigger the transpex's autodarkening function, giving Bernice's view of the buildings and the sedan-hover car some distance away a suitably melodramatic sheen. The sedan seemed even darker through the monochromatic filters, a snub-nosed, car-shaped black hole that absorbed light and threatened to engulf their flimsy craft.

'Hold on,' breathed Mphahlele, although there was nothing

within grasping distance. Bernice toyed with the idea of closing her eyes, but couldn't bear the thought of *every* diary entry about their escape from the marina being a work of fiction.

Assuming they escaped at all.

Extract from the diary of Bernice Summerfield

From standstill, the sedan flew at us like ... well, like a thing that moves from zero to bloody fast in the blink of an eye.

Alex pushed down with the control column, and we ducked underneath them. As I craned my head around – cursing, just for a moment, the restrictive energy harness – I just caught the back of their vehicle jamming down on the rear of our own. There was a clicking sound, audible within the canopy, as something peeled away from our hover's rear-end.

'Thought you said they didn't want to scratch their paintwork?' I queried.

'Looks like they've changed their minds,' said Alex.

'I hope they've not hit anything important.'

'Me too,' said Alex, his eyes fixed on a miniholographic display of our relative positions just in front of the canopy. 'Look,' he said, pointing, 'they've got an inertial vectoring system. Allows them to pull cool stunts like turning on the spot with minimal loss of forward momentum.'

'Yes, I've noticed that,' I said.

'And it's strong, too.'

'So, you're telling me we're going to end up as sushi-sized pieces down in the marina, then?'

'All this could be to our advantage,' said Alex, flipping the hover over and spiralling away as the black car *whizzed* (look, I know that's not a very good word: it should be 'roared' or 'screamed', but the more I think about it, the less

109

accurate those words would be. Hover cars don't scream, or roar, or even shout. You can hold your foot to the floor for as long as you like, but you're unlikely to get more out of them than an embarrassed whisper) underneath us.

'Why's that?' I asked. (I said this while trying to locate my stomach. Half of it seemed to have jumped at my tonsils; the other half lay squirming at my feet. A charming image, I think you'll agree.)

'Most people aren't used to inertial vectoring systems,' said Alex. 'Those two don't look like they *own* that vehicle. Seems to me the boss has let them have a play for a few hours. So, there's a couple of things that might take them by surprise. For example, when the AI control protocol decides they are overcompensating during a full-power thrust-and-turn manoeuvre blah blah blah blah blah blah blah blah blah blah.'

If it's possible for your eyes to glaze over when your mortal life is in danger, mine did at that point.

'Just show me,' I said, as the sedan geared itself for another run.

Extract ends

The two vehicles had ascended high into the sky. To those that watched them from the marina, the craft looked like little more than mating insects, the larger, darker car (the male) making aggressive darting runs through the intricate dance of the more vulnerable female.

Suddenly the female stood still. It seemed that the courtship was over – she had agreed to the advance of her powerful suitor, and was waiting for the final moment of contact.

It was easy to imagine the black male looking very pleased with himself as he charged forwards, towards the acquiescent, weaker partner.

Extract from the diary of Bernice Summerfield

We ground to a halt – if that's the right way of putting it –
hundreds of metres above the marina area. We didn't fall – I
could feel the vibration from the engines keeping us up –
but we weren't going anywhere, either.

I looked across at Alex. 'This is part of the plan, right?' I
asked nervously.

He didn't answer, his hands moving over a pad of controls. He seemed to be doing a series of calculations, the
results playing out on the miniholographic display. But then
I remembered the chunk the sedan had taken off the back of
our own craft, and I wondered if something was the matter.

I didn't say anything else. I didn't want to be a distraction. In any case, out of my side of the canopy, I could see
the black hover car hurtling towards us.

Somehow, it seemed worse knowing that it was going to
hit me first.

I closed my eyes.

Post-It note over the previous extract

I stared at the ship as it came. I couldn't really tell how fast it
was going – it just seemed to be getting bigger all the time.

Just when I thought it was close enough to touch – when I
could see every ghastly inch of the two grinning buffoons
under the canopy – we shot upwards almost vertically.

The black craft followed, still getting closer. We couldn't
outrun it, hadn't Alex said as much? The sedan was just
beginning to nudge its nose towards us – towards me – when
Alex pressed a control in front of him.

The hum of our engines died to nothing.

We began tumbling, like a pebble dropped out of heaven.

Without turning around, the sedan came after us.

Alex's hands moved over the instruments. The engines

surged into life again, and the craft flipped on to its back before executing a twisting, vaguely horizontal arc over the ocean. I hadn't realized how low we'd got, how quickly. All of this must have happened in under five seconds.

Extract from the diary of Bernice Summerfield (continued)

I looked behind us, and the black sedan flipped over on to its back, then clipped the water.

It sank in seconds.

'Hurrah,' I said, or words to that effect.

'Cool, eh?' Alex's grin was as wide as the Cheshire cat's. 'Wanna know how it was done?'

'Not really. I –'

'You see, a big craft like that is fundamentally unstable. The inertial vectoring gives it a computer-aided stability, but if it blah blah blah blah then it blah blah blah blah blah. Do you understand?'

'Yes,' I said with a smile, watching his big, well-muscled hands moving over the hover car's controls, thinking only about . . .

(Sorry, I'm off for a cold shower.)

Extract ends

Marginal note next to previous extract

I still don't trust him. No, really. I don't.

'It doesn't make sense,' said Bernice. They were flying high over the city now, waiting for the air traffic to diminish before descending.

'What doesn't?' Mphahlele barely looked up from the hover's instruments. Bernice had yet to see him switch his vehicle over to computer control, though she knew it came with a perfectly serviceable one. It made their travelling more exhilarating, though the downside was that conversation could be stilted at times.

'What the young man told us yesterday. About the government being behind some sort of cover-up. I mean, what's the one thing that is true of any political party in power, anywhere in the universe?'

'That they're corrupt?' ventured Mphahlele.

'No. Well, yes, possibly. I meant that you can guarantee that they will take delight in the misfortunes of their adversaries. Party-political *schadenfreude*.'

'I still don't follow you.'

'This lot have only just come to power, right? So why would they be interested in covering up poor planning decisions made by a previous administration? If anything, they'd love to get the sort of ammunition that Lizbeth could provide.'

Mphahlele rubbed the back of his neck as he considered this. 'Well,' he ventured, 'like the guy said, I don't suppose you'd want to frighten your richest supporters and potential voters. Maybe they can just do without that level of hassle.'

'No,' said Bernice. 'No, I don't think it's as simple as that.'

'Then you're right, it doesn't make sense,' said Mphahlele. The hover car was starting to come down through the clouds, little vortices of cold air spiralling upwards as it fell. 'Unless . . .' he began, in a quiet voice.

Bernice barely heard him above the hum of the engines. 'Unless?' she prompted.

'Unless the current lot have made the same mistake.'

'Any process is only as effective as people's underlying belief that it will work.' Bernice turned the statement over in her mind. She had first come across the idea in a book about magic tricks when she was a child. She wondered if everyone goes through the phase of wanting to make things appear – clothes, money, boyfriends – and disappear –

teachers, rivals, acne ... The manual of magic had suggested that sheer bluff and bravado were the prestidigitator's most powerful tools, that if something is done right out in the open with as much self-confidence as possible then it is much more likely to succeed.

Making king marbles appear out of thin air hadn't exactly allowed Bernice to win friends and influence people. But she knew all about the importance of self-belief.

The trouble with cloak-and-dagger scenarios, she thought, was that they involve daggers. After recent events at the marina, she wondered how qualified she and Mphahlele were to give Lizbeth the kind of help she needed. 'I'm not suggesting that we run out on her,' she said, 'but if we did the wrong thing at the wrong time, or the right thing at the wrong time, or just about any other combination of time, space and intervention, then we may end up being buried in polystene ourselves.'

They were walking along the riverbank inside the western enclave on the outskirts of the city, close to where Mphahlele had his apartment. Efficient filtration had turned the water back to its natural aquamarine: Bernice could see for many metres into the glassy depths where, close to the pebbly bed, huge fish as big as tuna and electrically coloured like neon tetra swam lazily.

'The only thing that is required for evil to succeed is that good people stand by and do nothing,' said Mphahlele.

'Taking the moral high ground doesn't necessarily give you the best view of the situation,' Bernice replied. 'And, in any case, doing the good thing isn't inevitably doing what's most effective.' She ran through the options available to them. 'Now, we can't tell the authorities about the problem ...'

'Yeah,' Alex agreed. 'The authorities *are* the problem. Besides, without proof we have no power to change the situation.'

'It's getting the proof that's going to kill us!' Bernice

said. 'Whoever's behind this has already cautioned Lizbeth, and now we too have been warned.'

'*Warned?* They tried to kill us, Benny!'

'We don't know that for a fact.'

'I wasn't prepared to give them the benefit of the doubt. Anyway, I thought *you* were the one who reckoned our lives were at risk.'

'You know, Alex, I'm tempted to think they haven't bumped us off yet because your death or disappearance would cause a stir . . . Mine too, maybe,' Bernice added with a modest cough. 'Interplanetary repercussions and all that. My creditors would be up the wall!'

'So that's one advantage we have on our side,' said Mphahlele, as they stepped under a perfumed tree. 'But our suspicion that the government is covering up information relevant to public safety is nothing more than that. The possibility does exist that we're wrong, or even that we've been fed misleading information.'

Bernice shrugged. 'Whenever I've lifted up stones in the past I've found nasty wriggly things underneath, Alex. And so have you. Admit it.'

'I admit it,' he said, surprisingly. 'But what are you saying, Benny? One minute you're advocating caution, the next you're suggesting that we go in with our guns blazing.'

'I don't know *what* I'm suggesting,' said Bernice. 'I suppose I'm just playing devil's advocate.'

'So am I. I'm just seeing if we can brainstorm our way to a more reasonable, and safer, solution. But I think we can't. It's obvious that Lizbeth's excavations are threatening to uncover data of profound importance – data which will prove damaging to the Dimetan government and its relations with other worlds. I think we're being dissuaded from pursuing the matter any further –'

'Oh well, so in that case –'

'So in that case, if only to protect ourselves with

knowledge, I think we need to dig deeper. Which is where you come in.'

Mphahlele outlined his plan with a suavity that made Bernice think he had worked it all out beforehand, together with the twists and turns of her logical, though increasingly desperate, arguments not to go ahead with it. But ultimately Bernice was forced to concede, not because Mphahlele was cleverer, but because he was right.

They came to a small, cosy inn where a weir tumbled the water in a wide cascade to a deep pool. Above this was a transpex seating area; people seemed to be floating above the water where the giant neon fish gathered in kaleido-scopic crowds. Mphahlele bought Bernice a very expensive cocktail, told her that she was a brave and beautiful woman, and toasted her certain success.

'Bullshit smells the same on any world, Alex,' Bernice said. And she wondered if she should have read the magic manual more carefully all those years ago. She would have given anything to disappear at that moment.

At least his name was not Mas-ta-ba-gal-gal-al-kharatani or Shad-la-wa-na-na-na-whatever-it-was. Mphahlele assured Bernice that she could call him Katri.

Once Bernice had been given her instructions, she real-ized two things immediately. Firstly that the whole situation was vastly more complex and dangerous than she had estimated, and secondly that Mphahlele must have been working very effectively behind the scenes to arrange the meeting.

'They say that a person has as many faces as he has friends,' Mphahlele had said in the honeyed tone which Bernice had come to recognize as being his most dan-gerously persuasive. He had treated Bernice to a devastating smile. But cynicism laced through with fear makes a sober-ing combination. The first cocktail and the second had no effect. And neither did Mphahlele's charm.

'So which face am I to wear in front of Katri?' Bernice had wondered.

Mphahlele told her. And she had laughed to stop herself from screaming.

Bernice had always assumed, rather naïvely, that wheeling and dealing of this sort went on covertly, perhaps in old abandoned warehouses or way out in the country – or even wayer-out at some distant deep-space rendezvous. But no. The Far Horizons Hotel lay in the Aljuan Hills outside the city, which was discernible as a faint hazy shadow on the skyline. The place had a five crescent rating from the Dimetan Tourist Board, plus recommendations from several off-world organizations. It was constructed largely of huge seamless sections of a delicate transparent substance which was neither glass nor transpex, subtly tinted to lend the land and the sky a rich and vibrant tone. The effect had not been overdone – the colours did not look false, but more natural than reality itself, as though the doors of perception had been cleansed. Bernice couldn't help but be impressed.

Bernice arrived by hover car and made herself known at reception. The receptionist was a pretty Dimetan girl, but it was a desk drone that escorted Bernice upwards through several shining levels of the building to the private balcony where her meeting with Katri was to take place.

He stood up as Bernice arrived; a tall, gangly humanoid half a metre taller than her. He cupped his huge bony hands around Bernice's in the standard Bantu greeting.

'I am,' she said, 'pleased to meet you – Katri?'

'Actually Katrianadmanijadhimashamali.'

'Right.'

'But Katri for tonight. I would not wish to embarrass you by standing upon etiquette. And – Bernice?'

'Benny for tonight. Likewise,' she told him, trying to lighten up, trying to relax.

Katri smiled and half closed his eyes, a hooded look that might have been one of appreciation or offence. Bernice reminded herself that most of the Bantu delegation were non-human and that she should keep things simple.

They ordered drinks and Katri eased back into his seat and stared out through the almost nonexistent substance of the window into the glorious Dimetan evening. He seemed lost in his thoughts, giving Bernice the chance to look around and admire all over again the hotel's astonishing architecture. It was like sitting in a castle of soap bubbles.

Snacks arrived with the drinks. Bernice tucked in, watching as Katri picked delicately at a dish of what looked like greenish lichees. The massiveness of his hands struck her again, together with the flash-panic thought of the damage those hands could do if he so chose.

Katri popped the lichee thing into his mouth and chewed slowly. His skin had the dark sheen of a native American. The veins beneath spread in strange patterns, like circuitry. He was doing nothing, saying nothing. But even so, Bernice was frightened.

Bernice swigged another gulp of beer to stop her mouth from becoming dry.

'It is customary in such circumstances,' Katri said at last, 'for the buyer to make the first approach.' Bernice realized that he was helping her, but his mouth inside looked black when he smiled, his eyes hooding over even more.

'Yes, yes of course. I guess I'm not very good at this . . .' Bernice put a brake on her tumbling words, realizing how easily she might put herself and Mphahlele at risk.

'Or, you're very good at it.' Katri's smile grew wider and more knowing. 'I have never known Alex Mphahlele to act clumsily in such matters.'

'Well.' Bernice chuckled ambiguously. 'You must realize, Katri, that this is purely a, ah, fact-finding mission. As you possibly know, Alex acts as an intermediary for many peoples, including the Dellahan Network.' Bernice wasn't quite sure what the last bit meant, but it sounded good. Dellah itself was strictly neutral, but perhaps Katri would be swayed by the idea of some sort of faction that wanted to wrest power from the ruling sultans. 'They have expressed an interest to Alex in liaising with the Bantu Cooperative over the possibility of purchasing some of your defensive technology –'

Katri laughed suddenly, so that a little fleck of the lichee-like fruit spat from his mouth and landed on the table's white cloth.

'Forgive me, Benny. It's just that I always find euphemism so ridiculously amusing.'

'It wouldn't do for us to be overheard, Katri.'

'No, no indeed,' he said, controlling himself. Yellow drops of ichor had appeared at the corners of his eyes, mirth-tears which he swiftly wiped away. 'I apologize. I have to say that I'm also delighted by your façade of naïvety in this process. My dealings are usually with hard-nosed businessmen or, more offensively, their drone representatives. Talking with machines annoys me tremendously.'

'Me too. Now let's get down to business. You have something we want, Katri. And we have money to spend.'

'Tell me something I don't know.'

'Not until you tell me something *I* don't. We on Dellah aren't interested in pulse-beam weapons or singularity bombs – old hat, you know. Our interest would be in weaponry of a more subtle nature.'

'Ah.' Katri nodded sympathetically. 'The quiet revolution.'

'Well, yes. Therefore, before we eat, I'd like to look at the menu . . .'

'Nicely put,' Katri said. 'The difficulty is that I would not wish to be in the centre of a conflict of interests. Dellah and Dimetos,' he added.

'But our respective alliances are at peace.'

'Today is not tomorrow, Benny. And you are taking your role as the innocent a little too far. Any deal with your "network" will have political ramifications. And you know well enough that the Bantu delegation is here at the express invitation of the Dimetan government. It can be no secret to you that our presence is not entirely diplomatic. The Dimetan authorities aren't interested in simple courtesy. We expect a generous offer for our services from them imminently –'

Katri loomed forward, cobra-like, and Bernice flinched back.

'So better it, Benny, and we'll talk.'

'I still don't know what you can do for us, and wonder, perhaps, if you're a shopkeeper with old stock on the shelves.'

Bernice was playing her role well and to the limits of her bravado, but, even so, she tensed herself to either apologize or to run away. Astonishingly, the black skin tone she had noticed inside Katri's mouth was spreading through his lips, down over his jaw, upwards into his cheeks; the equivalent, perhaps, of an angry flush.

As they had talked the sun had set over Dimetos and the sky had turned darker. It was rather like sitting in the crystal depths of an elaborate chandelier. Katri's impatient hand waved suddenly and the golden orange sunset was back, replayed from the data stored in the molecules of the hotel's transparent material.

'You test protocol to the limit,' Katri said. The repeated sunlight made his face clearer; the black flush was fading. 'I am still suspicious about many things – your true allegiance, for instance, not to mention your motives.'

'For goodness' sake, Katri, I'm not asking you to show me the blueprints of your latest weapons technology, or to demonstrate the – whatever it might be. All the Network wants is my recommendation to buy Bantu!'

'That's reasonable. And in a few months' time you will be able to see the weapons in action at our new facility, here on Dimetos.'

'In a few months I'll be long gone, together with my offer.' Bernice made it sound final.

Katri shrugged, then drew Bernice's attention to the white tablecloth. The speck of lichee that had been lying there was gone, and as she looked up at him, puzzled, something happened which Bernice could not entirely comprehend.

Katri changed. Not just his expression but, only for a moment, his whole face and musculature shifted out of true; swirling, becoming, returning. Katri again.

Bernice doubted the veracity of her vision for a moment, but knew intuitively that she had seen something. It was beautiful control, to weave the change and then unstitch it inside a second; a flickering proof that was terrifyingly effective.

Katri lifted his glass and downed his drink, then stood, smoothing the creases out of his stylish square-cut purple tunic. At that moment, he was huge, imposing, utterly alien. When he gazed down at Bernice she was again reminded of a cobra.

'Your intelligence denies, but your emotions remember,' Katri said. 'We will sell to the highest bidder, Bernice. Tell that to Alex Mphahlele and your Network. But keep what you have witnessed in your innermost heart.'

He turned to take his leave. Bernice reached out and gripped his arm – his lean, powerful arm in her slight fingers – and she fancied she could feel the very cells of his body dancing in a surge of Brownian motion.

'I thank you for being forthright with me. And I wish to say that, even if perhaps you haven't earned our custom, you have earned my respect – Katrianadmanijadhimashamali.'

Bernice watched him descend the stairs away from the balcony with a strangely elegant loping walk. Then she sat for a while, pondering, while the sunset happened for the second time before the image blinked out to reveal full night and a pair of blue moons hanging like Christmas baubles in the wide Dimetan sky.

Feeling quite exhausted, Bernice sipped the last of her beer, pushed her chair away, and followed Katri's path towards the lobby.

Bernice realized afterwards that she wasn't particularly alert to anything at that moment. Therefore the fleeting image of the face barely registered. By the time Bernice paid it some conscious attention, he had gone, and she was left not knowing whether Karl Csokor had been spying on her or not.

'Are you sure?' Mphahlele wanted to know.

'Of course I'm not sure,' said Bernice. 'I told you, I only caught a glimpse.' She paused, flustered by Mphahlele's intense questioning and niggled by the worry that she had already let him down; that the meeting with Katri should have gone so very differently, and she was the only one to blame for that.

'I've never trusted him,' said Mphahlele, flexing his big fists under the table. He and Bernice sat at a simple street-side café opposite the Far Horizons hotel. The waiter had brought two steaming glasses of Repareet coffee to them some time ago, but neither had touched their drinks.

'Of course you don't trust him,' said Bernice.

'I don't mean *that*,' snapped Mphahlele. 'It's got nothing to do with jealousy, Benny. Believe me. But . . . think back to when we met him at the ball. Can you honestly tell me that you warmed to the man? That you didn't find him . . . sinister?'

'I'm not sure what I thought of him,' said Bernice. 'He was rather charming, and I can understand what Lizbeth sees in him, but . . . well, he seemed very sad somehow.

Tense or something.' She finally took a swig from her glass. Like all Repareet coffee, it felt cold on her lips, but was warm in her mouth. It tasted faintly of vanilla and liquorice. 'No, you're right. I don't trust him either.' She placed the glass down on the table, watching the cogs turning behind Mphahlele's eyes. 'So, what do we do now?'

'Well,' said Mphahlele after a long pause, 'I suggest you return to the hotel. Think of a reason. The most important thing we can do right now is link Csokor to the Bantu traders.'

'Why?'

'The Bantu Cooperative are here after being invited by the government; the government are trying to keep Lizbeth quiet; Lizbeth is intimately involved with Csokor . . . If we can prove that Csokor is working for the Bantu delegation, we must be some way to seeing the whole picture.'

'Very neat,' said Bernice, with a hint of sarcasm in her voice. 'A circle of intrigue!' She stared back at the hotel. There was a regular procession of expensive fliers coming to rest just outside the entrance; they disgorged their rich passengers, before sinking through a house-sized slot in the road into the underground parking matrix. 'But you're right, of course.'

A big black sedan drew up outside the hotel. These craft weren't exactly two-a-penny, and Bernice couldn't help but remember their experience earlier that day.

Mphahlele glanced across at the hover car and nodded. 'Maybe things are just starting to fit together. Maybe –'

He swung his head around to look over his shoulder. The waiter drone had come up behind them. Silently. Bernice had no idea how long it had been there, hovering, its optical units twitching like compound eyes on stalks.

Mphahlele made an animal growling noise, and the drone scurried back into the café building.

* * *

The young Dimetan girl was still behind the counter at reception. She was half-turned away from Bernice, engrossed in a conversation, a simple voicelink device held against her cheek. Bernice stood, patiently.

'Yeah,' said the girl, 'I've heard hot-metal branding is all the rage again. Yeah. It was in that immersion flick. Brutal, yeah?' By now the young woman's back was to the entrance.

Bernice had glimpsed the girl's badge earlier, and it was obvious that she was starting out at the bottom of the heap. Her uniform was smart enough, but her shoes – presumably her own – were scuffed. Bernice came to the conclusion that she wasn't being deliberately ignorant – but she was making a big mistake.

'Oh, it's amazing what you can brand,' said the girl. 'Yeah, you tell that to your father. That should make his hair stand on end. Yeah.'

Bernice tapped her on the shoulder. 'Excuse me.'

Immediately the young woman dropped the voicelink unit to the counter and swung round. Her face was red with shock. And fear. 'I'm sorry,' she said, her voice little more than a squeaking whisper. 'I didn't realize you were waiting.'

'That's fine,' said Bernice. Her voice was soothing, an attempt to put the girl at rest. And win her confidence. 'I'm looking for my friend, Karl Csokor. Is he here?'

'At the moment I'm unable to divulge information of that sort,' said the girl, a little confidence returning to her voice.

Bernice smiled. The young woman had been well trained. 'It's business,' said Bernice. 'Important news.'

The girl looked lost, jammed between well-drummed procedures and a very real knowledge that most of the hotel's clientele would wipe her off their feet as much as look at her. Bernice knew the girl didn't want a confrontation, so she played her trump card. She didn't want to come over as the big bully, but sometimes there was no alternative. And, given

124

the events at the marina earlier in the day, Bernice decided that maybe it was time to do a bit of stamping and shouting herself.

'Listen,' said Bernice in a slow, frosty voice. 'We don't want the management to find out that you're using their comms budget to talk to your friends, do we? Now, just tell me where Karl is. If he gets funny, blame me.'

At last the girl relented, and checked a list on a discreetly hidden screen in front of her. 'Yes, he's here.'

'Is he in his room?'

The girl's hands hovered over the readout, indecisive for a moment.

'Come on,' cajoled Bernice. 'He's a businessman, right? So I'm here on business.' Then she considered the type of business the Bantu Cooperative engaged in, and the secrecy seemed to make more sense.

The young woman relented, but there was no reply from his room. 'Would you like to leave a message?' asked the girl.

Bernice nodded. A second holographic display appeared in front of her, shimmering slightly, waiting for her to input a message. 'But I think I'll take it in person.'

Bernice walked towards the main hotel elevator. The woman at the reception desk went to say something, but fell silent.

Bernice had noted Csokor's room number from the display, and she strode into the lift with the confidence of someone who was just starting to believe in the game they were playing. Rococo metal doors eased close and a computer-modelled three-dimensional face appeared in front of her. It smiled broadly. 'Floor, madam?'

'Twelfth.'

'Very good.'

The reception vanished into darkness, the lift rising so smoothly there was no sense of movement whatsoever. The synthetic face made a show of *not* staring at Bernice while still looking alert and ready to deal with any problems. 'Twelfth floor,' it announced when the elevator came to rest. 'Have a nice day.'

'Whatever,' said Bernice, pushing through the metal doors, and running straight into Katri.

He looked, if it was possible, even more pensive than before, his great hands folded together at the front of his tunic, his head bowed, so that he looked less strikingly tall than usual. 'Terribly sorry,' he breathed.

'My fault,' said Bernice.

There was an embarrassed pause. Bernice knew that some sort of explanation was in order, but she was unwilling to betray her hard-fought sense of cool. Katri eventually broke the silence. 'I am pleased to see you again.' He gestured Bernice away from the lift, where a number of suited guests and their luggage-dragging drones were gathering. 'You returned for something?'

'Yes.' Bernice realized that outright denial wouldn't wash – what reason *did* she have to return to the hotel? – but struggled for a convincing lie that did not involve mentioning Karl Csokor. 'I . . . I wanted to apologize.'

'Really? For what?'

'I might have been . . . over-strenuous in my argument.'

'Over-strenuous?' The detached amusement was audible in Katri's voice again, but now it was mixed with something else. He spoke even more slowly than before, as if weighing up something of great importance. 'I do find your idiom most appealing.' His hooded eyes glanced around. 'If any apology is forthcoming, it should be from my lips, Benny. I said more than I meant.'

He spoke as though he had already incriminated himself in some way, but Bernice struggled to recollect anything out of the ordinary in what Katri had earlier said. 'I don't understand,' she eventually blurted out.

126

Katri glanced around him. He suddenly seemed nervous of crowds, of the very fabric of the hotel itself. 'There is a club in the city that might amuse. Let us go there, and I will be able to tell you more about what you want to know.'

And without another word he swept back towards the elevator. After a moment's thought, Bernice followed.

Katri's hover car was waiting for them underneath the hotel. The subterranean chamber was full of hoverlimos and ornate fliers. They were just about the most obscenely enormous vehicles Bernice had ever seen. Not so much big as *long*. She reckoned it would take a week to clean just one of them by hand – by which time, the front would be dirty again. And before her sat hundreds of them, all gleaming and polished and perfect, and in every colour of the metallic rainbow: gold, sparkling umber, silver, splashes of rose or champagne.

Katri's hover car was small and dark in contrast. It was not especially clean, its lines utilitarian rather than aesthetically pleasing. Built to do a job, and do it well, but not to excite in the process.

Bernice looked around for Mphahlele. He said he'd stay close, but she hadn't seen him since talking to the girl at reception. Then again, he did seem to be rather good at hiding in the shadows. His passion for skulduggery certainly seemed to exceed her own.

Katri clicked his watch, and the doors of the car slid open. Bernice was not sure she could trust Katri, but it seemed too late to back out now. She climbed in, just to show willing.

Katri, settling into his own seat, instructed the hover car's onboard computer to bring up a holographic map of the city, with their present location and eventual destinations picked out in red. 'That's where we're going,' he said. 'A lot of our clients have requested this venue. I think you'll like it.'

'As long as my backers and I are impressed by what you're selling,' Bernice said, slipping back into her role,

'I'd be prepared to discuss matters anywhere.'

'Really.' The word wasn't a question or a statement – there was no emotion or thought in the word whatsoever. It was a noise made to fill in a gap in the conversation. Something had changed about Katri. Bernice was sure of it now. When faced with this inarticulate, distracted individual it was hard to remember the charm and confidence – and the anger – he had displayed some hours previously. He was bothered by something, and was completely failing to hide it from her.

Katri switched off the AI-driver, preferring, as Alex had done, to pilot the car himself. The hover car rose into the air and Katri lapsed into silence. Bernice passed the time by turning over in her mind their previous conversation. Her interest had been piqued by the Bantu negotiator admitting that he had said more than he meant to. Whatever it was, it seemed to have rattled him. She wondered if his superiors had been monitoring their conversation, and that they'd ticked him off for some indiscretion. But what could it be?

They flew low over one of the poorer areas of the city. These regions were dotted around the capital, shanty towns of squalor thrusting up through the opulence like dark cancers. Bernice looked down, and caught glimpses of long lines of washing stretching between the ramshackle buildings, and of people hurrying through the shadows. She wondered if the mystery she had uncovered had any bearing at all on their lives. She somewhat doubted it. Conspiracies involving old maps, rich people's houses and weapons traders would seem esoteric to them: their only concern was the constant struggle for food, warmth and employment.

Just for a moment Bernice considered asking Katri to let her out here. She wondered if it wouldn't be for the best if she spent her remaining days on Dimetos helping the needy, leaving Lizbeth to sort out whatever mess it was that she had discovered. Bernice knew she was no saint, but she had a brain and a pair of hands, and so perhaps could help on a practical level, fixing roofs and filling out job applications.

And then Katri spoke and she put these thoughts to one side. And a voice in her mind said: *Thus does distraction make cowards of us all.*

'I apologize for being poor company,' he said, with a nervous sideways glance. 'I have a lot on my mind.'

'That's OK,' Bernice replied. 'I'm not here for the high life.'

They were now at the street level of one of the nicer commercial districts, swooping past hotels and clubs that looked like twisted sculptures, and sculptures that were as big as the hotels. Myriad lights studded gleaming façades. A floating advertising platform, complete with male and female dancers, skipped past, pumping out music.

'Even so,' continued Katri, 'we do like to entertain.'

'I can't argue with that,' she said.

'Of course, we both know this is all window-dressing – or, to change the simile, the glitter-cream atop an Olarkian sundae. It is a shame that we have to do such things to cover over our inadequacies and failings.'

The deep regret in his voice caused Bernice to look at him more closely. 'Failings?'

'We're beings of flesh and blood, are we not, Benny? Prone to errors and misunderstandings, exaggeration and conceit. We're so very fragile, on all levels.'

Katri had one hand on the controls of the hover car; the other was fiddling with something set to one side of his seat. Bernice caught a glimpse of a polished metal spheroid, with recessed controls for impossibly small fingers. It seemed so very different from the angular black framework of the rest of the car that she was surprised she'd not noticed it before.

Katri turned to Bernice, his eyes wide. 'I'm so sorry,' he said in a whisper.

Bernice pulled the manual door release just before he detonated the bomb.

SONG TO THE SIREN

Extract from Dimetan Infobase (Level Four), as requested by Professor Bernice S. Summerfield

The Bantu Cooperative has enjoyed – some would say suffered – a long and chequered history. The first reference comes in 2011 CE, with a political movement that championed the rights of the oppressed in southern Africa, Earth. Resentful of perceived governmental failure, the Bantu Independence Group (BIG) was able to buy land and build its own model communities under the watchful eye of sceptical national authorities. This, at least, has always been true of the Bantu Cooperative: a suspicion of any system of authority, other than its own.

Despite this partial embrace of capitalism (which, it has been argued, sowed many of the seeds for future decisions that would so radically impact upon the Cooperative), by 2044 the BIG existed in (abbreviated) name only as a small holding company, lacking any political or social motivation. Olle Ahlin became chief executive in 2067, and immediately set about expanding the group. He had the money to achieve his aims. In the 2040s, Ahlin had invested in solid fuel systems when most had turned to alternative technologies; his reward was to become one of the world's richest men by the 2060s. He ensured that the BIG ruling council consisted almost entirely of nationalists and fundamentalists from regions such as Scandinavia and central Africa; once more, the BIG had a political emphasis, although until the 2070s and 80s it was not clear what that agenda might be.

The BIG sent out many of the first sub-light-speed vessels and, freed from the constraints of operating on Earth, it began to colonize. Ahlin's final address to the ruling council, a year before his death in 2099, stated the new credo most clearly: 'Our metal glove of military and economic strength contains within a hand of compassion and hope. As we create our own laws and systems, so we become accountable to the people who live under them.'

Commentators on Earth were less elegant in their summation. 'The BIG are imperialist terrorists, acting inappropriately beyond any natural jurisdiction. If we could stop them, we would.'

As far as Earth was concerned, the BIG vanished from the scene in the early 2200s. In fact, they were colonizing and subverting whole swathes of the galaxy, much as the newly named [information deleted] were doing elsewhere. With each passing generation, the Bantu Cooperative, as it was now known, became more militaristic in structure. In time the Cooperative became a loose alliance of dominated worlds, maintained, supported and governed by countless alien races. It established a complete economic and trading system where everything worked to the benefit of the Cooperative.

Wisely, the Cooperative had concentrated on a region of the galaxy that Earth was unlikely to become interested in. As Emah-ji-ji-Ke-gege, the first non-human leader of the Bantu Cooperative put it in 2397, 'Earth has the richest pickings. However, we make better use of our more meagre resources.'

Covert links were established with various Earth organizations, most notably [information deleted] and the [information deleted]. A chance diplomatic encounter with the dragon people, some hundred years before their war with the Earth Empire, led to the Bantu Cooperative co-funding a pre-emptive weapons creation programme with Terran personnel. It is not known whether the Bantu peoples and the dragons ever went to war, but this preparation speaks volumes of the Cooperative's unwillingness to leave anything to chance.

Protected from Earth by light-years of buffer space, and Terra's absolute indifference and distraction by war, the Bantu worlds flourished until the early 2500s.

Defeated in war in 2511 – the exact details, and even the name and nature of the aggressor, are hard to establish – the Bantu Cooperative re-emerged as a purely commercial body in 2543. Many of the structures remained from before, but its emphasis was now on weapon development. So successful has it been in this field that many of its employees do not even know of its former life as a pan-world imperialistic body; still less its obscure origins some hundreds of years previously on Earth.

Extract ends

The hover car fractured, listed to one side, then exploded in a fireball of heat and oily smoke.

Mphahlele was out of his own vehicle and running before he'd fully taken in what had happened.

Boiling-hot shards of plastic and alloy fell like hail on to the sidewalk. Passers-by were screaming, holding their arms over their heads against the debris that rained down. A couple of service drones were already circling the smoking hulk warily, their warning lights pulsing.

There wasn't much of the vehicle left when Mphahlele got to the fiercely burning angular pyre. A little distance away was a charred pile of rags that might have been a body, but was probably just some shredded hover-car fragments. Flames flickered across the wreckage, engulfing what remained. It was as if they were obeying some external authority, searching out what was untainted and consuming it utterly.

Someone groaned from the side of the road.

Mphahlele turned, pushing his way through the excited crowd that was gathering there.

Bernice lay face-down in the gutter, her back and legs blackened by the blast.

Impulsively, Mphahlele reached to roll her over.

There was a cut across her forehead and a bruise the size of a fist at the side of her face. Her eyes were little smudged slits, clamped shut; her breathing was irregular but strong.

'Benny?'

She twisted her head to one side, as if keen to avoid the sound of Mphahlele's voice.

'Benny? It's OK. You're all right.'

Her eyes, shockingly pale and damp, flicked open. Her lips moved, but they were bruised and dry. She paused, gathering together the last of her energy. 'Is he ...?' she began, before slumping into Mphahlele's arms, exhausted.

Mphahlele shook his head slowly.

With a whimpering sigh, Bernice's eyes closed again.

Mphahlele pulled Bernice closer to him, waiting for the emergency services to put in an appearance. Even as he scanned the crowd he noticed that the debris was vanishing before his eyes, the flames completing the last of the job. Whatever technology had destroyed the hover car was advanced enough to obliterate every last piece of evidence. Only Bernice remained, thrown free by her hurry to escape and the blast that engulfed the vehicle.

Mphahlele looked up as sirens sounded from a few blocks away; medical vehicles were coming, preceded by a rapid newscast flier. The latter was already disgorging reporters and camera drones.

A number of hover cars made their way slowly down the street, its occupants gawping at the mass of people but denied the pleasure of any actual wreckage. Mphahlele's attention was drawn to one in particular, a dark vehicle with gunmetal reflective windows. Only in the back was the transpex clear, the rear seat containing one individual. Their eyes locked, just for a moment.

Karl Csokor.

The man turned back to the front of the craft, and it accelerated away.

Mas-ta-ba-gal-gal-al-Kharatani wiped a serviette across his thin lips.

'I'm not disturbing you?' queried the man who stood to one side of the table, wringing his hands nervously.

'Of course not,' Mastaba replied, positioning his cutlery precisely on his plate. Almost immediately a waiter cleared the table and retreated back into the shadows. 'Though the cuisine at this hotel is magnificent. I must compliment whoever chose this establishment. It is an excellent temporary base for our work here.'

'It was Csokor, sir.'

'Ah. I should have guessed.'

'It's Csokor I wished to talk about. It's important.'

Mastaba nodded slowly. 'As befits the primary asset of the Cooperative. Go on.'

The man settled into a chair, leaning across the white linen that covered the table. 'You see, I have reason to believe he is no longer taking his medication. And I can't stress how important those drugs are to him at the moment.'

'You have proof of this?'

'No. The tablets are disappearing, but I don't believe he is ingesting them. I've heard that he is simply flushing them away.' The man paused, glancing into the eyes of the leader of the Bantu delegation. 'I always said it was a risk giving him even this measure of autonomy.'

'We cannot keep him in chains for ever,' said Mastaba coldly. 'The Cooperative works best by liberating the true potential in people. That does, however, mean that sometimes mistakes are made.'

'I heard about Katri's blunder.'

'Indeed? Well, I have just this moment been informed that he has tried to make amends in the most brutal of ways.'

'The girl . . . ?'

'Summerfield will recover soon. I am told that the authorities hope to hold her in the med centre for no more than an hour or two.' Mastaba picked at some crumbs on the table. 'I can see the logic of what Katri had planned, but it lacked finesse. It is as well that he bungled even his own death.'

The man rose to his feet. 'I just thought you should know about Csokor.'

'Thank you.' Mastaba looked about the almost empty dining room with a bitter expression. 'One rogue element we can handle. Two is another matter entirely – especially when the individual concerned is Csokor.'

Extract from the diary of Bernice Summerfield

When is a door not a door? I told the naff old joke to Alex and he didn't understand it.

'How can it be a jar?' His big handsome face looked serious; not puzzled, but decidedly concerned for my mental health perhaps.

'Ajar, one word. It's a pun, Alex. Oh, forget it . . .'

After what I'd seen Katri do at the hotel, I was in a mind to doubt that he had taken me to the club and then self-destructed the vehicle. When I first met Katri he had seemed too strong for that, much too obviously in control. Was it really he who had exploded the bomb? Would the Bantu Cooperative risk the scrutiny of the public by pulling such a stunt? Fact is, I knew I'd seen Csokor at the Far Horizons, and Alex had spotted him after the explosion. How does the saying go? Once is happenstance, twice is coincidence, three times is enemy action. Csokor was cropping up a little too frequently, during too many critical moments, for me to think of him as an innocent bystander . . .

If it *was* Karl Csokor, said the devil on my shoulder. If Katri – and by implication the Cooperative generally – could morph at will, by whatever means, then our whole frame of reference was meaningless.

I looked back at Alex across the width of his lounge as he poured drinks and brought them over.

'But if a door's been opened a little, how come it's not then a door?'

'Alex,' I said, 'just shut it, will you?'

He will never understand why I broke into a spontaneous fit of giggling immediately afterwards.

We brainstormed until our heads were in a spin. What kept coming back to haunt me, even as we talked about cutting-edge science and the destruction of worlds, was the little bit of lichee fruit that Katri had spat on the tablecloth, but which had vanished a few moments later. It seemed deeply significant, a little jigsaw-puzzle piece that would somehow complete the whole picture if only I knew where it fitted in.

Generously I thought, Alex accepted I'd seen Katri do *something* at the hotel. We batted around the idea of telepathy, hallucinogenic drugs, nanotechnix, AI-optics, morphic field technology (whatever that might be), hypnotism and its variants, genetic engineering, and all kinds of combinations of these. The answer, we felt, must be in there somewhere.

'And it will be sophisticated. The Bantu Cooperative

would not be strutting their stuff if they didn't have a product worth selling. And they must have convinced the Dimetan government already, to get clearance for their new weapons facility.'

'So we're back to square one.' Alex swirled his brandy around in its eggshell glass. 'If the Cooperative are so technologically advanced, why try to turn you into hamburger with a suicide bomber? It's so – uninventive.'

'Well let's be thankful for small mercies,' I said, slightly miffed. 'Even using such a conventional method the Bantu Cooperative nearly succeeded.'

'If it was the Cooperative,' Alex replied, 'and if they really wanted to succeed, and if you were the intended target . . .'

'Oh great. With all these ifs and buts there's only one thing for it then,' I told him. He frowned. I held out my glass. 'More brandy, please.'

Extract ends

Mphahlele manoeuvred the hover car with practised ease through the complex skeletal framework of the parking matrix. Huge structures like these, made possible by the use of ultralight, super-strong polymers, were evident throughout the industrial and more heavily populated areas of Dimetos City. The planet's geologically unstable surface made subterranean work or living spaces an uneconomical proposition: in recent times at least the Dimetans had gone for height and lightness.

In the end, thought Bernice, it just means that you can't bank on finding street-level parking outside your office or home. So much for progress.

Bernice closed her eyes as the onside wing of the hover car came within millimetres of a guide rail. She was remembering the many bumps and scrapes that had punctuated her own driving career, and had noted previously the pristine condition of Alex's vehicle.

'After the first dent, you don't worry so much,' she said, half to herself. Mphahlele chuckled softly. There was a gentle breath of hyperdraulics and the whining-down of motors as the car came to a cushioned halt, swaying gently on its rockers as Alex flicked off systems and remote-activated the courtesy software in the matrix to provide light and guidance for them to find their way out.

'The biggest structure can hold fifty thousand vehicles,' he told Bernice casually as they stepped into a televator made entirely, Benny suspected, of the same glassy substance as the Far Horizons Hotel. 'You can see it from here on a clear day, like a crosshatching of tiny lines over on the south side . . .'

Bernice ceased paying attention at that point. The televator was not only dropping swiftly downwards, but slipping alarmingly away to the right. It was a severely disconcerting sensation, exacerbated by the fact that they seemed to be riding inside nothing at all: the televator's surface was non-refractive, optically perfect, invisible, and only the lack of wind-buffeting told Benny's brain she wasn't falling freely through space.

'Can we go back for my stomach?' she quipped as the cubicle came to an infuriatingly tame halt within the apartment block where Lizbeth Fugard lived. They were looking out across a spacious atrium, beautifully stocked with vegetation including spectacular cascades of orchid vines. The door slid back and Bernice and Mphahlele stepped into the perfumed green coolness, Mphahlele leading the way to Lizbeth's apartment.

'What if Csokor's with her?' The thought brought a flare of near panic into Bernice's chest, even as she regretted saying such a tactless thing. Mphahlele looked at her darkly.

'We play it by ear. Since we don't know precisely how Csokor fits into the scheme of things, I suggest we keep anything we say light on detail. We're puzzled, we're nervous, we're concerned for the safety of both Lizbeth and Karl . . . The Dimetan government seems to be trying to put a stop to our investigations, and is leading us to suspect the involvement of the Bantu Cooperative, who we feel are trying to implicate Csokor in turn. We don't believe that, of course, although Katri's actions against you are indicative. If it was Katri. And if his actions were against you.'

'Alex, that's really dumb.'

He grinned. 'Which is exactly the impression we want to create.'

They turned a corner to be greeted by a page drone. It flashed a pixelated image of Lizbeth across its display screen, bade them welcome, and escorted them along the final two corridors to their destination. Bernice wondered if the drone were also covertly checking them for weapons.

Perhaps it was fall-out from the bomb attack and the two hours spent in the med centre, having her bruises bled away and her cuts grafted back together. Perhaps it was simple paranoia, a state of mind that Bernice knew only too well even when nothing was going wrong. But Lizbeth's use of a page drone unsettled Bernice. It was as if Lizbeth was putting up barriers, in all sorts of ways. Bernice wondered if it was time to bite the bullet and move all her stuff into Alex's apartment. After all, they were spending most of their time together now, even if it wasn't for the reason Lizbeth probably imagined. And Lizbeth herself had Karl Csokor. Bernice hadn't come all this way just to play gooseberry.

Lizbeth was waiting just inside her open door as Bernice and Mphahlele came into view. Bernice gave a little sigh of resignation when she noticed how attractive Lizbeth managed to look in her casual leisure wear and ponytailed hair. Her expression, however, was not so laid back. She was glaring razor blades at Mphahlele while hardly deigning to notice Bernice at all. Benny wondered what Csokor might have been saying to her, recalling Sartre's powerful epithet that words are loaded pistols – yet *they* would pass the page drone's safety scans every single time.

'Hello, Lizbeth –' Bernice began tentatively, but Mphahlele waded in, walking right up to her and past her into the apartment. Bernice thought that perhaps he'd seen her in this mood before.

'We'd like ten minutes of your time, Lizbeth. After which you can throw us out if that's what you want.'

'That's just what I intend to do unless you've got proof to back up whatever outrageous claims you're about to make.'

'Well . . .' Mphahlele kept his voice calm, his body language suggesting that he too was having difficulty taking in what had happened. 'We could start with Katri's exploding hover car, and Bernice's narrow escape from it.'

He spoke so convincingly that Bernice herself was tempted to buy it, weaving a tapestry of intrigue and lies that portrayed the four of them – himself, Bernice, Lizbeth and Csokor – as unwitting puppets in a high level powerplay of money and politics.

'Without wishing to patronize Karl,' Mphahlele went on, 'it occurs to me that he was invited to Dimetos for the express purpose of taking the blame for the crimes of the Bantu Cooperative on this planet.'

'He's just an independent businessman,' said Lizbeth hotly. 'He's not about to take the blame for anything.'

'Look, we're concerned about Karl too, Lizbeth,' Mphahlele lied beautifully, becoming conciliatory as he saw her face soften. 'However things stand with us, it's clear to me that you have a certain fondness for him. At the very least, you wouldn't want to see him wrongly implicated in what's going on, would you?'

'Whatever that might be,' Bernice echoed, reading Lizbeth carefully for clues. 'Point is, if the Bantu delegation or the government were prepared to sanction my assassination, then God knows who's safe in the city right now.'

Lizbeth looked away from her visitors, her arms tightly folded, standing with the city as a backdrop beyond the room's large window-wall.

'Do you really think Karl is so stupid that he'd let himself be manipulated like this?'

'Not stupid, but unknowing,' Bernice replied quickly, sensing the storm that was coming. 'As we all are. I mean, be honest, Lizbeth, we still don't know who filled the trench, or why –'

Then she saw the shift in Lizbeth's averted gaze, swiftly veiled, to be replaced by an anger she recognized.

'Karl would never be so naïve and you know it!'

The barriers were going up and Mphahlele shrugged his shoulders with a sigh.

'Lizbeth, please, be reasonable –'

'Reasonable? You know what I think? I think that underneath you're blaming Karl for this. You've already made him the scapegoat; condemned him because, I don't know, because of who he is, or the fact that he likes me –'

'This is absurd!'

Bernice touched Alex's arm to forestall his outburst. 'You don't have to do this, Lizbeth,' she said.

'You think he's in it up to his neck. Helping the Bantu delegation, plotting against the government, trying to harm you –'

The rage had risen; Lizbeth's face was flushed and her eyes, bright as mica flecks, were looking out on a different reality. She was losing control. Bernice had seen hysteria before, and its onset: that wonderfully sexist Freudian term that so casually labelled so many people's pain. In Lizbeth's case, Bernice guessed, the fury was the energy of misplaced betrayal of Mphahlele and their unborn baby. Her guilt must be unbearable.

Mphahlele began to deny Lizbeth's assertions, trying to talk over her ranting. But that wasn't the way. For all his skills in diplomacy, he was inadvertently leading her to the brink and encouraging her over.

Bernice acted quickly. She gripped Mphahlele's arm to shut him up, then said, just as loudly as was necessary, 'No point arguing, Alex. She's only like this because she thinks we're sleeping together.'

The effect, instantaneous, was just what Bernice had anticipated. Lizbeth's flow of accusation stopped dead as effectively as if Mphahlele had delivered an open-handed slap to her face. And in that hurricane-centre, in that moment of vacuum when Lizbeth's emotions were disabled, Bernice went up and hugged her close, and whispered in her ear that they would never hurt her.

Then she stepped back.

'Come on, Alex. She'll be all right now . . . Call us if you need us, Lizbeth. Any time. OK?'

Lizbeth, starting to shake with the onset of shock, nodded compliantly. Bernice and Mphahlele walked towards the door.

Lizbeth watched her two friends, whom she loved so much in their different ways, letting themselves out. Bernice glanced back once as if to reaffirm her promise.

When they were gone, Lizbeth moved over to the panoramic wall overlooking the city. It had been a key selling point when she'd been searching for just the right place for her – and Alex – and . . .

She spoke a single keyword and the wall opened silently, letting in the cool air of the evening. There was a little balcony and a rail which felt cold under Lizbeth's hands as she gripped it, steadying herself and bracing herself against the awful shivering inside.

So many people out there. Such a swarming, vigorous, fertile sky –

A police car swooped out of the heavens on a long parabola, a spinning jewel of lights. It swept by, trailing its ululations, and the wind-wake of its passing washed against Lizbeth like a refreshing wave. She gasped as the breeze caught her and fluttered her hair.

She wondered where the police car was going, and why. Then she wondered which of the hundreds of moving dots in the busy airlanes marked the vehicle in which Bernice and Mphahlele were travelling.

Did she believe what Bernice had said? She was too shaken to decide. But looking down now, hundreds of metres to the night-crowded streets, Lizbeth realized that for the first time that day she could do this and not think of jumping.

'I'm impressed,' Mphahlele said. Bernice thought he didn't sound it. His voice was full of gratitude and hurt. He flicked a switch and put the hover car into autocruise mode. It rose smoothly a hundred metres, then levelled out.

'It was nothing really.' Bernice sounded matter-of-fact. 'It's called a biolinguistic intervention. We all get through the day by running little subroutines in the way we think and feel and behave. Sometimes things get out of hand and negative feedback sets in – Lizbeth may have been convincing herself we were lovers for days. That belief was linked with an expectation that we'd deny it. The way to break the loop was to bring it to light, and then modify the program to make Lizbeth more resourceful.'

'It sounds very logical.'

'It's powerful,' Bernice said. 'Next time you go to shake hands with an ambassador, instead of actually shaking his hand, take it and bring it up before his eyes and make some positive suggestion. Do it quickly and smoothly. You'll be amazed at the effect. Or, try this: as someone begins to greet you, say "Hello, how am I?" It's like a whiff of tranquilliser.

Move into their confusion and say whatever you need to say to help the meeting along . . .'

They sailed on through the night. At one point Mphahlele spoke quietly to the guidance controls in the vehicle: the hover car tilted and dropped, the stars swinging round them in a slow pivot.

'Where are we going?' Bernice wanted to know. 'Some exclusive restaurant perhaps, so you can thank me for calming Lizbeth down?'

'Maybe later.' The craft was busy making attitude adjustments as it drifted over the spacious grounds of what Bernice recognized as the government buildings where Lizbeth worked. 'First I'd like us to check out a few things . . . What troubles me, frankly, is that everything Lizbeth accused us of thinking about Karl Csokor might yet turn out to be true.'

Bernice decided that even her biolinguistic sleight-of-hand wouldn't have gotten them past the smartlocks protecting Lizbeth's office. Luckily Mphahlele knew, and was known by, both the human and electronic guardians of the building. In the reception lobby he chatted amiably with the night watchman and with the desk drone who, despite its friendliness, insisted on hand-print and retinal-pattern identification before allowing them to proceed.

'That's the trouble with drones; you can't ask after their kids,' Mphahlele said with a broad smile as they walked the quiet corridors towards their destination. More ID verification was necessary, and Bernice was required to provide a voiceprint for records, before the final door was opened to admit them to Lizbeth's office.

Machinery talked quietly in the dimness, carrying on the routine work of organizing data while its human controllers were absent. As Bernice had expected – and in complete contrast to herself – Lizbeth's workplace was wonderfully organized and neat. And this seemed to have nothing to do with any installed tidyware programs; Lizbeth was simply meticulous.

Bernice gave a little sigh, reflecting that perfectionists are never happy –

Then shrieked as something snaked out and touched the back of her hand.

She lunged sideways, away from the thing, catching her left hip on the rounded corner of a tabletop, tumbling off balance into a pile of box files stacked beside Lizbeth's desk.

'I am sorry to have startled you.' The robotic helper sounded demure and precise and, actually, pretty sincere. 'Is there any way in which I might be of service, ma'am?'

'Yes,' Bernice said as embarrassment brought a flush to her face. 'Tell me honestly, how am I?'

'That'll teach you to sneak about like a common burglar.' Mphahlele came in from the adjacent room and dismissed the drone with a code word. He tutted as the little device tucked itself tidily into a niche. 'More trouble than they're worth, if you ask me. Five years ago there was a government initiative to buy for universities, libraries, and various departments in the government itself. They were intended for secretarial and administrative duties. Being semi-autonomous, they can get on quietly with the minimum instruction. Or so the theory goes. But if you run a quirky filing system like I do – in other words, one that's useful rather than logical – having one of those damn drones around is a nightmare.'

Mphahlele's tirade had allowed Bernice to clamber up and check for damage without feeling even sillier than she did already. 'Well, I agree with you completely. But maybe the drone can help us find what we're looking for.'

'Oh, no need for that,' Mphahlele said airily. 'I've already found it. Or at least, something that gives us a useful lead. Come on, it's through here . . .'

He led Bernice into the next room, an annex of the main office which was much more obviously Lizbeth's personal space. There were some ornaments on the shelves and a notice-board which was an untidy jumble of reminders, mottoes and other visual bric-à-brac – like the spare room at her apartment, this was Lizbeth's only concession to chaos. And, Bernice noticed, there was another framed photograph of Alex and Lizbeth on her desk; nothing holographical or fancy, just a flat image of them smiling, his arm around her shoulder, both looking happier than Bernice had seen them since her arrival.

Mphahlele ignored the snapshot, or pretended he hadn't noticed it: he was busy with a palmtop, cueing-in some data sequences that flickered between shots of Homam, bits of Lizbeth's videolog and scrolls of technical information which, Bernice assumed, were being summarized by Lizbeth in her video abstracts.

'This can't all be to do with the dig,' Bernice said.

'Clearly not.' Mphahlele pointed to something on the screen. 'This bit, for instance. Something to do with an electronic spider?'

'Ah,' said Bernice. 'I'd almost forgotten about that.'

'You hadn't mentioned it to me.'

'I wasn't sure I could trust you before,' said Bernice. 'And then I forgot. Sorry.'

Mphahlele shrugged. 'Looks like we're not the only ones interested in electronic information, then,' he said. 'Wouldn't surprise me if the bug wasn't sent to see if there was any interesting data stored at the flat. All other avenues exhausted, try the home. It's standard procedure.'

He pulled a seat across for Bernice, then stood beside her and issued some voice commands to the palmtop. 'We'll take a couple of copies of the rest of this material. Personal security,' Alex added with a cold, hard smile. 'I'll also transfer the data to a stasis bank, and give it a time code so that if we, er, aren't around in two weeks' time, the information will proliferate throughout the Dimetan web.'

'It's that serious?'

'Watch,' Mphahlele said.

The sequence, crisply edited and capably presented by Lizbeth, took fifteen minutes to play. Essentially her thesis – her accusation – was an extension of what the minister's son had told Bernice, namely that the Dimetan government was knowingly allowing a number of building projects to go ahead, including the construction of the Bantu weapons testing facility, on ground which was geologically unstable, mainly as a result of the extensive mining carried out by the EB Corporation in the past. Over the years, Lizbeth surmised, scores of similar projects had been allowed, the government passing off structurally dangerous sites as prime land. And it wasn't only the Dimetan people that had been fooled. The planet for some decades had attracted off-world attention with billions being invested in redevelopment of various kinds.

'If she didn't know what was going on before,' said Mphahlele, 'she does now.'

'And if the news leaks out, Dimetos could be bankrupted within weeks.' Bernice looked up at Mphahlele and saw the sombre glow of grave responsibility in his eyes.

'The government would be forced to resign. I mean, it wouldn't affect me, but for others . . . well, the political uncertainty might be as damaging as the geological weaknesses of the planet itself.'

'Shit,' Bernice said with feeling. 'So that's why Lizbeth was threatened, and why the excavation was filled in – to scare her away from finding this out, or at least to delay it.'

'But the government didn't anticipate Homam's expertise in reprogramming the buried digger drones to continue their work underground. Lizbeth had the jump on the authorities and put the picture together before they could intervene further. In her own way, she's been trying to protect us by keeping *us* in the dark about this.' Alex sighed and shook his head. 'The bitch always was headstrong . . .'

They watched the rest of the presentation in shocked silence. The sequence concluded with a brief sparkle of rainbow lights which Bernice recognized as a 'clamshell': terabytes of sensitive information fractally enfolded and deep-coded within the molecular framework of the data crystal itself. This was a standard added safeguard, something Bernice had used herself to verify the integrity of data and protect it from corruption or misuse. The clamshell could never be opened except under special circumstances designed by and known only to the person who had implanted it. It amounted to a high-tech version of a wax seal on a private document – but a seal which also contained a copy of the document and all other significant information.

Lizbeth was being as clever as she was careful, Bernice realized. Which was an indication of how terribly frightened she must be.

Mphahlele reset the palmtop and did what he could to erase any trace of their use of it. He extracted two small crystals from a recorder attached to the device and passed one over to Bernice.

'I'll wear it always,' she smiled, fluttering her eyelids in a failed attempt to lighten the bleak scenario.

'Make sure you do.' Alex sounded deadly serious. 'But it will only confer full protection when certain individuals know about it, and know what we know.'

'Government ministers?' queried Bernice, tucking the crystal into a locket around her neck.

Alex nodded. 'And, I'm tempted to add, members of the Bantu delegation.'

'I'm still confused about that. I can't imagine the government wanting the Cooperative to know all about this, so perhaps they're as much in the dark as the rest of us. In which case, why did Katri try to kill me?'

'I don't know. Perhaps Katri was a maverick in some way we don't yet understand. But our immediate concern is not to answer that question –'

'It's not?'

'No.' Mphahlele switched off the desk light and indicated to Bernice they should leave now. 'After what we've seen, Benny, I think our main problem is how to stay alive.'

LET ME WATCH YOU MAKE LOVE

'Being a diplomat, Benny, I refuse to walk like Daniel into the lions' den.'

'But,' reasoned Bernice, 'somehow we have to confront the Cooperative with what we know.'

'Don't you understand how dangerous that is?' Mphahlele persisted, sticking to the same arguments he had used ever since they had left the government site. Bernice thought Mphahlele was being totally paranoid: rather than riding into the city in his hover car, he had sent the vehicle home in auto-return mode, and called a cab. He had not been pleased when Bernice had suggested that the taxi driver might be a government spy.

'Alex,' Bernice said reasonably, 'not that long ago, you were more than happy for me to go traipsing into the hotel to meet the Cooperative. What's changed?'

'The stakes.'

'Tell me, what's the best form of defence?'

'In this case, it could be running away. And in your case, I suggest back to Dellah. Both of us have our careers to consider.'

'Sure. And on the way back to Dellah, the cruiser can be safely vaporized, the "accident" being blamed on an engine fault, or pilot error, or any one of a hundred other unverifiable factors!'

'You said I was getting paranoid.' Mphahlele nodded. 'But you may have a point.'

'And that same point applies if I stay on Dimetos,' Bernice added. 'If I'm low profile I can be wiped out and it won't even make the headlines. I don't want my death to be a half-column news item tucked in next to the weather forecast –'

'You'd rather go out in a blaze of glory?'

'I'd rather not go out in any kind of blaze. Alex, see sense. If the Cooperative is part of the puzzle, by facing them off we're telling the Dimetan government that we know what they're up to. You said as much yourself. If all this is news to Mastaba and his friends, we're still protected because then they'll be on our side.'

'You are assessing an alien psychology from a human perspective,' Mphahlele replied. 'Also, making this move constitutes a state of change in a finely balanced situation. What you intend doing, Benny, is tactically dangerous.'

'Yeah, where have I heard that before?'

They were approaching the centre now and the hover car was descending towards one of the illuminated landing parks.

'It all comes down to the fact that I travelled to Dimetos to help Lizbeth. And although the position has changed considerably in a short time, that part of it still applies. She's still at risk. She still needs my help. I think going to the Bantu delegation will improve our position.'

The vehicle settled on its stasis fields and the canopy lifted away like beetles' wing cases. Mphahlele and Bernice strode swiftly across the lawn towards the hotel where the Bantu Cooperative was staying.

'After all I've said!' Mphahlele complained, his voice rising angrily. 'Despite the threat to your safety, you're still going ahead with your hare-brained scheme!'

'Yep.'

'But why?'

'Because I feel like it,' Bernice said, fed up with battling over the same ground.

Mphahlele placed himself in front of Bernice, forcing her to stop. 'Very well,' he said. 'But I insist that you take precautions.' He reached into his jacket for a black metal case. From this he took a small transceiver, which he fitted inside Bernice's locket alongside the data crystal. Then he attached a small speaker to one of Bernice's drooping earrings.

'Where did you get this from?' asked Bernice.

'Spies R Us. I never go anywhere without this stuff.'

'What sort of diplomat are you, Alex?'

'You don't need to know. Now, test it out,' he instructed, pointing. 'Walk over there and say something.'

'I feel silly.'

'So you'll tell that to the mortician, will you?' Mphahlele said.

Bernice scowled, then did as she was told, reciting poetry from the Early Ikkaban period until Mphahlele bleeped a signal through the transceiver when she was several hundred metres away. Bernice guessed that either the device worked fine, or he was bored stiff with early Ikkaban poetry.

She walked towards the hotel, Mphahlele pacing her at a discreet distance. As Bernice reached the elegant entrance portico, she whispered a reassurance that she'd back off if anything looked at all suspicious –

But events had already overtaken her anticipation of them.

Alex heard her message just as Karl Csokor appeared from a side alley adjacent to the hotel. He began walking quickly down the street, his eyes dark and staring.

* * *

'Where are you going?' whispered Bernice.

'Sorry. I've got to find out what Csokor is up to.' Mphahlele's voice at her ear was beginning to dwindle away to nothing.

'Don't be so bloody stupid,' snapped Bernice.

'I beg your pardon?' This voice was loud and unfiltered by technology.

Bernice turned, and saw an elderly woman watching her closely. With her diamond-studded dress and hat of jungle egret feathers the woman looked like some sort of exotic and aged poultry. She had two moggy-tiger hybrids on leads of golden rope.

'What are you looking at?' snapped Bernice, cupping the earring closer to the side of her head to try to make out what Mphahlele was saying.

'Are you quite all right, dear?' asked the old woman.

'I'm fine.' Bernice frowned, banging the side of her head. 'Look, haven't you ever seen someone talking to themselves before?'

The woman harrumphed, and disappeared down the corridor.

With a crackle of interference Mphahlele's voice rang out in Bernice's ear again: '– think he's going to Lizbeth's apartment,' he said.

'What?' said Bernice. 'Sorry, couldn't hear you for a moment then.'

'I was apologizing for leaving you in the lurch,' said Mphahlele.

'I need you *here*,' whispered Bernice, making her way towards an elevator.

'Sometimes,' said Mphahlele, with what sounded like a sigh, 'sometimes you've just got to make a snap decision.'

'That's what I'm going to do to your neck when next I see it,' said Bernice.

* * *

Alex Mphahlele turned down the input volume on his transceiver. He hadn't taken the decision to leave Bernice lightly, but she'd proved she could look after herself. Lizbeth was another matter entirely. If the exploding hover car was Csokor's handiwork, then Mphahlele had seen more than enough evidence of the threat the man posed. And the person closest to Csokor at the moment was Lizbeth.

Mphahlele followed Csokor at a safe distance, ready to become an anonymous tourist at the merest turn of his head. But Csokor had walked straight to a parked hover car without looking around, leaving Mphahlele to break into an undignified run towards the back of the hotel for his own.

'Come on, come on,' breathed Mphahlele as the energy harness for a moment stubbornly refused to engage, the security protocols cutting off the engines. When everything was ready, Mphahlele pushed the car into the air and, swerving to avoid a couple of kids out for a high-speed deathride, set off in pursuit of Csokor.

Thankfully, Csokor had not changed course, his own hover car – smaller than the black one Mphahlele had seen him in earlier, but no less impressive for that – skidding over the roof tops and penthouses in the direction of the city's western downtown area.

Lizbeth's apartment. It just had to be.

Mphahlele knew the various routes so well. Watching Csokor fly between the same buildings and take the same short-cuts that Mphahlele had done so often in the past was almost an intrusion in itself. This was the sacred route home from work, when home had been Lizbeth's place, her rooms and her bed. And now a man who sold weapons for a living was treading the same path.

Mphahlele could feel his pulse quickening, and he fought to control his anger. He'd let his own car drift a little bit too close to Csokor's sunburst-coloured vehicle and, not wanting to draw attention to himself, he turned down towards some warehouses in order to take an alternative route to Lizbeth's apartment.

What if he lost him? Well, if Csokor's destination *wasn't* Lizbeth's apartment then, for the moment at least, Mphahlele didn't greatly care *where* he was going.

And if it was? What would he do then? Wait in the hover car, a boiling mess of anger and frustration? What was the alternative – spying on them?

Without prompting, he imagined watching Csokor taking Lizbeth in his arms, peeling back her blouse, running his lips over her neck. That glorious chuckle Lizbeth made when she was aroused; the way her pupils dilated and her mouth suddenly seemed so very moist: all those sensations that had once been his – theirs – Mphahlele in an instant projected on to Csokor.

He pushed the image away with a mixture of self-loathing and jealous hatred, pounding his fists into the hover car's instrumentation.

He dipped the vehicle down towards street level, and turned the corner that would bring him to Lizbeth's apartment. It looked like Csokor was already there, having spurned the nearby parking matrix for the last bay right outside the tower-block entrance. Mphahlele brought his own craft to rest half a block away, and sat watching the building intently, as if its façade of chrome and frosted glass would tell him all that he needed to know.

What if Csokor stayed in there all night? How long would Mphahlele wait outside?

He flicked the volume of his link to Bernice a little higher. She was talking to someone now, a woman – one of the Bantu delegates, possibly. Everything seemed to be fine at her end.

Csokor and Lizbeth suddenly appeared in the tower-block foyer. His arm was draped around her slender shoulders. He helped her into the hover car, and seemed to spend a few moments switching the controls over to Lizbeth.

Then Csokor eased himself into his own seat, and the transpex seals clicked into place. The hover car darted into the air.

Mphahlele set off after them.

It was a kind of dream, one part of Lizbeth said; a dream of comfort and peace, of safety and of never having to be frightened or hurt again. It felt like coming home.

They drove out into the hills beyond the city, to a private, quiet place where they could stroll and talk, simply be together. Lizbeth thought this was an important thing, allowing her to get a perspective on her feelings for Karl. She had settled the hover car close to a stand of oriana trees, their delicate paper-lantern fruits glowing with a yellowish bioluminescence: the whole dell was filled with gentle veils of such light. It looked so romantic, though Lizbeth had sense enough to realize the shallow transparency of romance when set against what was happening inside herself now.

'You're very lucky to have such beautiful scenery close by,' Karl commented. He walked a few paces away from Lizbeth and their vehicle, to stare out through the orianas at the broad swathe of the city below in the distance. It was a galaxy fallen to earth, the farthest stars sparkling madly on the horizon, shimmering through distant layers of unevenly heated air.

'I'm luckier than many.' Lizbeth came up beside him and slid an arm naturally and comfortably through his own. 'This is regulated land. You need to pay to come here. The place is wrapped in low-level surveillance fields which read your ID as you approach. If you don't carry the right smart-cards, you don't come in.'

'How do they stop you?' Karl wondered. He sounded slightly alarmed, and Lizbeth smiled.

'An unauthorized hover car will begin to lose power; you have time to turn round and fly on out of here, of course – but if you carry on the car's regulators will cut in and deposit you at the base of the hills. Oh, and you automatically get booked for the trespass and fined.'

'What happens if you try to walk up here?'

'Alarms trigger in one of several security stations in the area, and the wardens come and get heavy-handed as they explain the rules to you all over again. But you needn't worry, Karl. Offworld visitors have automatic access as a courtesy. It's only the poorer native Dimetans who can't enjoy the beauty of their own planet . . .'

Lizbeth caught herself sounding bitter, and shut up. She didn't want it to be her fault if the occasion failed to turn out as she'd fantasized it many times now since Karl had suggested the date.

The date. It made her want to giggle. This was no school-girl crush. But neither – she hesitated before admitting it – was it the same kind of clear, bright and passionate love she'd shared with Alex. That had been good; that had been so good and true while it had lasted. Yet if things were finished between them now, well, so be it. But what she felt for Karl was different – different, actually, from any emotion she'd experienced before or could name. And perhaps, Lizbeth reflected, part of the excitement for her and the anticipation was this quality of not knowing. Karl was a mystery, a dark continent he had invited her to explore by the offer of his company. As they turned their backs on the city and walked slowly amongst the trees, Lizbeth thought maybe that was it: Karl was so attractive because being with him was like setting out on a holiday, and the days and months and maybe the years ahead glowed with his companionship and promise.

'Are there any sites you've excavated near here?' Csokor wanted to know. Lizbeth wondered if he was just making conversation, being polite. If so, he needn't. Simply being here with him, knowing he wanted to be near her, was enough.

'No. The latest digs are towards the eastern fringe of the city. As far as I'm aware this region has never been worked . . . There may be relics, possibly very early Eurogen Butler stuff, and it would be good to do some preliminary surveys to find out . . . But one day, not now. Funding, time, resources. You know how it is.'

Lizbeth looked up into Karl Csokor's eyes and saw them shining with a strange, unreadable light. The sense of his sheer difference struck her again very strongly. How odd, then, that she should feel so close to him now, as though she had known him for ever.

'And would you like to excavate sites on other worlds, like your friend Summerfield does?'

The idea of it made Lizbeth's breath catch. Benny had many qualities she admired, not least the gutsy way she took up any challenge. Lizbeth had always regarded herself more as the deskbound academician, earning her accolades by dint of sheer intellectual effort. She had routinely felt more comfortable with a screenful of stats than making leaps of the imagination as she held a just-unearthed potsherd in her hands. Benny didn't mind trudging knee-deep in mud, but Lizbeth had never really contemplated doing that, or enjoyed it when she had to. But as to the future? Well, why not? Why shouldn't she do just what she felt like doing; be exactly who she wanted to be?

'Do you know, Karl, I think I would.' The note of determination in her own voice cheered Lizbeth enormously. 'Yes . . .' Her mind was leaping ahead into the future, envisioning herself breaking the seals of a tomb of some alien king beneath a faraway sky. It was, for the brief moment the image existed, exhilarating, a reminder of her true aspirations before events had conspired otherwise.

They had strolled some little way from the hover car and

the oriana grove, moving out of the trees' natural glow on to gloomier ground. Lizbeth's foot caught on a stone and she stumbled suddenly. Karl tensed as he supported her and stopped her from falling.

'Karl, I'm not sure I –'

'We could go on a bit farther,' he insisted. 'I'd like to see the stars . . . It is such a wonderful night.'

She couldn't argue with that. After the recent rains, this spell of fine, warm weather was welcome, and the balmy, sweet-scented summer nights were one of Dimetos's finest and most delicate treasures.

The land rose more steeply, and there was a narrow track, just visible, twisting up through the rocks and billowing purplish tufts of velvet heathers. Their musk was very strong in the windless air.

Csokor took the lead, guiding Lizbeth along until they reached a flat limestone shelf that formed a natural vantage point giving a wide prospect to the south. Of Dimetos's two natural satellites, only one, the minor moon, was visible low down in the east, like a dim, bluish coin lying on the bottom of a pond. Its light did not detract from the splendour of the stars, swarms of them dusting the heavens, gathering to a bright nucleus, like a ghost moon.

'It's lovely, Karl. Thank you for suggesting it.'

Lizbeth had wanted to go on and say what a welcome change this was to having her head buried in a book, or bent over some screen digesting data. It was true that the dig, together with all of the other recent complications in her life, had taken their toll. After losing the baby, and then Alex, she had felt emotionally drained, so that the world looked dull and grey and pointless, reflecting her mood. To do this now, to take time simply for herself, to sit and gaze at the stars, was no luxury, she suddenly understood, but an absolute necessity for survival.

Her own thoughts, drifting slowly through, were making

her uncommunicative. And she could see the same had happened to Karl. He was staring upwards, his mouth slightly open, letting the starlight pour in. Lizbeth realized that her eyes were adjusting to the night, becoming sensitive to the dimness ... And yet surely the dark was playing tricks on her? As she studied Csokor more closely, it seemed as though his skin was moving; not obviously, but with a subtlety suggesting that the very cells were teeming like a busy hive, second by second maintaining his overall form.

It was an absurdity, of course. And as Csokor moved, shifting his weight to lean on his left hand, the illusion was lost and he was just Karl Csokor again, handsome and exciting and silvery beside her.

'So many different planets out there,' he murmured. 'So many unique and alien peoples . . . each with their own story of becoming.'

'You mean mythology?'

He glanced at her with his fathomless, haematite eyes.

'Mythology makes it sound like a product of the imagination. But the core stories of all races, of their creation and final destiny, must have some basis in truth . . .'

It wasn't an idea Lizbeth had ever really considered, not deeply anyway. But it occurred to her now that if her job was to bring to light the pages of a people's history, then somewhere there had to be a first chapter, and a first page of that first chapter, lying buried deep down in the stones of the earliest times.

'Well,' she said, 'perhaps . . .' Profound discussion of this or any other topic – with the exception of their own future – seemed out of place.

Csokor grinned at her suddenly and Lizbeth felt uneasy. The minor moon, rising higher through the haze, cast him in a cold light. He reached and picked up a small round stone that lay between them.

'We are each of us unique, Lizbeth. You'd accept that of course?'

'Of course . . .'

'And what makes us so? Tell me – why am I Karl Csokor and you Lizbeth Fugard, so that even if there existed a million other Csokors and Fugards, none of them would be just as we are, now, in our individuality?'

'Our – genes?' Lizbeth suggested tentatively. This was ridiculous. Even as Csokor was taking her through his pantomime, for whatever obscure reasons, she felt the echoes of her schooldays, of lectures in the headmaster's office, of playing the game of guessing the right answers –

Csokor made a sound of derision. 'Our genes! Simply psychobiological instructions programmed to unfold at various times through our lives, or else lie latent until the circumstances are right. They are the dumb and blind envelopes of meaning. Within exist the messages. But who wrote them, Lizbeth? And how are they rewritten to cope as the universe evolves?'

'I'm afraid,' Lizbeth said, 'you've lost me . . .'

'I've lost you!' It was almost a sob. Csokor reached out to touch Lizbeth's cheek, her chin, and she found herself cringing away, frightened now as the nature of the experience changed. No longer the stern headmaster and the slow-witted pupil, but, unbelievably, the spider and the fly.

'Karl, why are you being like this? What's got into you?'

'Beneath the genetic pattern, Lizbeth – what shapes us?'

'The – collective unconscious –'

He laughed aloud, a harsh bark. 'A crude and obsolete concept.' He held the stone up closer, turning it in front of her eyes. Lizbeth saw it was limestone, weathered at some point out of the bedrock and rounded to a pebble by the blind lapidary of an ancient sea.

'There's something else, beneath all we've said; a force that tells the rocks how to be themselves, the same force that maintains every expression of such rock throughout its history . . . built into the basic fabric of things, Lizbeth, an imperative finely targeted, infinitely precise. This stone is the only one of its kind, uniquely itself once born from the matrix of the limestone.'

'Karl . . .' Lizbeth noted the brink of panic in her voice. 'I want to understand this – and maybe I do. I've heard of things like this, ideas . . . morphic fields, spread through space and time . . . I think Benny mentioned something of the sort . . .'

'Now you are beginning to appreciate the power of what I'm telling you, Lizbeth.' Csokor hefted the pebble in his hand, tossed it once, twice, then regarded it curiously, losing himself in his thoughts. And as his attention shifted, Lizbeth glanced carefully around herself, planning the moves of her escape.

'It's more than that, of course. The Bantu Cooperative have begun to tap the forces of the morphic fields – oh, and what delightful nightmares they will suffer because of it! But just imagine, Lizbeth, fields that encode mythologies, as you would call them: instructions that reach across the light-years and down the great spans of time from one epoch to the next. What would it be like to be a part of such a magnificent destiny?'

'I . . . I don't know.'

'Yes you do, Lizbeth. Listen carefully to yourself. In your deepest heart, don't you hear a word whispered endlessly to remind you of your true and secret nature? Shiga, Shiga, Shiga . . .'

Lizbeth could make little sense of Csokor's words, but the name was tantalizingly familiar. Lizbeth's mind flickered desperately through the books she had read, the lectures she had listened to, the huge input of knowledge that at the time she had thought to be trivial and quite inconsequential. Shiga. Shiga.

'The Narayayan people of Thuba Castelani!' The answer bloomed in her head like a redemption. 'One of the cycle of destruction myths from the Thuban Zone. I remember now, Karl. The Shiga was a creature out of space, some terrible malevolence that wiped out the Narayayans. The Shiga, awesomely powerful but mean in its ways – it destroyed in order to live, but then hid itself in the flesh of other beings, waiting through the centuries until it grew hungry again . . .'

She felt pleased she'd remembered, though that small satisfaction was wiped away by the import of what Csokor seemed to be saying.

'Karl, I'm confused. The Shiga myth marks the earliest record of Thuban storymaking, like Earth's Gilgamesh. It's a metaphor – it's Yin-Yang, the balance of the forces of good and evil. The Shiga and . . .'

'And Asan, last of the Thuba Castelani race, sole survivor of the Shiga's horrific evil.' Csokor said it quietly, though his expression was tortured. He eased back with a sigh. Lizbeth became very still, not wanting to provoke him.

'You can't imagine, Shiga, the frustration of seeking you out each time you re-embody the flesh of some unknowing host.'

'Wait, you called me –' Lizbeth interrupted, but Csokor seemed not to hear.

'I only have my instincts to guide me, you know . . . And sometimes I find you again swiftly and the killing is easy. But then again it may take centuries, for you can be so elusive, so very clever . . .'

Lizbeth tensed, ready to run. Csokor's words were a madness that promised only violence. All trace of the man she had been so attracted to seemed to have faded. 'I'm sorry, Karl, but . . .' What was the old advice, humour madmen or stay clear of their crazy delusions? Lizbeth couldn't remember. 'I've got to go,' she said in a quiet voice.

Csokor still wasn't listening. 'Of course, you will help me finally, Shiga. Because one day when I destroy you, you'll stay dead. The obliteration of the Narayayans is a teaching tale, one of perseverance and the nobility of revenge. You must understand that, so that you don't go down into the darkness in ignorance.'

It was utterly impossible, and no trick of the light this time. Csokor's hand seemed to melt like a powder over the limestone pebble, dissolving it away into dust. Then, suave as a master magician's artistry, the powder gathered itself back into fingers and skin, reached into Csokor's robes, and emerged with a long-bladed knife.

'Anything more sophisticated would have triggered the security systems in your apartment, Shiga,' he said, almost apologetically. 'But then again, there is a certain rightness, and a wonderful irony, don't you think, in so simple a means of slaughter.'

Lizbeth lashed out with her foot and kicked the knife away. It clattered down among the rocks.

He lunged for her with a howl, but Lizbeth was already on her feet and running. She leapt over the larger stones on the path, finding her way by instinct and fear.

She ran with the image of Shiga, destroyer of worlds, in her mind. It was a monstrous shadowy thing, harpy-like but in other ways beautiful beyond imagining.

She dared not imagine Csokor at her back – his driven eyes, his fixed expression. Her breathing was harsh and ragged now, blocking out any sound of pursuit.

As she ran through the oriana grove, she turned to look for Csokor, hoping that she might spot him as a tiny figure still struggling up among the rocks.

Instead, she screamed at the sight of the looming, surging mist that came sweeping towards her, as silver grey as his eyes, ghostly with the form of his face and its smile of vengeance.

IN PRAISE OF TEARS

Extract from the diary of Bernice Summerfield

At first, everything seemed to go alarmingly well. Which, I reckon, is reason enough to get nervous.

I strode into the hotel reception, and asked to speak to Mas-ta-ba-gal-gal-al-Kharatani *now*, if not sooner. When the young woman behind the desk (a different one; I hoped they hadn't sacked the other girl, or taken her away to be used as a human carpet or something) started to prevaricate I snapped, 'I know his secret. I need to talk with him.' I then gave her a knowing wink, as if she ought to know the secret, too.

Mastaba turned up soon enough.

I've always been taken with the idea that the quickest way to clear a lecture theatre is to shout at the top of your voice 'Quick! The secret's out!' Of course I've never tried it, but the point is, everyone has a secret. And, it seems to me, the more important you are, the more secrets you have. And I reckoned that Mastaba must register at least 8.7 on the skeleton-in-the-closet-ometer.

Even so, he greeted me warmly, almost purring like a cat. 'So good to see you again . . . even if you do employ a most

165

melodramatic method of getting my attention.'

The leader of the Bantu Cooperative delegation on Dimetos was flanked by four dark-suited figures. One was (almost literally) an ape; the second was a human, augmented to such an extent that he really did seem as wide as he was tall. The other pair were small and tall, and looked strangely familiar. It was Laurel and Hardy, fresh from their swim in the marina, no doubt.

Which either meant that Mastaba was wanting to put his cards on the table or, more likely, that he was keen to remind me of the pitfalls that awaited anyone who crossed him.

Extract ends

'We needed to talk,' Bernice said.

'Indeed.' Mastaba forced his lips into a sly smile as he waited for Bernice to make the first move.

They sat at a small, round table in a quiet area towards the back of the hotel. Fronds of palmlike trees concealed them from scrutiny, but the four thugs patrolled the area relentlessly, trying not to look conspicuous. Although, Bernice thought, they wouldn't have looked any more conspicuous if they'd had 'I am not a sinister goon' stamped on their foreheads.

'I'd like to be very honest with you,' Bernice said, after concluding that she knew so little of the truth that lying about *that* would only get her still more confused.

'Honesty is policy, where the Bantu Cooperative is concerned,' said Mastaba.

'I know that you've been trying to kill me.'

'No,' said Mastaba immediately. 'No, that is not quite how I see it.'

'Our hover was deliberately attacked at the marina.'

'The truth is, friends of the Cooperative asked us if we would – how can I put this? – assess your abilities under pressure.'

'That sort of pressure I can do without.'

'As you say. Unfortunately, my minions were somewhat overzealous in their pursuit of you.'

Bernice could sense the tall man and the fat man shrinking still further into the shrubbery. She paused for a moment, reflecting on Mastaba's sudden openness. Such incriminating truthfulness does not come without a price or an agenda, somewhere. 'Hang on a minute,' she said. 'What's to stop me recording this and going to the security forces with your confession?'

Mastaba laughed. 'To my mind, there are two reasons why that would be a most precipitous course of action. Firstly, you won't be able to, because we've scanned you for recording equipment and the like, and have found only a simple two-way transceiver. We've been blocking all outgoing signals since this conversation began.' He paused, the sort of self-satisfied smile on his face that Bernice really felt like rubbing off. With the broken end of a bottle, for instance.

'Secondly?' she prompted.

'I am afraid that the Dimetan security services are among the very best friends the Cooperative has on this planet.'

'Meaning: they put you up to all this?'

'Meaning: that they would hardly prosecute us for following a governmental agenda.'

'Neat,' said Bernice. 'So, the minister's son . . .?'

'Dealt with,' said Mastaba, as if he was referring to a memo that needed shredding. 'The friends of the Cooperative really are most grateful to you. They had been aware of security lapses for some time. In following you, they were led straight to the culprit.'

'What happened to him?' Bernice asked. In her headlong pursuit of the truth she had almost completely forgotten that individual lives were at stake. She remembered the young man's charm and warmth: for all his faults, and unlike her current company, his heart seemed to have been in the right place.

'I do not know. That at least is not of my concern.'

'And yet you're happy to supply some thugs to do the job?'

'If this comes to light, far better that the security services are not directly involved. Sometimes friendship means a willingness to be a scapegoat.' He paused, drumming his fingers on the tabletop. 'Of course, I use the word "if" merely to make a point. I am sure that none of this will ever come to light.'

'Which is why Katri tried to kill me.'

Mastaba shook his head. 'Again, I feel the reality is rather different from your perception of it. *You* took it upon yourself to meet Katri again. We initiated nothing.'

'I bumped into him in a corridor.'

'Yes, I know. You were looking for Karl Csokor, were you not? Anyway, Katri took it into his head to try to kill himself – and you – with one of our weapons.' Mastaba spread his hands wide on the table, palms uppermost as if to show that he had nothing to hide. 'I cannot think why he did that.'

'Oh, come on! You didn't order him to try to kill me?'

'No.'

'I don't believe you.'

'Believe what you will. The Bantu Cooperative prefers alliance to conflict.'

'But conflict is good for trade.'

'Perhaps.'

'Before he detonated the bomb, he spoke of personal failure – that he had said something to me during our first meeting which he should not have.'

'Really.' Mastaba tried to sound bored, but Bernice was unconvinced by his acting skills. Only later did she realize that he was using reverse-psychology to get her to say what she knew.

'I think it was something to do with your weapons testing

facility.' It had suddenly occurred to Bernice that this was the only thing that seemed to connect what Katri had discussed to the revelations that Lizbeth had uncovered.

'No one is supposed to know of that.' But Mastaba's eyebrows were arched like those of a delighted teacher when a pupil finally comes up with the answer to a complex question.

'Katri blurted it out. That soon the people I represent will be able to see your military technology in action, at a purpose-built location. And I think that you put pressure on Katri to eliminate me, after he inadvertently revealed that you were building this R&D centre here on Dimetos.'

'I reminded him of his error. I said no more than that.'

Bernice didn't believe Mastaba, but he seemed unwilling to do other than protest his innocence. 'Tell me about the weapons testing centre,' she said.

'It does not officially exist, so I'm afraid I cannot tell you anything.'

'I thought we were laying our cards on the table.'

'In the games we play, it is always wise to keep one or two in reserve.'

'Fine,' Bernice said, rising to her feet in feigned anger. 'Then you won't want to know what the Dimetan authorities are keeping from *you*.'

'I already know that,' said Mastaba.

'Ah,' said Bernice, taken aback. 'That wasn't supposed to happen.'

'No?'

'No. You were supposed to act all grateful, and then we'd come to a deal where we trade information.'

'I don't do those sorts of deals, Ms Summerfield. And certainly not when there is nothing on the table that I want.'

'Oh.' Bernice couldn't work out why Mastaba didn't just wind up the conversation there and then, and send her packing. Perhaps with a bullet in the small of her back, for good measure.

'I, too, am grateful to you,' said Mastaba at last. 'You see, the moment that our friends in the government said they were interested in Ms Fugard's work, but wouldn't tell us why, we became suspicious. There were important gaps in our knowledge and, it goes without saying, that can be rather bad for business.' He paused, waiting for a couple of tourists to pass by. 'We found out about the maps when you did. Our ears and eyes are everywhere, observing good and evil deeds alike.'

And with that, a small ant scuttled across the tabletop. It was the colour of quicksilver.

'The spider . . .' said Bernice.

'Unlike Mr Mphahlele, we weren't able to access Ms Fugard's data at her office, so we tried other means. And, as I said, we were observing you anyway when you met that poor, foolish boy.'

'So, now you know.'

'Now we know. We know that our weapons testing centre, which was supposed to be "presented" to the Dimetan people as a *fait accompli*, is being built on a site that the idiotic government is no longer sure is safe.'

'In my experience, politicians much prefer to ignore their mistakes and hope they'll go away than admit to them.'

'Well put,' said Mastaba.

'Tell me about Karl Csokor,' said Bernice. 'He's working for you, right?'

'Correct,' said Mastaba. 'But that's all I'm going to tell you.'

'You're not going to tell me your entire plot before you shoot me, then?'

'Who said anything about shooting you, Ms Summerfield? Although I will admit that I am surprised you are interested in Csokor. Unlike Katri, he has always been a model member of the Cooperative.'

'Until now,' Bernice said. 'I saw Csokor after the car blew up.'

'I sent Csokor and some of the others out to look for Katri and your good self.'

'I don't remember them stopping to help.'

'They didn't want to get involved.'

'And yet Csokor *has* got involved – very involved – with Lizbeth.'

Mastaba could not hide his surprise. 'He was under no orders to interfere with Ms Fugard or to continue his observation of her.' He paused, sighing deeply. 'I wondered if it would come to this . . .'

'Csokor is romantically involved with Lizbeth,' Bernice continued. 'I'm not sure she's safe. Tell me about him, or I'll go to the press with what I know,'

'As I said, you know *nothing*.'

'I've got proof that your employees have tried to kill me, and that your friends in the government have interfered with a legitimate scientific exercise.'

'None of that sounds especially incriminating to me. Bar the odd bruise, it seems to me you've got very little proof of anything.'

'The evidence that Alex and I found in Lizbeth's office – evidence that you've admitted you have been unable to get hold of – could bring down the government at least. Do you want to get mired in all that?'

'Very well,' said Mastaba. 'Csokor is of a rare shape-changing species. In addition, he has a certain . . . charisma about him. A charm, if you will. I've seen him change people's minds as if at the flick of a switch.'

'Which is why he works for you. He'd make an excellent negotiator.'

Mastaba nodded. 'Amongst other things. His chameleon abilities are invaluable. Most races respond best to a familiar face.'

Bernice remembered the physical change that had come over Katri, and wondered if he had been similarly equipped. 'Where is he from?' Bernice asked.

Mastaba paused, as if formulating a careful response. 'He says that he comes from –'

There was a sudden explosion of sound at Bernice's ear. She had forgotten that Mastaba had only jammed the outgoing signals. During most of her conversation with the Bantu leader, Mphahlele seemed to have turned off his own unit. Now it was back on again, transmitting loud and clear. *Very* loud and clear.

Bernice could hear that Mphahlele was running, and, somewhere in the distance, someone was screaming – she couldn't immediately tell if it was a man or a woman.

And Mphahlele was saying – shouting – 'Benny! Benny! Get over here! Csokor's gone nuts, and he's attacking Liz –'

And then the whole thing cut off.

Bernice paused for a moment, ignoring every part of her mind that screamed at her to *do something!* She didn't know where Mphahlele was, how she could get there, or what she could do to help.

She glanced up. Mastaba was watching her closely. Bernice had missed what he had said when the transceiver had suddenly reactivated, and it looked as if he had lapsed into silence when he had realized Bernice was no longer listening.

'Right,' Bernice said as calmly as she could, trying to force her beating heart to slow to a normal rate by sheer concentration. And trying to forget the terrifying screams. 'I'm afraid this conversation will have to wait. It seems that your obedient servant Csokor has gone mental in the head, to use a technical term that I'm rather fond of. He's attacking Lizbeth Fugard. Now, I need something from you that can track him, take me there, and – what phrase would you use? – neutralize him, if I have no other option.'

'Why should I help you, Ms Summerfield?'

'Come on!' Bernice snapped. 'One of your employees is about to murder someone in full view of many witnesses.' That wasn't strictly true, but Bernice was grateful that Mastaba wasn't to know that. 'The authorities will *have* to investigate. And the person in question isn't just anyone, but the very woman whose research the government were so keen to keep from you. There will be repercussions if she's harmed, Mastaba. I promise you that.'

'We do not wish to see our good relationship with the government destroyed,' said Mastaba, thinking aloud. 'Having said that, we are only allowed to keep civil vehicles in the hotel. Local by-laws prohibit –'

'Oh, bollocks!' Bernice exploded. 'Don't give me that. You're here to sell weapons. You're not telling me you've brought no product samples with you?'

Mastaba paused, his hands drumming on the table again. 'Very well,' he said. 'I think we have just the vehicle you're looking for.'

Extract from the diary of Bernice Summerfield

It was squat, black and murderous-looking; some alien bug bristling with sensors and nasty weaponry that curled neatly into its shell. 'Wow,' I said softly, an expression of admiration that came out before I had time to begrudge it.

'I suggest you use the scarab merely for conveyance,' Mastaba said with an evil twinkle. 'We wouldn't want you destroying a sizeable portion of the continent.'

He handed me a silver smartkey, and as I took it I looked into Mastaba's eyes and read the secret message there: that little or none of this was happening outside the frame that Mastaba and his colleagues (and perhaps the Dimetan government) had constructed. That even if Csokor was out of control, it could be a design parameter the Cooperative would use to see how we reacted.

'You've got full AI capability.' Mastaba chittered some fast commands in his native tongue and the attack vehicle stirred, seeming to come to attention as a clutch of systems blinked on and the ship's micromotors powered up. The smartkey grew warm in my hand, and when I opened my fist its metal had spread over my palm like hot solder.

'Oh, and we've incorporated nanotechnix into the package too. Don't worry. The nanocules that have already entered your body have a limited lifespan. The problem was that organic pilots were reacting about a thousand times too slowly to take advantage of the scarab's AI drive systems: it's a bit like working with someone who answers your questions an hour later. At least this way the ship can use its insight circuits to assess your responses before you make them.'

Mastaba touched the vehicle and a wing of metal lifted like a bract uncovering some lovely elegant seed.

'All very impressive, Mastaba, the perfect sales pitch,' I said. 'But I've gotta dash. A friend of mine might be dying.'

He gave me a barracuda grin. 'Oh, I think you'll find the transport will get you there in plenty of time . . .'

I jumped into the close and cosy cockpit and felt the leatherite seat moulding itself to my body. Around me lights were sparkling in complex patterns, visual analogues of the scarab's busy superspeed selftalk. Without me having to say anything, the ship lifted like a gazelle priming itself to run –

Then it leapt and the underground vehicle park became a blur.

OK, I admit I made a little girlie squeal and tried to gasp out some clumsy instruction for the AI systems to avoid the walls and ceiling – by which time we were already out into open sky and the lights of Dimetos City were dropping away behind like a bagful of diamonds tumbling into fathomless darkness.

I began to think about how to locate the source of Alex's transmission: my earring was transmitting sounds of high drama again, and it occurred to me that a ship as advanced as the scarab would surely possess a decent tracking device . . .

The attack vehicle stopped dead, paused, and shot off again an instant later at about ninety degrees to the east. At the same time a gentle womb of force contracted around me, so that all I felt was a slight and fleeting disorientation as my inner ear concluded that something interesting had happened. Simultaneously, a warm gush spread through my body, an electrochemical reassurance that everything was all right – a natural reaction, or had the teeming nanocules inside me deliberately triggered the endorphin release from my brain?

'How long until we reach the transmission source?' It was a long shot, I know, hoping the vehicle spoke contemporary, colloquial English –

'Madam, we are here.'

The ship was in my eyes and in my seeing; in my head, and in my understanding.

'Oh. Well done . . .'

The inertia dampers engaged a second time. I looked down at the city lights and was instantly annoyed.

'Bloody hell, we haven't left the suburbs yet!'

The ship reassured me with another endorphin balm, and I realized with some embarrassment that I was staring at the stars, millions of them, bright and blazing freed from the polluting city-glow.

'Above' me, startlingly close, a range of hills and swathes of woodland swung into view. I heard a scream, intimately near, not just from my transceiver: the scarab's acoustic scanners were operating, picking up the sounds of Lizbeth's fear – and Alex's too, and his anger, as he battled with Csokor.

The world somersaulted high and wide and searchlights

dazzled on, catching the action in raw brilliance – Lizbeth lying sprawled at the edge of a grove of odd-looking trees; Alex furiously struggling with a figure that must have been Csokor inside some kind of milky fog.

Alex gave a grunt of pain, swore, and stumbled backwards, falling heavily into the dust. His opponent (Csokor, or something other, something new to the equation?) emitted a shriek that was truly beyond the capabilities of any human or Thuban throat.

'She is not yours to let live. The Shiga's destiny is to die at my hand.'

That was weird enough. But then the real insanity began.

The fog that had surrounded them both began to coagulate, gathering itself and oozing into Csokor's body like a timelapse sequence run backwards. It was hard to believe. Easier to react to.

I wanted something disabling, not to destroy but perhaps to delay.

The scarab, almost static in the air like a weightless dandelion puff, dipped closer to earth, putting the thought in my mind that stun grenades would be best for the job.

'You sure about that, ship?'

'Yes, madam.'

'Enough of the madam, if you please.'

'Certainly, sir –'

And they launched, bumph-bumph, with lovers' sighs, fist-sized oval pods like little comets trailing their tails of tracer light.

The first came down midway between Csokor and the spot where Alex was lying: the pod, impact-sensitive, disintegrated instantly and let loose a bloom of sound and smoke and blinding radiance. Alex curled foetally with a shrill scream. Csokor, buffeted backwards, regained his balance and came on holding what looked like a knife.

The second grenade hit him solidly on the left shoulder,

176

and he went spinning away in a whirl of shredded clothing, crashed against a rock and lay still. A second later, that sickening fog started to rise around him and, unaccountably perhaps, I felt he was more dangerous now than ever before.

'Get me down, quickly – get me down!' I shouted at the scarab, needlessly, of course. It had already picked up my adrenaline surge and interpreted it and acted accordingly: I was at zero metres before I'd finished yelling.

The ship touched ground and opened to let me leave, like a protective fist uncurling so I could go free. But it was still doing its work: even as I hurried over towards Alex, its multiple sensors were scanning the scene across the frequency range, its weaponry poised. Waves of reassurance washed through me again and again as the nanocules inside fulfilled their function. I felt like crying, for all kinds of reasons.

'Sir, we have alerted the authorities. An air ambulance and the enclave wardens are on their way. Will there be anything else?'

'Yes,' I said. In seconds the scarab turned my thoughts into a detailed series of instructions, complete with flight path and objectives.

It was bizarre to be speaking with a vehicle that had the engines of a starship and the manners of a Victorian English butler. I wanted it to stay, but my chemistry said differently. The scarab hummed softly and started to rise.

'Ship, do you have a name?' I asked. But it was already a star in the night-time heavens, then a splinter of diamond, then nothing at all.

The sky was empty. It felt like a lifelong companion was leaving.

Extract ends

Bernice noted that the stun grenades had lived up to their

name as far as Mphahlele was concerned. He was out cold, possibly concussed. Something told Bernice to touch his brow. She did so and understood with a powerful surge of factless knowledge that his injuries were superficial, though requiring treatment. Smiling delightedly, she looked at her right palm and the smartkey which had been controlling the nanocules, peeled it off like tinfoil and dropped it to the ground, where it degraded away within seconds.

Mphahlele would be all right, and the air ambulance was already approaching beyond the grove. Bernice left his side and hurried over to where Lizbeth was lying, weeping uncontrollably.

'Don't let him near me!'

'Shh, shh. It's OK now. I think . . . Lizbeth, I think Karl's dead. One of the stun grenades struck him direct. I didn't want it to, but –'

But what? Bernice wondered. It seemed odd that the scarab's perfect control of itself should lapse and misguide the stunner. Perhaps Thuban physiology was different – evidently so, given the miasma that had surrounded him, but which seemed now to have been reabsorbed.

The air ambulance broke out from above the trees in a burst of light and engine noise: several drones dropped from the craft on cushion fields, scurrying quickly about once they were down to survey the scene and assess the situation. Bernice had heard from somewhere that such outriders were known affectionately as hot spot bots.

She let them do their work, staying with Lizbeth and comforting her as the ambulance landed and the Dimetan paramedics deployed. Two of them checked Mphahlele and Csokor, a third, an elfin girl, came over and ran a hand-scanner over Lizbeth's crumpled form.

'Shock, bruises. How do you feel?'

'Shocked and bruised,' Lizbeth said, with a flash of humour that Bernice greatly appreciated.

The paramedic smiled. 'Glad to hear it, if you know what I mean. My name's Zaniah and I'll be staying with your friends on their way to the med centre ... What's been going on here?'

Bernice caught the panicky look in Lizbeth's eyes. She said, 'Is knowing a matter of medical necessity?'

Zaniah shrugged. 'Just nosy.'

'Glad to hear it, if you know what I mean ...'

Zaniah's smile moderated. She nodded, her sterilene jump-suit crackling as she glanced over her shoulder. 'I'll check on the others for you. Back soon.'

Bernice watched Zaniah move towards her colleague and Mphahlele, then helped Lizbeth sit up against the coppery trunk of one of the orianas.

'Her question was impertinent,' Bernice said. 'But also valid. What *has* been going on here?'

Lizbeth told her as calmly and with as much detachment as she could. If it had come from anyone else, Bernice would have called it neurotic at the very least. From Lizbeth it sounded bizarre but plausible.

'When he was inside the cloud, he seemed to be so many things,' Lizbeth went on, trembling slightly as the memory hit her again. 'For a few moments he looked like the man that had stalked me, but then he was a stranger again, then Karl, then a creature I didn't know at all, a monstrous thing.'

An explanation popped into Bernice's mind. Some years before, a biopharmaceutical company called BioTek had devised an organo/synthetic hologen capable of re-creating schizophrenic delusional visions in people otherwise sane. The hologen, a heavier-than-air gas compound with the appearance of dry ice, directly affected the eyes and optic nerves, producing semi-externalized imagery directly from the most ancient parts of the brain.

'Monsters from the id,' Bernice concluded as she explained the idea to Lizbeth.

'Do you really think so?'

'Who knows? I remember reading that BioTek did some development and field testing of the drug, but then the whole thing dropped out of the public eye. Maybe the Bantu Cooperative bought out the technology and turned it into a weapons system. Pretty effective too, if your experience is anything to go by.'

'Benny . . .' Lizbeth reached out suddenly and gripped her arm. Bernice thought it was because one of the paramedics had pulled a sheet up over Csokor's face, just prior to the drones stretchering him away to the air ambulance.

'Benny, I'm as human as you are. You believe me, don't you?'

'Course I do.' Bernice felt dreadfully sorry for all this, for everything Lizbeth had suffered with Mphahlele, and now with Csokor, the mad man with his pledge, not of new love, but of terrible ancient hatred. A man who had let the black dreams of history metastasize in his own mind to the exclusion of all else. She was saddened by the fact that her own assistance had been anything but effective. And by the feelings she had for Alex Mphahlele.

'Of course I do,' Bernice repeated, to convince herself a little more. Csokor was inside the big medical transport now, while the drone team were efficiently fitting Alex up to a standard lifesigns monitor array as they moved him aboard.

Zaniah wandered back over, casually friendly now that the situation was under control. 'Mr Mphahlele will be fine. I guess he'll be unconscious for the next hour or so. Then he should rest overnight.'

Bernice nodded. 'What about the other one?'

'No ID on him that we could find. He's dead. Um, possibly one of you could supply some background to the incident –'

'No problem,' Bernice said brightly. 'There are implications, if, er –'

'I know what you mean.' Zaniah beamed at them.

'So we'll drop by the hospital later,' said Bernice. 'I think, right now, Ms Fugard also needs to rest.'

'Sure.' Zaniah went through the formality of having Bernice swipe her ID card through the reader, Lizbeth's datafile having been downloaded automatically during the handscan. 'Right, I think that's all.' She returned to the air ambulance, which whisked her away.

'I'll take you back in Alex's hover car,' Bernice said, helping Lizbeth to stand. 'What about the one you came in?'

'Karl's.'

'We'll leave it. Not our problem.'

Lizbeth didn't argue as she allowed Bernice to lead her towards Mphahlele's vehicle parked nearby.

'You will stay with me, won't you, Benny?' The note of desperation in her voice was obvious and deep.

Bernice voice-activated the hover car's systems including the home-James software to allow the craft to autocruise back.

'Of course.' She smiled darkly. 'But I reckon the powers that be won't let me leave even if I wanted to. I'm in this up to my split ends, and that's no exaggeration.'

Lizbeth's face twisted into an expression of gratitude and pain. She settled back and closed her eyes, quickly lapsing into a shallow and much-troubled sleep.

Bernice stared through the transpex, watching the clusters of oriana fruit, shining palely like hollow Hallowe'en pumpkins, dwindling into the distance.

Then her attention turned inwards as she thought of many things, and so failed to notice another craft lift like a stealthy shadow out of the grove and pace their ship as it flew back to the city.

IT'S A WONDERFUL LIFE

Max Rucca looked up as the senior pathologist, still dressed in formal suit and head scarf, breezed into the operating theatre. 'Who's the stiff?' It was the same old question, always asked with the same air of indifference.

Max had been working in the pathological sciences department of the city's med centre for six months. He had become used to the terrible black humour of the morgue, but he still could not see the dead as the senior clinicians did – as commodities or currency, to be dealt with as efficiently and soullessly as possible. It was, he supposed, a very necessary defence mechanism: the job could not be done if one paused to reflect on the life led by the individual, on the sorrow caused by the death, whether untimely or expected – not that either context made grief easier to cope with.

Max felt for the person who lay on the slab in the brightly lit centre of the room, denied even the privilege of individuality. To the pathologist, Ryte, on the other hand, this was just another stiff, another stack of biological components to examine and consider. He – it – was noteworthy only in as much as his sudden arrival had interrupted what had probably been a rather grand dinner party.

Max shook his head, forcing out a reply to Ryte's

question. 'No details have been given,' he said while continuing his prepping of the body. 'Sorry we had to call you in. The place has been swarming with security officers and government officials. They want to know exactly what happened, and they're not prepared to wait for long.'

'Of course they're not.' Ryte pulled a large green smock over her trouser suit. 'And a virtual post mortem wouldn't really cut it with them, would it? Forgive the pun.' She laughed as she removed some gloves from their packaging. 'Shame, though. The last one I performed was the highlight of the party. Picture the scene: lavish food atop a groaning table, and I'm elbow-deep in a computer-modelled corpse. Broke the ice, I can tell you.' She reached over to the drone that hovered at her side, and instructed it to begin recording her PM notes. It stamped the recording with a tamper-proof date and time marker which sounded to human ears like a burst of feedback, and then everything was ready for Ryte to begin.

She pulled a cloth mask over her nose and mouth. It contained a filament microphone, her voice sounding un-muffled as it emanated from a speaker built into the drone.

'Subject is a male humanoid, indeterminate – indeed, changeable – skin colouring. This appears to be a residual chemical process as no cardiovascular motion has been detected. The nervous system is dormant.' Ryte looked the corpse up and down, prodding here and there. 'No evidence of any puncture wounds or bruising.'

She glanced across at Max, who was also examining the body. He ran a gloved hand across the soles of the feet; the skin looked clean and unwrinkled, like a baby's.

He nodded in agreement. Just another stiff.

'The sectional mapping scan has given us a pretty clear idea of what's going on here, but I'll open up immediately below the ribcage and have a quick look inside, just to be sure,' said Ryte, reaching for a maser scalpel. She held the tip just over the body, setting a tiny gauge on top of the device with her thumb. 'We'll begin by revealing the muscle tissue,' she said quietly, as if to herself.

Max watched intently as the tip of the scalpel glowed green.

The theatre door crashed open.

Max clutched his chest and turned, trying to conceal his shocked surprise. There were two of them: one in an expensive-looking silver-grey suit, the other in informal country attire. They walked in as if they owned the place.

'What the hell are you doing?' exploded Ryte, her flushed cheeks just visible behind the mask. Max allowed himself a sly smile.

'Just reminding you of the need for a rapid conclusion,' said the man in the casual clothing. Max suddenly noticed the badge he wore on his shirt, and the ministerial designation beneath the governmental logo. Which meant that he *did* own the place, in effect.

'I'll get on a lot quicker without interruption,' snapped Ryte. 'And for heavens' sake, put on a mask or something. This is an operating theatre.'

'But he's dead,' said the man in the silver suit. Max and Ryte exchanged resigned glances.

'We're not staying,' said the minister. 'Just thought it might be helpful if you knew the context of how this man died.'

Ryte shook her head. 'That's the last thing I want. *I'll* decide on cause of death. I don't need government bullies putting ideas into my head.'

'No bullying,' continued the man. 'It's just . . . these are very unusual circumstances.'

'I'll be the judge of that.'

'And he worked for people we are keen to maintain good relations with. A sudden and unexplained death –'

'Get out,' snapped Ryte. Max wondered for a minute if she was going to aim the scalpel at the two men, but they turned away, leaving the door to close behind them.

Ryte swore, but even the microphone struggled to pick up her words. She glanced back at Max. 'Now, where were we?' she asked rhetorically.

The green light again appeared on the end of the maser device. Ryte gently eased the beam on to the body.

The two men strolled through the medical centre corridors. The lights had dimmed and the wards were silent but for the low hum of machinery. Only an occasional nurse drone crossed their path.

'What do we do now?' asked the man in the bright grey suit, his nose wrinkling at the sharp, antiseptic smell that seemed to be everywhere.

'We wait.' The minister pushed open a door, revealing a brightly lit computer room. From here the medical systems of the entire centre could be monitored. There was a single doctor on duty, dwarfed by the wall-covering screens, his face obscured by a book. The controlling software would alert him if there was a problem quickly enough.

He glanced at the men, then returned to his novel.

The minister adjusted the controls beneath one of the displays.

The woman's clear voice came through a speaker built into the screen: '– external evidence of tissue damage to any of the major organs. Some necrotic tissue attached to the kidneys, but it seems possible that –'

The minister lowered the volume a little, smiling at his companion. 'We can hear the pathologist's conclusions from here. No point watching all the gore if we don't have to.'

'I'll be glad when we're through,' said the suited man, fingering his collar. 'Can't stand hospitals.'

'Don't tell me: they're full of ill people.'

'Yeah. Who is this guy, anyway? Why's he so important?'

'If you don't understand now, you never will.'

'Yeah, but ...' The suited man lapsed into silence for a moment, watching the lights from countless read-outs splashing droplets of bold colour over the room's spartan furniture. 'How are you feeling?' he asked at last.

'Fine,' said the other man automatically. Then he caught the real intent behind his companion's words. 'Why do you ask?'

'I was sorry to hear about your son.'

The minister's warning look was like a distant rumble of thunder. 'Don't,' he said quietly. 'Just ... don't.'

The suited man sighed, inclining his head to one side as he tried to read the back of the doctor's book. 'Sorry,' he said at length. 'Just want the time to pass.'

'We'll be away from here soon enough. We've just got to –'

A terrified scream fractured the air. The doctor dropped his book to the floor; all three men jumped to their feet.

For a moment it was impossible to establish where it had originated; then, with dumb disbelief, the minister nudged up the volume of the autopsy report.

There was another shrill cry, which collapsed into choking silence.

The government men ran from the room.

The man's skin swirled like fog. His eyes were blank, then dark, then full of blinding light. Finally, everything ... *settled*. Only then did he remember to stop screaming.

The pain subsided, helped by the anger he had unleashed. His mind, for a moment, was empty. Then came a rush of contradictory information, more than his consciousness was designed to cope with:

I left the woman behind. Why? I can barely remember. It was long ago ... But I feel the emotions again, surging over me, wave after wave ... But I can name few of them now.

186

So much has changed. I remember the black ships as they descended, and the pain that they brought. My world, dwindling into infinity. Then years of movement and torture and biomechanical tampering; unending, unremitting decades of pain, with scant hours of senselessness in which to prepare for the next ordeal. Then, one glorious day, I remembered nothing . . .

Induction was the proudest moment of my life, though I knew many viewed the Cooperative with contempt. But what better way to explore my Thuban heritage than to swear obedience to the unarguable tenets of the Bantu creed? I remember the modest ceremony in an uncluttered room; militaristic flags pinned to the walls, simple plaques commemorating the founders. With the ceremonial dagger, I pledged myself to the Cooperative, and they to me. An undying devotion and dedication. I lost myself in true selflessness. And then my journey began . . .

I am Asan, last of the Narayayans. My purpose is to find the Shiga, to love her, and then to abuse that love by ripping out her heart, and choking the breath from her throat – to re-enact what that once great creature did to my entire race. With each death, she dwindles; as each passing life falls from her, her ability to resist dwindles. She resurrects, as do I. She tries to flee, but I am always at her back. Watching, waiting – and, when the time is right, I fall in love, and then I kill her. Again and again and again. Until she dies . . .

'Who am I?' he asked.

He let the doors close behind him, and breathed deeply, his face showing disbelief and fear. Then he held out his arms. The sleeves of the light jacket were a little too short, leaving much of his well-muscled lower arms exposed. He stared at his wrists and hands as if amused by something. He watched as a miasma seeped from his skin. Muscle tone changed, bones began to re-form. Within moments the jacket fitted him perfectly. It was as if he had always owned it.

He paced the corridors, still buttoning up his shirt. The incision had been deep, but the violation he had felt was beyond expression. He rubbed his lower chest absent-mindedly, feeling organs pull back into place, cells knitting together, ribs restrengthening their protective cage. Anything could be mended, in time.

Well, almost anything.

He was approaching the reception area when a voice halted his progress. 'Excuse me, sir?'

It was a security officer, a firm-faced man carrying a slim palmtop.

'Can I help you?'

The officer broke into a smile, as if delighted by such simple politeness. 'I was just wondering if you were with the government delegation?'

The man nodded. 'Yes, though I'm off to attend to matters elsewhere now.'

'All sorted, then?'

'Indeed.'

'I heard the screams,' said the security officer. 'Wondered what the hell was going on.'

'It's quiet enough now,' said the man. He nodded curtly, and walked towards the exit.

Just for a moment there was a crackle of silver energy around him, but the guard had already turned away.

The government men pushed open the door to the operating theatre. The room beyond was in a terrible mess, machines pulled over and the slab-like table resting on its side. A hand reached up from the clutter of smashed fibre optics and plastic fragments, the fingers set in an ironic wave.

The suited man clattered over the synthetic scree, pulling at the wreckage that surrounded the arm. The hand was resting against a storage locker and the attached body was motionless. 'It's the woman,' he called over to his companion. 'The pathologist. I think her neck's been broken.'

The man in the casual clothing had spotted a second figure, a pale beacon in the shadowy corner of the room. It was a young man, stripped half-naked and, seemingly, dropped on the floor again from a height. His arms and legs stretched away from his skinny-looking body in random directions. His white skin, peppered with small bruises, was clammy to the touch.

'Damn,' said the minister. 'He's gone.'

'Who?'

'Our merchandise.' It was a different voice, from the doorway. Three enormous figures stood there, dressed from neck to foot in black. It was impossible for the moment to establish which of them had spoken.

'Sorry?' said the minister, getting to his feet and striding over towards the newcomers.

'How far did you get with your analysis?' The central figure spoke, his head swinging around to gaze upon the minister. 'The Cooperative does not appreciate attempts to back-process our technology.'

'Your name's Sharat, right?'

'Correct.'

'Well, as we told your leader, Sharat,' said the minister, 'we were about to carry out a standard post mortem. We were as puzzled as you were by the unexpected death of your employee. As you are our guests on this world, we felt in some way responsible.'

'Responsibility does not explain why you ignored Mastaba's request *not* to perform the autopsy,' said one of the Bantu delegates.

'Or why our attempt to follow the body from the scene of the accident was . . . interrupted . . . by your own security forces,' said Sharat.

'We put an immediate cordon around the hillside,' said the Dimetan in the silver-grey suit. 'I'm sorry if you were . . . inconvenienced.'

The delegates from the Bantu Cooperative stood motionless in the doorway, three slabs of deeper darkness against the twilight of the corridor beyond.

The minister held his hands up, a calculated gesture of openness. 'Look. You can see we weren't trying to keep anything from you. Our only concern was the unexplained death of your employee. We want to ensure it does not happen again.'

'He was not our employee,' said Sharat. 'Or, rather, he was that and more. We suspect that you already know this.'

The minister shook his head firmly. 'No. No, I wasn't expecting any of this.'

'I am told that Mr Csokor has something of a history of mental illness,' said Sharat, as if noticing the two corpses for the first time.

'And a history of coming back from the dead?' queried the minister.

Sharat smiled lightly. 'Excuse me. We must retrieve what is rightfully ours.' Then all three delegates turned as one and walked back down the corridor.

Alex Mphahlele ebbed – vaguely – back to consciousness. There appeared to be a myopic film over his eyes, and his throat was locked solid, as if something had crawled into his throat. And died there.

He pushed himself up with his elbows, staring in panic at his blurred surroundings.

'Wha–'

His voice faded to a croak after a single syllable, but it was enough to attract the attention of one of the ever-vigilant med drones. It skipped over towards him, emitting some sort of sensor field to check on Mphahlele's life signs.

It was like being gently tickled all over.

Mphahlele scanned the room – a hospital ward, clearly. He didn't remember being brought here, but maybe if he worked backwards from his present location ... Yes, a blur of corridors and speed lifts, some sort of air ambulance. A hillside. He remembered the smell of damp ... grass? Something sweetly scented, as if with herbs. A camomile variant, possibly. And he had rested there, just for a moment, breathing in the perfumed, dewy moisture. Rested? No, he'd been knocked down ... thrown down, hit by ... some sort of attack vehicle, like a rounded beetle.

And Csokor. Yes, it was all there now, every piece, in the right order. Csokor had been screaming some incredible mythological madness at Lizbeth, threatening to –

Lizbeth.

Mphahlele sat bolt upright just as a human nurse appeared on the ward. Her eyes were on him, unflinching with their *don't even think about it* stare.

Mphahlele ignored her and rolled over – every fibre of his body screaming in protest, and just for a moment he wasn't even sure if he had cried out in pain – and reached for the bedside cabinet. His fingers scrabbled at some sort of lock; he was so confused he couldn't even work out if it needed a retina print or a password or just a plain, solid key.

His vision flashed to white – he definitely cried out this time – and he wondered if his eyesight was giving up the ghost again. Then he smelt something – a cologne, perhaps, but somehow utilitarian and splashed with flowers at the same time – and strong arms began to ease him back towards the bed.

The nurse looked down at him. She was a being from heaven, dragged down by the cries of a starving man in the desert. A halo of short dark hair, eyes the colour of dew-encrusted apples, lips like candy and sugar, a just hinted-at cleavage to drown in. For a moment, in the junky madness of painkillers and pain, Alex Mphahlele thought he had found love.

Then something like sanity washed over him, an anti-adrenaline buzz of sudden calmness. He swore under his breath.

'You see?' said the nurse. It was as if she had been talking for an age. 'You're not fit for anything.'

'I wouldn't say that,' said Mphahlele.

The nurse tutted and got to her feet; the last fragment of the spell was ripped aside. She was nice, yeah – but nothing special. Not like Lizbeth.

Then he remembered why he'd nearly fallen out of bed, and what was at stake – that Lizbeth was relying on him, even if she didn't realize it yet. 'Nurse?' he said. Inside his skull, his voice sounded like a startled bullfrog.

'Yes?'

'The man who was brought in with me . . .' He remembered that much; arriving at the same time as Csokor. Or Csokor's body, at least.

'Yes?'

'He's dead, right?'

The woman looked puzzled, and turned away from him. Then she glanced over her shoulder. 'Well, you know what they say about rumours of death . . .'

Mphahlele slid from his bed, pounding on the bedside locker.

Lizbeth slumped into an enveloping armchair. It wheezed like an asthmatic old man, sending up an invisible plume of Always Smell New fragrance. For once, the scent was irritating, and Lizbeth stifled a sneeze. But then, anything and everything seemed to irritate her at the moment.

Her apartment – with its little luxuries and wilfully imposed idiosyncrasies – had felt like home for months, but now it was violated. It was like the desecration wreaked by a petty thief, but the damage was entirely internal. She had let a monster into her rooms and into her life, and he had betrayed that trust with . . . what? Violence and insanity, at the very least. She looked around at the personal space that had once offered security but now seemed full of vengeful, violating ghosts.

Thank God Bernice was still around, a reassuring presence in a world turned upside down. Lizbeth watched as her friend fiddled about in the kitchen, making drinks or something. An auto-pilot response to unexpected adversity. Well, this might be par for the course for an adventurer like Bernice, but it was something new and frightening to Lizbeth. She wanted her old life back – a life before governmental conspiracies and cover-ups, before inhuman boyfriends with sudden revelations of insane mythologies. She thought, just for a moment, of Alex's strong arms around her and the simple protection they offered. Then she pushed those feelings away.

Lizbeth looked up as Bernice handed her a cup of something hot and sweet-smelling. 'Why do you think the knock-out weapons killed . . .' Lizbeth sighed, her voice fading to nothing. Even now, she couldn't bring herself to mention Csokor by name – if, indeed, that was his name. It seems like he'd lied about most things – or been guilty of deluding himself, which, perhaps, was worse.

'Maybe he's even less human than he appears,' speculated Bernice. 'I guess the Bantu Cooperative only test their merchandise on bog-standard humans or the more common human derivatives or equivalents. Each species will react to things differently.' She took a cautious swig from her coffee. 'This is going to sound so inadequate, but I'm sorry all this happened.'

'My taste in men, eh?' Lizbeth forced a smile. 'I suppose whatever-he-was counts as a man.'

'Barking insanity is part of my preferred definition of

masculinity,' said Bernice.

'Insanity . . .' Lizbeth turned the word over in her mind. Yes, of course Csokor had been mad – it really was as simple as that. He was a twisted and sad individual who quite possibly was not responsible for his actions, and – though any death is regrettable – perhaps it was as well that it had all ended as it had. Yes, it was some sort of merciful release. And she was fine, wasn't she? She'd looked into the eyes of a madman, and lived to tell the tale.

Then Lizbeth remembered those eyes, burning with hatred and desire as Csokor told his story of the Shiga, of the reincarnating quest to love and destroy that spanned a thousand worlds and ten thousand years. Eyes that flickered like flames, fuelled by truth and self-loathing – eyes that *believed* every word he said, because they felt like the truth.

'I suppose,' said Lizbeth in a quiet voice, 'that what he said would explain a lot of things.'

'Sorry?'

'This story about me being the Shiga. It might explain why I had a miscarriage. Humans and Shigas don't mix!' Lizbeth's laugh was brittle and carried little warmth, as false as an undertaker's compassion.

'Oh, come on,' said Bernice. 'Some things just happen. That's all there is to it.'

'Nothing *just* happens,' said Lizbeth. 'The madness that drew me to Csokor – that must have come from somewhere.'

'Earlier,' said Bernice, '*you* were the one who was adamant that you were human, that Csokor was just deranged.'

'But who's to say I was right? Have you ever looked inside yourself, Bernice? Seen the heart and lungs and ribs that would prove that you are human?'

'Now you're just being silly.'

'Am I?' Lizbeth placed the cup on a table. 'And if we can't really be sure what we are biologically, who's to say what the truth is up here?' Lizbeth tapped the side of her head.

'The scarab homed in on just one unusual life sign,' said Bernice.

'But you weren't looking for two, were you?'

'Well, no. But the point is –'

'The point is I'm just not sure about anything.'

'So you believe all that bollocks about the Narayayans?'

'*No*. No, of course not. What Csokor said is absurd. I pity him. It's just . . .' Lizbeth got to her feet, pacing the room in confused frustration. 'Oh, I don't know, Benny. I haven't felt this worried since . . .'

'Since?' prompted Bernice.

'It doesn't matter,' said Lizbeth. 'Some other time.' She turned towards the door. 'Come on, we'd better go and check that Alex is OK.'

Bernice nodded. 'Built like an ox, though, is our Alex. He'll probably be conscious by now. Flirting with the nurses already.'

Lizbeth caught a glimpse of the sudden, resigned *why can't I keep my big mouth shut* look on Bernice's face just before the apartment's main screen chimed the arrival of a guest in reception.

'Who is it?' Lizbeth asked.

The screen dissolved to show a grinning black face. Lizbeth fought back the simultaneous temptations to laugh and cry and whoop for joy and dive for the sofa.

'It's me,' said Mphahlele, shoving his eye right up to the tiny page drone down in the foyer. That part of his face ballooned in size, like a face in a trick mirror or a cartoon character about to explode.

'We were just talking about you,' said Bernice.

Mphahlele smiled at this. 'I *like* being this popular,' he said.

'They let you out pretty quickly,' said Lizbeth, keying

in the sequence that would start the lift moving to her apartment.

'Yeah. They said I'm fine.' The screen clicked off, but moments later the voice continued, for real, from the hallway. 'To prove it, I'm here.'

Mphahlele strode into the room, still smiling.

Then the delight vanished from his face, like someone switching off a light. 'You thought you could evade me so easily, Shiga?' he asked.

Mphahlele's form faded, became something less substantial, a generic humanoid shape of plasma and fibre and flickering light. The mist stabilized momentarily, and from it came Csokor, his eyes bright with fury.

Bernice threw herself at Csokor; a bludgeoning fist shattered into her face, knocking her unconscious. In one sweeping, impossible movement, Csokor was upon Lizbeth, hands around her throat. 'Time to die again,' he said.

High above the surface of Dimetos, the scarab was daydreaming. Unlike most organic beings, the attack vehicle's mind was constructed as a parallel consciousness; it could attend, quite deliberately and simultaneously, to many hundreds of different tasks. So that even as it primed its weapons systems to take out the designated target quickly and cleanly, a different part of its mental field was reciting Antaren poetry, another was pondering a number of advanced equations of quantum chronodynamics, and yet another was reflecting on its encounter with the creature called Benny.

She had been . . . 'interesting' was the word that came to mind; a wonderful complexity, a bundle of contradictions so disparate that the scarab was led to wonder how she managed to function at all. Certainly her psychological landscape was more varied and colourful than those of the scarab's own creators. The attack vehicle's origins on the planet Rho Menkaliah were clear in its memory, together with the impression it had gained at the time of the Menkaliahn engineers and programmers being a dull and boring bunch. They were driven solely, it seemed, by the challenge of ever-greater technology, striving endlessly to produce the perfect machine. It was a grail quest and nothing more, the scarab mused as it updated its holomaps of the Dimetan terrain in light of a fresh landslip it had just spotted, together with a number of other more minor changes. Nothing could be perfect, because perfection itself was the supreme abstract, beyond definition, let alone realization . . .

A tiny malfunction in one of the attack vehicle's subsidiary guidance systems made itself known. Instantly the scarab's multimind deployed half a billion routine maintenance nanocules to sort the matter out, and less than a millisecond later was informed that the repair had been completed.

And even this capability, projected almost to infinity, the ship reflected, would fail to achieve perfection. Because the scarab had come to realize that it too was a bundle of contradictions, knowing clearly then that it had learnt this important lesson from Bernice. She was many kilometres away now, right on the limits of her implanted nanocules' transmission range. There were only a few million of the machines still active inside her, mainly the clean-up squad ensuring that the swarms of dead nanocules whose job was now done were being safely ingested by the body's own natural defences. In another ten minutes the scarab's presence would have left her entirely, and all links would be broken. But even before then, of course, the scarab itself would have ceased to exist as it completed the final requirement of Bernice's program directive.

Strange that, thought the ghost in the machine. Strange that a being with such compassion for life should not regard the scarab itself as alive. I think, therefore I am, the ship told itself. But although I think, am I alive? No scientist or philosopher had ever really got to the bottom of that one – and the ancient question still remained unanswered. What *is* the difference between a live rat and a dead one?

An image of Bernice chuckling about this puzzle slipped into the scarab's reverie. And perhaps from its deep subconscious the solution now presented itself. Life is not just animation or the ability to reason or reproduce. Or even, the vehicle considered, to construct an emotion it recognized as regret for all the things it had never been or done ... Life surely is the capacity to be alive, and to be uniquely alive, complete in oneself, ever growing but always whole, moment by moment re-perfected.

The scarab experienced a certain glow of pleasure at having come to this rather clever conclusion. Bernice was alive because of her rage, her fear, her humour, her essential self-like-ness; far more truly alive than the Menkaliahn technologists intent on their dead and passionless mission, or the Bantu traders who purchased their wares. For both, life was what happened while they were making other plans ...

The scarab wondered where it had heard that before. And if there had been time, it might have searched through its colossal database for the source of the memory. But time was its most limited commodity just now and, besides, its primary consciousness was being distracted by other matters.

The target described earlier by Bernice had appeared over the horizon, a complex of girders and panels set amongst a circlet of granite hills. That was good, allowing the energy of the destruction to be contained and the damage radius limited.

Applying a sizeable fraction of its mentality to the task, the scarab performed half a million simultaneous functions to ready itself – not to die, it thought a little wistfully, but simply to end.

At ten thousand metres high it stopped dead, tilted on a pivot of force and plummeted downwards, accelerating on a geometrical curve. Through the screaming air it unfurled its arsenal, pulseguns, pods of omegaviruses more effective than the strongest acids, a gravity net to help concentrate the force of the attack ... There was plenty more where that came from, but the scarab judged its strike would be effective enough. Besides, it had been brought up to be economical.

Its last act before unleashing enough energy to power a small planet was to scan for life-signs in the valley below. It found some surveillance drones, organic lower forms, a number of verminous mammals, nothing more highly advanced than a Dimetan scrubcat. Good enough. *Mens sibi conscia recti* – a mind conscious of the right.

In its first and final moment of life, the scarab felt satisfied.

A hypothetical person standing on the site of what was to have been the new Bantu Cooperative weapons testing facility would have noticed nothing until the penultimate second before impact. The Dimetan equivalent of summer cicadas were chirruping among the satinbrush; somewhere far off a scrubcat yowled a mating call, which went unanswered; the stars were out, the minor moon sailing high through veils of misty cirrus, while the glow of its larger companion was strengthening by the minute beyond the hills.

Then, perhaps, a sigh that might have drawn the onlooker's eyes upward. And was that a shadowy wing streaking obliquely across the constellations, so stealthy, so unbelievably fast? Maybe not. The mind might easily have dismissed it as an illusion.

Then the sun came out, belying the fact of the night. Ten suns. A hundred. Anything alive in the strike zone before that instant was gone now. Steel and silicrete were melting, tree trunks were spontaneously combusting in a series of loud detonations as their internal sap flash-boiled and the pressure exploded the wood. Rocks cracked and shattered, scattering shrapnel. There came a dull thunder.

Then the scarab dived into its own cauldron of flames, timing the self-destruction of its engines to coincide with the moment of reaching ground zero. There was a titanic eruption as the attack vehicle smashed through the earth and underlying rocks, plunging deep into the old mineshaft over which the weapons facility was being built, the enormous energy of its momentum carrying the incandescent ball of fire and light it had become hundreds of metres down through the crust of the planet.

Seconds afterwards, a plume of blinding superheated gases and vaporized rock surged upwards, broke the surface and burst high into the air, slowly dispersing and cascading down as waves of liquid flame lapped against the ring of hills before fading. Minutes later there was only a rash of small fires burning in the valley. By morning, there would just be smoke curling out of the char.

Something had dropped from space on that scented summer night. And its name was oblivion.

Extract from the diary of Bernice Summerfield

I've never really been able to describe accurately what it feels like to be unconscious, and then to come round. On this occasion the whole unpleasant experience was made worse by the shock of seeing the dead walk.

After Csokor had struck me – bloody hard, I can tell you – I remember hitting the floor and then nothing else for a while. There's a gap in my life; it could only have been a few seconds, but enough time for Csokor to step over me, catch Lizbeth as she desperately tried to escape him, and lock his fingers firmly around her throat.

I heard the screams first, just before my vision switched on. Then sensations crashed back in a rush: the sting of a carpet burn on my left forearm, a churning oily nausea that made my stomach clench up, and the mother of all headaches, a real blaster, like the punishment of a hangover without the pleasure of getting pissed. Oh, and I'd bitten my tongue too and it was bleeding over my hand.

I turned over. The headache shifted and got worse, throbbing above my right eye. Everything had a bright fringe of grey and red, the furniture, pictures, houseplants, all viewed as though through a poorly ground lens. Csokor and Lizbeth seemed to be struggling in slow motion, her strangled cries reaching me out of synch with the movement of her lips.

Karl Csokor, clone, revenant or avenging spirit, was in the process of murdering her.

She had told me about him, what she thought she had seen him become, and to be honest the intelligent and rational part of me had not been able to believe her. But this was not rational, and no degree of intelligent thought could understand or explain it.

He roared at her – he actually roared like some furious predatory animal, the sound filling the room to bursting, as his already greyish skin turned a darker shade of pale like some thunderous leaden sky.

Lizbeth screamed and lashed out, I think catching one of his eyes with a fingernail. Csokor howled and broke his grip momentarily, allowing her to turn away from him and stumble towards me, her face ashen, lost in its own private terror.

I scrambled up and dropped back down on to one knee. My balance was gone; it was like trying to stand on a raft pitching in a four-metre swell. Lizbeth saw me and I could see the hope of salvation light in her eyes. But much help I could be against a monster on the loose . . . He had died, for God's sake! I had seen the medics pronounce him dead, seen him taken away in a black bag –

'Lizbeth!' I stood up and grabbed for her, thinking I might drag her out of the room and slam the door and we'd run together along the yellow brick road and take the second star on the left and straight on till morning.

Our hands touched, then he reclaimed her, smothering over her with some filthy grey shawl that wasn't smoke, wasn't flesh, but seemed to be something between both. Briefly she was enfolded in his membranes, dragged back as bony hands broke through the veil and wrapped round her neck once again.

I searched round for a weapon – any damned thing! – but there was a clamouring then in the corridor outside.

I shouted out something incoherent and entirely unhelpful, to attract the attention of whoever it was, this impromptu cavalry.

They came into the room and my heart sank . . . Four or five of them, assorted off-worlders, but Bantu minions all of them, dressed in black, looking like they meant the kind of business that tended to be terminal.

On the other hand, the Bantu delegates I had met had been as fearful of bad publicity as the Dimetan government, and I was convinced that they would stop Csokor for this reason alone.

I turned towards Lizbeth, opening my mouth to speak, finding that words would not come . . .

It was not Csokor any more who was killing her, but Masta-ba-gal-gal-al-Kharatani. I caught the change just as it was completed, an obscene seething of Csokor's skin, right down to the flush of coppery colour that spread through in an instant. But Lizbeth had seen it all, and went still, held in a grip of awe more powerful than Csokor's clenching fingers.

'Mastaba' grinned as the thugs approached, and in one of the Bantu languages he chattered out a few words which made the others laugh; even I could tell they were richly laced with sarcasm. The Cooperative heavies hadn't noticed the transformation: as far as they were concerned, if Mastaba chose to throttle the life out of someone, then fair enough. He was their boss, after all.

One of the minions took hold of me and I instinctively back-kicked him hard in his balls. Except either he didn't have any balls, or they were kept somewhere else. He hardly budged.

Csokor gazed at me, and there was such profound passion in that look, such depthless emotion, that for a moment I had to turn my head away.

When I looked back, Lizbeth was trying to talk, but could not. Her face, purple and congested, was beginning to lose all expression as her eyelids fluttered closed.

Extract ends

SAY HELLO, WAVE GOODBYE

A woman lay on the floor, somewhere between death and life, a man's hands around her throat. Her attacker was crying and screaming like a lover in the throes of passion, surrounded by ashamed voyeurs made impotent by obedience and fear.

It is not surprising that only the mute witness, the dark-haired woman who had been bludgeoned into powerlessness, saw the tiny canister roll into the room.

It seemed such an unimportant detail.

Extract from the diary of Bernice Summerfield

A big grey cloud of gas poured from the blunt cylinder. It was like being in the front row of a heavy metal gig. I'd have laughed, if it weren't for the fact that my throat was still clogged with blood. And Lizbeth . . . she might not have been at death's door, but she was certainly in the right street.

The wall of mist flooded over us like a polluted ocean wave, prickling nostrils and tasting of rubber and cinnamon. Through the haze, I could see the Bantu goons coughing and retching, clawing at their throats, eyes popping like the guy in all those Laurel and Hardy films whose name I can never remember. My ears exploded with rending bursts of sound;

only later did I realize that I was listening to myself coughing my guts up.

If this gas wasn't doing us humans any favours, its impact on Csokor was even more dramatic. A moment before the canister's intervention, all eyes had been on him, as if he had been performing a solo drama in a theatre-in-the-round. But as soon as the fog swept over him – his own form, in the blink of an eye, blurring, ebbing, flowing – his hands jerked away from Lizbeth's neck. The unchecked momentum carried him backwards. He faded into, rather than hit, the carpet, but the result was clear enough: he was out cold, like he had been on the hillside.

All this happened in a second or two, of course. All this, and more. My mind was a jumble of a million voices, a thousand whispers asking inappropriate questions. Was this susceptibility a biological trait, an extreme defensive reaction to attack? Who had hurled the canister through the doorway? And what was this gas? Was it lethal?

That last thought seemed suddenly more important than the others, the neurons responsible for that gem of gut-wrenching, terrifying void-of-death insight having equipped themselves with a megaphone.

And, as I faded into unconsciousness, with the Bantu thugs falling around me like clumsily felled trees – and with another, tinier voice in my head saying stroppily, *Bugger! Not again!* – the thought came through once more.

What if this gas is lethal?

Extract ends

In the darkness, Lizbeth felt the pressure on her neck easing, replaced instead by the sensation of something being held over her mouth.

Mouth. Yes, that was important. A mouth meant a body, and a body meant a bridge between the inner world and the outer. Concentrate on that.

It wasn't a hand over her mouth. It was . . . not a fabric; no, something stronger. It encased her nose as well.

Nose. Mouth.

Breathing.

Yes, that's what she had to do.

Lizbeth's lungs began sucking greedily, and her world exploded in a blinding burst of light and confusion.

Mphahlele stood over her, gently holding the – whatever it was – to her face. Smiling. Grinning. But . . .

This was the real Alex. He had come and made everything safe, banishing Csokor, the man who had stalked her and dominated her nightmares and dreams for so long.

'Is he . . .?' she tried to say, but Mphahlele made a hushing sound and put his fingers to his lips.

'It's OK,' he said, bringing his face down against hers so that his lips almost brushed her ear. 'I found out about Csokor's escape from the med centre. He was obviously unstable and dangerous. I discharged myself, and borrowed some old anaesthetic equipment. I knew he was coming here.' He laughed. His skin smelt of honey. 'That's twice I've tried to save your beautiful ass in as many hours.'

'Leave her bum out of this.'

Bernice came over, holding a mask defiantly to her face. It was almost completely transparent, and merely softened her features, giving her jaw and mouth a glassy sheen.

Mphahlele rose to his feet. Only now did Lizbeth realize that he wore one too, flexing around his lower face to encompass an uninhibited grin. 'How are you feeling?' he asked Bernice.

She grinned back. 'Like there's an all-night rave in my head, and I've not been invited.'

'You'll get over it.' Mphahlele looked down at Lizbeth, his eyes wide with compassion. 'I reckon we'll all be OK now.'

Bernice shook her head firmly. 'I'm not so sure. I know I

need to get away from here. Possibly off-world. Pronto.'

Lizbeth coughed out a question. 'Why the rush?'

'Because the Cooperative are going to come here, and find their best boys snoring. They won't be impressed.'

'Better get packing,' said Mphahlele.

Bernice grinned. 'Almost done. Just need my toothbrush.'

Extract from the diary of Bernice Summerfield

I never like getting ready to leave. I hate packing, and I hate looking at things thinking, 'I may never see this again.' Still, the idea of another bunch of black-suited minions from the Cooperative turning up on Lizbeth's doorstep did aid my concentration.

Lizbeth kept asking – and I couldn't really blame her – what was going to happen to her. Surely the Bantu Cooperative and/or the Dimetan government would come after *her* the minute I left. I reassured her that I wasn't running away and leaving her up a certain creek without a certain implement.

We left the Bantu thugs and Csokor on the floor. I had no idea whether the latter was dead or merely unconscious, and, frankly, I had no desire to find out. In any case, I had a hunch that when Lizbeth returned, the apartment would be empty and swept clean. There wouldn't even be a fingerprint or dust-sized fragment of skin left to indicate the drama that had unfolded there.

Alex had his hover car ready for the off the minute Lizbeth and I clattered into our seats with my luggage. I took my last hurried look at Lizbeth's apartment block, and then in a blur of building and sky and ground, it was gone.

I wish now I'd been looking in another direction. I might have seen the Bantu craft following us. It brought us down to earth with a bump a few minutes later.

Extract ends

Lizbeth screamed. Mphahlele's hover car was lurching like a sleeper waking from dreams.

'The controls aren't responding!' shouted Mphahlele in frustration.

Lizbeth glanced behind; the big Bantu craft was almost close enough to touch.

Mphahlele's hover car crashed into the ground and crumpled on impact, sending chunks of cold grey earth and fractured machine parts flying high in the air. The nose buckled, the transpex canopy splintering like crazy paving.

The attacking insectoid craft came down gently over the ruptured hover car, alighting first on three legs, then six, then lowering its alloy carapace on to the stricken vehicle. The sensors and jamming equipment drooped like now-redundant mouth parts; the bug shell split down the middle to disgorge impatient occupants. They surrounded the wreckage of the hover car, shouting orders and nervously powering up hand weapons.

Last out of the attack vehicle was Mastaba, a grim expression on his face. Like he didn't really enjoy doing this sort of thing, but he had no other option open to him.

Lizbeth couldn't help but smile. Yeah, right.

The air crackled with potential energy as the guns turned in their direction. Bernice and Mphahlele were still pulling themselves from the smouldering remains of the vehicle; Lizbeth had been thrown free, and her back throbbed as if from the impact of a train.

Mastaba strode towards them, followed by a couple of anonymous-looking Bantu officials. He affected a bow, of sorts. 'I trust you are all unharmed.'

Bernice was on her feet now. Lizbeth couldn't help but admire her. She strode towards the Bantu Cooperative leader as if the henchmen simply weren't there, and stabbed an angry finger into the man's midriff. 'I'll make you pay for this, Mastaba.'

Mastaba smiled, savouring the moment. 'I think not.' He paused, casting his gaze around the wasteland in which they found themselves. Lizbeth knew they were just on the edge of one of Dimetos City's main industrial areas. And that murders could – and perhaps did – take place here without anyone ever knowing.

Mastaba revelled in the silence, in his superiority and the strength of his position. But he refused to speak immediately, like an official pretending to read a memo in order to remind the interviewee who was boss.

Lizbeth pulled herself to her feet, and, ignoring the pain, walked over to stand at the side of Bernice and Mphahlele. It was then that Mastaba chose to speak again.

'I knew I could not trust you,' he said, glaring at Bernice.

'The feeling's mutual,' she replied.

'The scarab was a splendid device. It performed well, even on the suicide strike you initiated. Potential buyers were impressed.'

'I had an idea you might be watching,' she said.

Mastaba nodded. 'It's rare my clients see the merchandise used in anger. Of course, it'll be rarer still now that the testing centre has been destroyed.'

'Then at least I've achieved something,' said Bernice.

'You have achieved far too much!' snapped Mastaba. 'You've wiped out a legitimate project that offered employment to thousands of Dimetans.'

'Cut the liberal-hearted shit,' snapped Mphahlele. 'We know what you deal in. You don't give a damn about jobs.'

'True.' Mastaba smiled, his own devil's advocate. He returned his gaze to Bernice and spoke more quietly. 'But the lives you put at risk –'

'I put no one at risk,' said Bernice. She spoke slowly, clearly trying to keep a lid on her feelings. And she was succeeding, thought Lizbeth, but only just. 'The scarab was instructed to injure no one.'

'If you say so. But then, the scarab was more than a machine. Perhaps it didn't obey your instructions to the letter.'

'It had more *soul* than you'll ever have.'

Mastaba smiled. 'I don't disagree with you.' He turned over a fragment of wreckage with his shoe, distracted for a moment. 'I can't let you leave, of course.'

'So you're not here to wish me safe passage back to Dellah?'

'Sadly, no. Although, as I have said before, without you I would never have found out what the Dimetan government were hiding from me. Your destruction of the weapons centre, on the other hand, is most regrettable.'

Lizbeth let the air whistle through her teeth. 'It was built over a bloody part-filled mineshaft, wasn't it? I'd have loved to have watched your little building vanish into the ground.'

'It was quite a sight,' admitted Mastaba. 'You should have seen the faces of my governmental colleagues ... Heard their feeble excuses.'

'Now *you* know what it's like to have the wool pulled over your eyes,' said Bernice.

'Oh, hardly. The Dimetan authorities told us that Ms Fugard was on the verge of uncovering something that, really, she shouldn't.' Mastaba stared at Lizbeth, his expression neutral. 'I'm told that you are making a habit of that, Ms Fugard.'

Bernice and Mphahlele both looked quizzically at their friend. Lizbeth fought back the embarrassment, struggling to maintain her poker-face. 'Aren't I the lucky one?'

'Lizbeth?' queried Bernice.

'*Later*,' she snapped.

'Later?' Mastaba chuckled. 'Such confidence in your safety is a pleasure to behold. You're misguided and naïve, of course, but it's a pleasure, all the same.' He clicked his fingers, and his henchmen restrained Lizbeth and the others, cruelly twisting their arms behind their backs.

'Why were you so keen to build here anyway?' asked Lizbeth. Despite the pressure on her shoulders, she spoke with a rhetorical smile, for she already knew the answer.

'We were led to believe it was a prime site,' answered Mastaba coolly. 'Dimetos is crucial to our plans for this sector.'

'No. Tell me the *real* reason.'

'Why should I do that?' queried Mastaba. 'I was quite forthcoming when I spoke to Ms Summerfield earlier – but at that stage, I was still hopeful of keeping a lid on this whole affair. I wanted to destroy the information you had amassed, before it reached the news media. A peace offering, if you will, to our partners in the government – one that would also keep our good name intact.' Mastaba walked around his three prisoners, clearly enjoying himself. 'But even the Dimetan government won't be able to explain away a crater the size of their parliament building. The truth will out. There will be repercussions.' Mastaba sighed. 'So you no longer have anything that I need.' He turned away. 'Kill them.'

Extract from the diary of Bernice Summerfield

At that point, I think I either swore or prayed. It might have been both. And I cursed myself, too. He was right, of course. My impulsive, spiteful programming of the scarab may well have invalidated the usefulness of the information stored in the locket around my neck.

What did I have to bargain with now?

Extract ends

Without warning, one of the Bantu thugs turned on Mastaba, gun raised. 'Stop,' he said, in a croaked whisper.

Mastaba was incredulous. 'What are you doing? Turn your gun away.'

211

'Answer her question,' said the man, wheezing, 'or I will kill you.'

The Cooperative guards were paralysed by this unexpected development, some even going so far as to lower their own weapons in an admission of temporary defeat. Mastaba opened his mouth to prevaricate further, but the man jabbed his gun into Mastaba's lean stomach.

'Do it.'

Lizbeth, Bernice and Mphahlele exchanged glances, baffled by this turn of events, but grateful for any stay of execution. It was only when Lizbeth turned back towards Mastaba that she noticed that the skin of the man holding him hostage was flickering and billowing, like marsh fog.

'Heritage,' said Mastaba. He turned his head to one side, as if that was all he was prepared to say.

'Heritage?' queried Mphahlele.

Lizbeth nodded. An awful stillness seemed to have descended. Her attention was fixed on the man whose gun was trained on Mastaba. 'The Bantu Cooperative has been to Dimetos before,' she said.

'When?' asked Bernice. She was looking at Lizbeth, but it was Mastaba who chose to answer.

'We were here when Eurogen Butler pillaged the planet.'

The man with the gun staggered for a moment, as if dealt a body blow, but righted himself before the other thugs could respond.

Bernice struggled to take this in. 'And your role was?'

'My predecessors also sold weapons, amongst other things. But I wonder if even they anticipated the genocide that resulted.'

'Genocide?' Bernice shook her head. 'No, hang on, there wasn't anyone here when EB hoved into view.'

'There was,' Mastaba said simply. Then he turned to Lizbeth. 'You asked why we were keen to come here. Well, surprising as it may sound, even gun-runners can ill afford a reputation as clumsy practitioners in mass slaughter. Our products are clean and safe, if used wisely. We can do without the unearthing of the past.'

'So that's why you interfered with my research,' said Lizbeth.

'Actually, it was the government who did most of the actual interference. But we too wanted the past to stay there, where it belongs, dead and buried. Compared to that imperative, the desire of the Dimetan authorities to hide from us the instability of the weapons testing site becomes less significant.'

'You were both working together, but hiding from each other the reason for your interest,' said Bernice.

'Just so,' said Mastaba. 'Our interests have a certain synergy. It is important that we can continue to work together.'

'Tell them . . .' said the man. 'Tell them about the genocide.'

'EB wanted the planet cleared, the intelligent life-forms shipped off-world. But the natives refused to cooperate. They were frightened of interstellar travel. Religious belief or simple weakness, I'm not sure. So the plans were changed. To genocide. The people proved strong in some ways, weak in others. Very proud and resilient, but very susceptible to even minor stun weapons.'

Something connected in Lizbeth's head. It was like the dawn of a great star. She stared at the man standing over Mastaba. 'Csokor,' she said in a hushed whisper.

The man screamed at the mere mention of his name. It was the most appallingly tortured sound Lizbeth had ever heard. His body came apart, literally collapsing in on itself to form a pale blue fog. From this a great red wave erupted, teeming points of light that flowed towards Mastaba.

The Bantu thugs, silenced for so long by the threat to their leader, finally tried to react; to run, shoot or bellow as their dispositions took them. All uselessly. The angel of death had been visited upon them, and as it swept in every direction it broke them, burst them, eviscerated them, cast them down into their own offal, which swiftly dissolved into the ground.

And somewhere, at the heart of the cloud, was a humanoid shape. Quite dead, as far as any standard medical assessment would conclude. But something inside him continued, urged on by hatred, betrayal and the lust for death.

The mist and corpse that was Karl Csokor enveloped Mastaba.

The Bantu leader had drawn some kind of beam weapon and was firing it wildly. The cloud lit up like a glo-bulb. Again Mastaba fired. Again. A stray reflection streaked by at a tangent and seared the side of Lizbeth's face.

Mastaba's hand clenched, his finger jerking on the trigger. And the beam drilled into the earth, because by that time the hand was severed and lying on the grass.

Mastaba reaped a whirlwind of his own creation. He shrieked briefly, once, twice, before his vocal cords unravelled and collapsed down into the dark, glinting mass that he had become.

Lizbeth turned away, revolted. Her body shook uncontrollably. Bernice was at her side, trying to hold her, to comfort her. 'It's all right,' she was saying. 'He won't hurt you, Lizbeth . . .'

Csokor discarded what was left of the Bantu leader and stumbled towards Lizbeth, his feet dragging. Amid the fog, Csokor's right hand lifted, open palm upwards, perhaps in supplication or a plea to be forgiven. And the flesh of his dead face writhed, attempting expression, and a cavernous noise emerged from his mouth – just meaningless sound, failed words that no longer had the mind to be spoken.

Lizbeth reached out and clasped Csokor's cold fingers.

'Let it end,' she sobbed. 'Let it end, and . . . rest.'

And he became a memory in front of her eyes: fingers turning to ash, crumbling down gently through the papery fragments of his body; becoming smoke within the smoke, that settled to the ground and was gone in only a few moments.

'He . . . he's gone . . .' Lizbeth said softly to herself.

Extract from the diary of Bernice Summerfield

Some of the Cooperative thugs survived Csokor's attack, as did one of the delegates. They struggled to their feet, looking about as dazed and shocked as the rest of us were.

Csokor had gone – died – finally. The remaining Bantu men were still armed and dangerous, as the saying goes. It didn't take the *de facto* leader long to realize this. 'What we have seen changes nothing,' he stated. 'Mastaba ordered your termination.' He had a gun in his hand, as if he proposed to do the job himself.

'Why?' I said, bravely (I hoped). 'You can't keep trying to obliterate what you don't like with still more force. You're only adding to your problems, um . . . what is your name, anyway?'

He told me, but I lost it after the fifteenth syllable. He almost flinched as he did so, perhaps because he could tell I wasn't persuaded by his attempt to pick up where Mastaba left off. I assumed that he was reasonably inexperienced, and I had to play to that.

'Look around you, Sharat,' I said. 'You've got a hillside littered with corpses. You've got a hole in the ground where your weapons centre was going to be, and a relationship with an incompetent government to salvage. Don't add to your problems by killing us. It will achieve nothing.' I realized that I was using similar arguments to those that Mastaba had used to justify our executions, but things had changed subtly since then. In fact, it seemed to me that the death of Csokor had changed quite a lot. 'Tell me about Csokor,' I said.

To my amazement, Sharat answered, but he addressed his words to Lizbeth. 'Csokor was a unique experimental being. He became mentally ill shortly after arriving on Dimetos. In part our own reprogramming of him at a genetic level might be to blame. But it was also because he recognized *you*, Ms Fugard. Or thought he did. Hundreds of years ago, he had . . . loved someone.' Sharat paused. His use of the word 'love' was cold and clumsy, like a businessman reading from a phonetic report in a foreign language. Which perhaps, in his own way, he was. 'I am informed that this love was spurned. And that person betrayed his world to Eurogen Butler, and in turn to us, to my predecessors. And he saw in you some similarity to his betrayer, to his unrequited love.'

'So he started following me,' said Lizbeth slowly. 'And he was then able to shape-shift into someone who I would find . . . attractive.'

'Mastaba always used to say that the ultimate weapon isn't the biggest bomb. It's misplaced trust.' Sharat smiled, his eyes faraway. 'We had hoped to keep him sedated until our experimentation was complete, but as you saw, things have escalated. The stress of returning to his home world. You see, one thing he told you was true. Somewhere, deep down in the core of his being, where even our scientists could not reach, he was an ethnic Dimetan. He *was* the last of his race.'

There was a little, rational part of me that felt a brief glow of satisfaction to see another loose end neatly tied off. But deeper down the old anger stirred, like the embers of an undying fire raked over by Sharat's words. What he'd said just boiled down to one more bleak chapter in another tawdry tale of exploitation. Whatever Csokor had originally been had ended up as a twisted mess, corrupted by the same crass commercial imperative that had riddled this world like a Swiss cheese and destroyed, near enough, the last traces of its original people. Another example of the survival of the shittiest, first law of the bungle.

'Hundreds of years ago,' continued Sharat, 'the Bantu Cooperative took Csokor – or Assan, as he was then known – away from Dimetos. "Saved him from Armageddon" is the phrase that Mastaba used. To them, he was merely a fascinating oddity, a relic of an extinct species. Like a . . .' He struggled to find the word he was looking for. 'Like a dodo, on Earth. Later, the Cooperative began researching and buying into morphic field technology and nanotechnical systems. The vision was glorious – a living being, wrapped around with billions of nanocules, each capable of slaughter; a being capable of blending in on any world or in any culture, living for years or decades or centuries until its pre-programming triggered it into action. A sleeping dragon, if you will, waiting for its command to destroy. Our predecessors tried to erase every trace of Assan's past life, and gave him a new identity. They worked on him, tirelessly. Years became decades. Eventually the scientists came to recognize that Csokor had an ability to control these various biomechanical augmentations. The original Dimetan race appeared to have the in-built capability of manipulating the morphic fields underwriting their genetic code, allowing them to change, not generation by generation, but moment by moment. We've been able to mimic such shape-shifting in a very crude way with technology. But to have it hardwired into the cells would be quite a breakthrough.'

'Except that you, and Eurogen Butler, had already exterminated every last trace of Csokor's people,' I said. 'Your laboratory rat was unique and irreplaceable.'

He didn't seem to pick up the bitterness in my words, but nodded sagely. 'Indeed. A short-sighted decision.'

And then – for no reason I could fathom at first – I thought of Katri, and the lichee, and the facial transformation. And then it dawned on me. 'You wanted to be able to mass produce the technology, apply its dubious benefits to any given species. Your work didn't stop with Csokor . . .'

'Oh, but Katri agreed,' said Sharat, picking up my inference. 'And bringing Csokor – Assan – here was our attempt at a – what is the word? – a dummy run.'

'But Katri couldn't handle the technology.'

'It seems not.'

At that moment, we heard the sirens – still far in the distance, but shrill enough to disturb our tête-à-tête.

'I would imagine,' said Alex, 'that the authorities have discovered Csokor's handiwork at the hospital. Two innocent corpses that simple corruption will not be able to sweep away. And they'll find us soon enough.' He pointed up at the dark sky, overlaid with a thin grey veil, the last smoke from the remains of his hover car.

I saw Sharat's finger tense on the trigger of his weapon.

'Don't do it, Sharat,' I said. 'You'll only make things worse.'

'Really?'

'Yes. Every scrap of data we have has been clamshelled in numerous locations, far beyond your reach. And the deadman's-handle subroutines I've encrypted with them will ensure that if I fail to key in my passwords on a regular basis, the data will transmit itself automatically right across the Dimetan net.' I rubbed the locket around my neck, as if to remind Alex that the idea had been his in the first place. 'We've got evidence of a governmental cover-up, of sabotage and intimidation, and the first archaeological hints of a pre-Eurogen Butler culture on Dimetos. It's a real can of worms. Killing us will only open the lid, so to speak.'

'There are ways of subverting clamshell programs.'

'Name one that's going to work in time.'

'Why didn't you tell Mastaba this?'

'Because I thought he'd shoot us anyway. But you don't have to be like him, Sharat. Make a new start. Let us go.'

Meekly, he acquiesced, without asking for proof of my claims or anything. He kept staring at what little remained of Csokor. I think he was only just realizing that he had witnessed the destruction of the Bantu Cooperative's most amazing piece of merchandise – and that he, as the senior survivor, would be held responsible.

Extract ends

'I've never understood why the government even allowed me to excavate at all,' said Lizbeth bitterly. 'They must have realized there was a risk of past mistakes being uncovered.'

She and Mphahlele were accompanying Bernice to the launchport. All were uneasy, as if a great weight had been lifted from their shoulders, but they had become so used to it that they couldn't believe it was no longer there.

'I said before,' said Bernice, 'and I think it's true, that perhaps they underestimated you. They really didn't think you'd uncover anything of interest – but the moment you did, they got very cold feet.'

'And doggedly refused to tell the Cooperative what was going on, which only made them more interested,' said Mphahlele. His hand rested gently in Lizbeth's; Bernice didn't want to read too much into so simple a gesture, but it was certainly a start. 'Knowing that you were somehow involved, they sent Csokor to trail you. And the moment he saw you, something went "click" in his head.' Mphahlele laughed. 'That's also true of me, of course. I think they call it love at first sight.'

'Oh, don't,' said Lizbeth. 'It's not funny. Poor Karl. No one deserves to live and die like that.'

'Or Assan, I suppose we should call him,' said Bernice. 'I guess that was the problem: he'd been brainwashed so much, he forgot who he was. Was he Assan, last of the ethnic Dimetans, or Karl Csokor, a Thuban who had elected to work for the Cooperative?'

'Or Asan, last of the Narayayans, dedicated to pursue Shiga the destroyer for ever,' added Lizbeth. 'The parallel in the names bothers me. Asan and Shiga are the protagonists in an ancient Thuban myth: what are the chances of Assan having almost the same name, and having lived a comparable life?'

'Astronomical,' said Bernice. 'But then, the coincidental similarities and differences between the shootings of American presidents Lincoln and Kennedy have been well documented. Alternatively, the other reading is simply this: we don't know for *sure* what Csokor's Dimetan name was, or what his background was. It's only hearsay, originating in a man whose mind and memories had been shredded and abused beyond words.' Bernice sighed. 'And I thought *I* was guilty of rewriting my past.'

'Could be a thesis in that,' said Mphahlele, catching Lizbeth's eye. 'I'm told the Thuban Zone is lovely at this time of year.'

'I'm told the Thuban Zone is always worth exploring,' said Lizbeth. 'Nice try, though.' She turned away for a moment, staring through the transpex as the launchport came into view. 'But to find such resonance in a myth that you come to believe it utterly . . .'

'But myths are only believable,' said Bernice, picking up Lizbeth's quiet words, 'because we feel they are, in some way, true.'

And then she shivered, because she didn't like the implication of what she was saying.

Bernice spotted the little clutch of Bantu representatives immediately. They stood on the launchport concourse, Sharat at their head, scanning the crowds eagerly. They swept towards Bernice, Lizbeth and Mphahlele with an air of casual arrogance. Normal service has been resumed, thought Bernice.

'*Don't*,' she said with firm finality. 'Just don't do anything to annoy me.'

Sharat smiled. 'My purpose here is simply to ask you, and your friend, to watch out for any mention of the Shiga in the work that you do. It is a powerful creature, incomprehensibly so. And inconceivably dangerous. Its mission, whatever that might ultimately be, does not take you or me into account, nor all the worlds we know and all we may love. The Shiga crushes worlds as we might tread on flowers as we walk towards our final destination. It doesn't even trouble to disdain us . . .'

'The Shiga's just a myth,' said Bernice.

'I have walked on Dellah,' the alien announced.

'And it rained, right?'

'Can you conceive of Dellah without rain? Without plants or animals or any living things? Can you imagine your current home as a sun-cracked dustbowl where only the hot wind moves, where nothing whatever remains – nothing, not even a warning, buried for some future archaeologist to find.'

'OK, you win,' said Bernice. 'I'll keep my eyes open. But, what if – and I *mean* "if" – I should find something?'

'Be very polite,' Sharat said, absolutely deadpan, 'and be prepared for a long journey.'

Extract from the diary of Bernice Summerfield

We settled down in one of the lounges that overlooked the furious activity of the launchport. Ships came and went against the backdrop of the city, and from here its true nature could be seen: an expanse of fairy-tale towers, surrounded by a black moat of shanty towns.

We didn't say much. For my part, I was nervous about the

flight, and about what awaited me back on Dellah. I couldn't work out why.

'Ah, I had hoped to find you here.' We all turned to see Homam walking towards us, hands held behind his back like a two-metre-tall schoolboy. His grin was even larger than I remembered it.

I shook his hand energetically. Frankly, compared to most of the creeps I'd encountered in Dimetos City, Homam Matar Sadalbari was pretty much on the side of the angels, and that was good enough for me. 'I'd hate to have gone off and not said goodbye,' I gushed.

'The feeling is mutual,' he said, 'though I understand that you've been a little busy just recently.'

'That's one way of putting it,' said Lizbeth.

Homam bobbed up and down excitedly. 'Word is beginning to filter out. Exploding hover cars. Strange events in the med centre. A big hole in the ground where a top secret building site used to be. There are already calls for ministerial resignations.'

Alex groaned. 'Looks like we'll be having an election sooner rather than later.'

'Yeah,' I said. 'I mean, forgive me for not leaping for joy, but . . . what did they say on Earth? Whoever you vote for, the government always wins.'

'Oh, don't be so cynical,' said Lizbeth. 'The next lot might be that bit more suspicious of the Cooperative.'

'Let's hope so,' said Homam. 'But, for the moment, every news channel in the city has their own slant on the whole Eurogen Butler-Bantu Cooperative-government scandal.'

'EB?' I queried. 'How do they know about all that?'

'I've not been sitting on my laurels either, you know,' replied Homam. 'The digger drones are still working hard, transmitting information. I keep having to reprogram them. My hunch is that the Cooperative have found a way of operating them remotely. More electronic spiders, I suppose,' he said, glancing in my direction.

'What are they looking for?' I asked.

'Believe it or not,' said Homam, 'the drones keep trying to find traces of early Dimetan culture.'

'Why?'

It was Alex who had guessed the answer. 'They're wondering if there's a trace of the Shiga on Dimetos, too. Because, if the Shiga's for real ... it would make one helluva weapon.'

Tears would come later, on the tedious haul home. As the final call to board sounded across the airy space of the departure lounge, I gave Lizbeth and Alex a big hug and got their assurances they'd take some time out for themselves; healing time, I called it, and I saw that my words had struck home.

'In a couple of weeks, I'll call you for an update,' I said cheerfully. 'By that time those digger drones will have come out at the antipodes . . .'

'As you saw, Homam has that side of things well under control.' Lizbeth smiled. It was a qualified smile. Maybe she was thinking that drone problems were so much simpler than the human equivalent.

'Yes. Good. Well, if I can I'll put in for some leave and come and visit you all again soon.'

A small, very irritated-sounding drone spun up beside me and absolutely insisted I board now, or risk missing my flight. I used that as the excuse I needed to leave.

In space, no one can hear you dream. I dreamt of planets united by respect and consideration for all life, joined by the urge of living things just to be, and in that being to fit into the greater plan – the one true program underwriting genes and morphic fields and matter itself.

It was a grand dream, and though I was the merest particle of flesh within that vast picture, I still felt proud, and profoundly content to be a part of it.

I awoke to the sight of stars, wiped tears from my eyes and ordered a double bourbon with ice from the comfort drone. I took a big guzzle of it and felt better. Around me was the quiet murmuring of passengers as they talked, a soft background susurration of clean air breathing through the recyclers; quiet light and a sense of calm competence as the ship streaked through space.

Beyond the portal, the universe lay waiting. There was no sense of movement at all, nor of the violence and horror that the Shiga symbolized, if not embodied. And it occurred to me then, as it had done so many times before when I'd held some ancient remnant in my hands, that the greatest wisdoms had all been spoken thousands of years ago. And among them, one came to my mind just then: that despite all our petty conflicts and schemes, our ambitions and the passion that attained them, *dis aliter visum*.

Heaven thought otherwise.

Extract ends

YOU ALWAYS HURT THE ONE
YOU LOVE

Dimetos seemed like a billion miles away. Which it was. And a million years ago, which it wasn't.

The Witch and Whirlwind was almost empty. Bernice sat in her favoured position at the bar, nursing a soft drink. The stool seemed so used to her presence that Bernice was sure it had by now moulded itself to fit her buttocks perfectly. The young man behind the bar appeared to barely realize that Bernice was there. She was part of the furniture, then. A mere nanocule in the greater workings of the university.

On her return to Dellah, Bernice had trawled puterspace looking for a definitive account of the Shiga. She found more information than she knew what to do with: if there was a deeper truth amongst all this fractured symbolism and mythology, it was difficult to spot.

She left the whole thing well alone for a few days, hoping that perhaps her subconscious would make the link for her. It hadn't yet.

Bernice glared at her drink, as if it was responsible for everything that had happened over the past few weeks. She glanced up as the bartender came over towards her. 'A Moni sherry, please,' she said.

When it arrived, Bernice gulped down the sweet wine. She imagined synapses firing, well-fuelled blips of electrical processing power jumping across gaps and reawakening whole swathes of her mind. Either that, or the sherry was unbelievably potent.

'That's better,' she breathed.

'Drowning your sorrows?'

The voice was quiet and strong, right at her ear. Bernice turned, scarcely believing that someone could creep up on her so quietly.

It was the stranger she'd encountered just before she'd left for Dimetos. The man very deliberately lit a cigarette with some sort of metal lighter that stank of ancient fuel. He puffed on it contentedly for a few moments, eyebrows partly raised as if encouraging a response.

'What do you want?' It wasn't one of Bernice's better ripostes, but it was the only one that came to mind.

'Word is you had a very unusual holiday.'

'I battled against fascists, uncovered a conspiracy. The usual.'

'Conspiracy is a very grand word to describe what you discovered,' said the man. 'If the news reports are to be believed, you stumbled upon . . . a straining in the relationship between two business partners.'

'Maybe,' said Bernice, imitating the man's non-committal style.

'Which reminds me,' he continued, 'how is Ms Fugard?'

'You know her?'

The man shook his head, the smoke spiralling around him. Bernice was suddenly reminded of Karl Csokor, of his unnerving abilities and his tragic and grotesque death. She forced away the image with a flurry of inconsequential distractions while she waited for the stranger to reply.

'I know *of* her,' the man said at last. He paused for a moment, scanning the bar intently, then abruptly turned for the door. 'You might want to ask her what *she* knows of this place.'

'Sorry?'

'You're not the first female academic archaeologist to work on Dellah.'

And with that, the stranger was gone.

Extract from the diary of Bernice Summerfield

At first I didn't have a clue what the man was dribbling on about. And then my newly recharged mind jumped to a few wild conclusions, and the colour drained from my face.

I ran back to my rooms, got Joseph to establish a governmental FTL link. It took a while, and it wasn't the most stable near-real-time connection I'd ever used, but it would do.

Eventually the Dimetan end of the link gave me access to Fugard's office, and then to Lizbeth herself. I had no idea what time it would be on Dimetos – early in the morning or late in the evening, if the sky through the windows was any guide.

'Hello, Benny,' said Lizbeth brightly. 'This must be important.'

I came straight to the point. 'What do you know about St Oscar's?' I asked.

There was a pause as the signal raced across the galaxy, and then a look of confusion gripped Lizbeth's face. She didn't try to hide it from me. That was pleasing. There was mileage in our friendship after all. 'Who told you?' she said at last.

'It doesn't matter.' And then I thought that I ought to reciprocate by being honest, so I added, 'Actually, it was the stranger in the bar. I don't know if I mentioned him or not.'

She nodded when my voice reached her. 'There's not much I want to say over this link,' said Lizbeth.

'It's secure,' I said as quickly as I could.

Lizbeth shrugged. 'So they say.' She paused. The hurt that time had not dimmed was still clear at the back of her eyes. 'But ... the simple fact of the matter is, I did an advanced research thesis at St Oscar's. This was about five years ago, I guess. I'd only just graduated.' She stared at the screen, and I wondered what she was reading in *my* face. 'I'm sorry I didn't tell you. I don't like hiding things from my friends. It's just that there didn't seem any real need for you to know, and so ... Oh, I don't know. Sometimes ignorance is safety.'

I smiled, remembering how Alex and I had come to the same conclusion about Lizbeth. 'Too late for that now,' I said. 'What happened here?'

'Let's just say that as part of my work I discovered something that I shouldn't have.'

'Story of your life.' I had a vague idea that Sharat had said something similar on Dimetos.

'Yeah.'

And that was all that Lizbeth seemed prepared to say, but I wasn't prepared to leave it there. So I pushed on with 'Tell me more ...'

She said nothing for some time, and it wasn't just the gap while the message was being transmitted. At last she said: 'There's nothing I want to tell you of all people, Benny. But the upshot was that I left Dellah with my tail between my metaphorical legs.'

'Which would be about the time you changed your specialization from ancient archaeology to industrial?'

She nodded, but refused to say anything else. I was about to apologize for disturbing her and terminate the link, when she changed the subject. 'While you're there,' she said, 'I may as well tell you about the latest research into the ethnic Dimetans.'

'Please do.'

'Suffice it to say, they had lived here for thousands of years before Eurogen Butler arrived. A complex and evolving society, with all the expected peaks and troughs of civilization and technology.'

I laughed. 'So there is real archaeology on Dimetos after all . . .'

A moment later Lizbeth laughed too, but, God, she sounded bitter. It was the sort of strange noise you make at a funeral when, frankly, there's less than sod all to laugh at. 'Eurogen Butler built over all the major sites in an attempt to obliterate the species from the historical record. And, more by luck than by judgement, the Bantu Cooperative were continuing that policy.'

I had an awful feeling in the pit of my stomach; a sense of what was coming. I resisted the temptation to look away as Lizbeth continued.

'As you know, the Bantu weapons centre was being built over an old EB mine. Unfortunately, it now looks as if below *that* there lay the most extensive of all the ancient Dimetan sites. Which, Benny, you blew into a million pieces.'

[FINISH]

Translator's note:
The Shahinitarazad Codex dating from the pre-Aludrai period of early Thuban culture is, though fragmentary, the clearest account we possess of the sidereal-mythological stories of the era, including those reproduced here. I am grateful to Christos Michaelides, Professor of Eschatology, the Grosvenor Datanetwork, based at Caph Beta IV, for his general assistance in my work of translation, and specifically for his useful speculations on the thematic links between Narayayan core myths and the Orion cycle of creation/destruction tales to be found throughout the Perseus arm of the galaxy. In time, a comparison will be possible between this mythology, and that being pieced together on Dimetos. Until that time, this translation, I hope, can happily stand alone.

Lizbeth Fugard, Professor of Sidereal Mythology,
Youkali University, 2597

> He who wants to see his time rightly must look upon
> it from a distance.
>
> Ortega y Gasset

1 – In those days even the planet was young, its name now long forgotten.[1] In the heart of that world's greatest continent, Asan, True Emperor of the Narayayans, was walking as he often did among his people. On this occasion, he had chosen to visit the town on market day, followed by his retinue of guards and advisers, and accompanied by Akiki, his betrothed. Despite the fact that Asan was well loved by the populace and felt comfortable among them, Yuanch'un his lieutenant stayed close by his side, ever vigilant for trouble.

Now it so happened that Akiki was passionately fond of jewellery, and although she possessed many fine pieces wrought from the rarest of metals, she had come to market in search of something rarer still, the fabled mirrorglass found only in the nearby Losun Mountains. Since Asan's interest lay elsewhere, in the delicious fish, fruits and meats caught and grown throughout the lush valley, he and Akiki decided to go their separate ways for a time, each accompanied by a number of well-armed protectors.

For the next hour, Asan, Yuanch'un and his men wandered through the extensive market, mingling with the crowds who smiled and bowed to the Emperor in deep respect. Presently, Asan happened upon a fruit stall that had obviously done particularly good business that day: the beds of straw upon the table were almost empty of fruit, the rest having been sold. All that remained were a few rather blemished pearl-apples and a thin clutch of andarin stalks, browning and starting to wither. Ordinarily Asan would

[1] Or deliberately deleted?

231

have simply passed by, but he found himself in an impish mood, so picked up one of the wrinkled pearl-apples, bit into it, and grimaced with distaste.

'Pah! Just look at this, Yuanch'un. This fruit is only fit to give to the pigs! Who would sell a nobleman such rubbish? Let the one who would seek to rob Asan come forward to justify himself!'

Several people and other traders nearby chuckled at Asan's teasing. The stallholder whom the Emperor was addressing had been out of sight, tidying up a pile of cloth bags. Now she stood up, much embarrassed, and bowed low in fear and humility.

'Forgive me, Emperor. Indeed, this fruit was to be given to the pigs, or to the beggars who come by at the end of the day. I was about to remove it from the stall, since you are right, it is not fit for my customers to eat. All I can do is apologize . . .'

Asan had fallen silent, though his mouth still hung open in admiration. The girl who had stepped out of the shadows was the most beautiful he had ever seen. Her skin was as unblemished as a cloudless sky, her eyes as clear as mountain pools. Her hair, long and golden – which was a rarity among the valley folk – shimmered in the sunlight. And her smile, as she caught Asan's frivolous mood and gazed at him coyly, was utterly perfect.

But even as she realized that the great Emperor of the Narayayans was only joking with her, Asan's demeanour had changed. He was now looking upon the girl with an expression she had seen before in other men, reflecting an extremity of passion and longing that neither she nor any other woman could ever satisfy. It was a look of dangerous love, and although the girl was young and only just into womanhood, she knew with a deep and ancient instinct that any relationship with someone possessed of such a yearning infatuation could bring nothing but unhappiness and pain.

'Tell me your name,' Asan demanded quietly, and she did so, feeling much afraid.

'Lord, I am Kaiagish,[2] only daughter of the fruit grower Kanryo.'

Asan nodded and handed over a small coin for the pearl-apple. 'Tomorrow, when you have better fruit to sell, I will come back for more.'

Kaiagish accepted the coin, for it would have been most improper to refuse, but as Asan and his minions turned their backs and walked away through the bustling crowds she felt despair overwhelming her, for Kaiagish knew her life, and the lives of her family, would never be the same again.

2 – Akiki too came across what she was looking for and yet had never expected to find. In one of the darker corners of the vast market she happened upon a trinket seller whose appearance, whose entire stall in fact, was grubby and run-down. Various cheap items lay piled untidily, one on top of another; ornaments, weaponry, bric-à-brac, oddments and bits of jewellery – hundreds of diverse objects, but nothing that seemed worth buying.

Akiki surveyed this array of junk with a disdainful expression, noticing that among all that drabness only the stallholder's eyes were gleaming and bright.

'Do you know me, trader?' she asked. The man, vast and slothful, shifted in his seat and inclined his head in acknowledgement.

'Then you know I am serious in my wish to purchase, and have money aplenty to do so.'

[2] The names 'Asan' and 'Kaiagish' (and variations of them) are, as one might expect, prevalent in Thuban myth. What is more surprising is that such names are found in tales associated with many Perseid cultures and religions. It is difficult to establish whether this onomastic repetition is merely the result of the ongoing popularity of these names, or whether we are witnessing the partial rewriting of earlier myths.

'Indeed, good lady.' The stallholder smiled rather revolt-ingly, and Akiki guessed there was much behind that smile for her to beware.

'I am searching for mirrorglass, the finest examples. Only a body-weight of it has ever been mined, I know, and most of that is of poor quality. I want . . .' Akiki's lips were moist with avarice. 'I want some that will shine!'

Naturally, she had never anticipated the stallholder actually owning decent mirrorglass, but a man like this would belong to a network of dealers; he would have many dubious con-tacts, someone knowing someone knowing someone who just might be able to procure, at a price . . .

The stallholder moved his great bulk, rose with a grunt and bustled about at the rear of the stall, pulling on something stuck beneath a mound of worthless rubbish. A moment later he turned to face Akiki, meanwhile polishing the object on the frayed sleeve of his grimy tunic.

'Perhaps – this . . .'

Akiki saw what he was holding and the breath caught in her throat, and her heart for a time beat more quickly. The trinket was no bigger than her tightly clenched fist, an ornate and mysterious polygonal shape made of some dark, bronzy metal, each facet inlaid with what appeared to be a flawless slice of the precious mirrorglass.

Akiki made an effort to bring her excitement under con-trol. She knew that the law of the market meant that the trader could refuse to sell her this or indeed any item, and that once he had given his decision, it was final. This was a long tradition throughout the land, one that even the wealthiest and most powerful must respect. Thus she did not want to seem too eager, or to indicate anything that might cause the stallholder offence.

'May I . . . ?'

The trader passed the ball across and laid it in Akiki's open palms. Both of them knew the value of the item; all that needed to be established was the cost.

Akiki slowly turned the artefact this way and that, trying to avoid actively staring into its many reflecting surfaces. Mirrorglass was a capricious substance, that on one day might show nothing, yet on another would reveal the deepest secrets and truths.

'My lady,' the trader reminded her, 'you should purchase the item before you use it.'

'Oh –' Akiki blushed at her mistake. 'Of course. Yes, I wish to buy.'

The trader made a small bow of gratitude. 'Then let us settle on a price . . .'

And so they negotiated while the life of the market went on around them, and about it the town and the land beyond, and the whole world in the infinity of space.

Finally an offer was made and accepted. The trader took Akiki's bag of money and wrapped up the ball in a plain cloth for her to take away. She thanked him, not too profusely, and moved to a quieter place the better to study her treasure.

The stallholder watched her leave. He had lived too long, and experienced too much that was selfish and mean, to feel any remorse for the fact that he had bought his future comfort and happiness with this woman's certain destruction.

Akiki found a quiet tent where just a few browsers had paused to rest. While her guardians refreshed themselves, she took out the mirror ball and tilted it, now up, now down, now right and now left, hoping to catch a vision of her future.

To her disappointment most of the facets were grey and obscure. Others revealed the merest flickers of imagery – perhaps Asan, though looking more furious than she had ever seen him; and was that her own face, wreathed in flowers and as pale as death? And once, just for a moment, a glimpse of a girl so breathtakingly beautiful that Akiki felt a helpless pang of jealousy and spite, without quite knowing why . . .

A little impatiently she tumbled the polyhedron about in her hands. And then was rewarded by a moving image of startling colour and clarity –

A little girl was playing in a garden, her bright yellow dress set against the backdrop of a black and thunderous sky. Like any young child, her attention leapt from one interesting sight to another, moment by moment – until presently she noticed something on a leaf nearby, leant closer –

And was astonished to behold two tiny beetle-like insects struggling together, locked in ferocious combat. These insects were unlike any that the little girl had ever seen before. One of them was pure white, with a small black dot marking the centre of its back. The other, equal and opposite, was utterly black, with a white dot marking its hard carapace.

The girl watched the battle going on: such a tiny conflict, beneath the attention of everyone but her, and yet so fierce and unrelenting. As the minutes went by, she came to feel sorry for the white insect. It seemed so clean and good, unlike the black beetle that looked sinister and dark.

The battle raged this way and that in a dance of subtle balances. Now the black insect was on top of the white, thrashing its many legs about. Then, after a huge effort, the white beetle gained the advantage briefly, before the black fought back and regained the ascendancy.

The girl had seen enough. She decided to act before the white creature was harmed or killed. So she reached out to separate the insects, intending to crush the black one under her heel. But she found to her surprise that they could not be moved. No matter how hard she tried, she was unable to draw the beetle-things apart, so closely and tightly were they intertwined.

236

She became so engrossed in her task that for some minutes she failed to realize that the dark thunderclouds were moving away. A warm shaft of sunlight on her neck eventually caused her to glance up.

One half of the sky was now clear and bright, the other half ominous with cloud. Perhaps the storm would come to nothing, or maybe it would gain the advantage and the afternoon would be rainswept and bleak . . .

There was no way of telling, of course. And then, understanding at last, the little girl left the two creatures alone, because the force that bound them was no different from that which made the day and the night, summer and winter, life and death, the stars and the spaces between.

3 – [The Shahinitarazad Codex is fragmentary at this point, and its continuity broken. Other sources – most notably the so-called Avalon Stone found on Omicron Canes Venatici VI – reveal a similar and possibly associated myth that allows us to speculate with some confidence that Asan's yearning for the peasant girl Kaiagish never abated. Indeed, if we accept Doctor San Quo Yen's thesis of a multiplanetary collective unconscious perpetuated through resonant space-time fields, then it may well be that the Omicron CV VI fragment picks up the very same story as that recounted in the Codex.

If this is the case, then we know Asan returned to the market as he had promised, but found that Kaiagish and her entire family had disappeared. Though he searched far and wide, his efforts were in vain. We can also deduce that he never stopped loving Kaiagish, and never forgave her for disdaining him. Indeed, his obsession with her increased through the years, overwhelmed him and became twisted and dark.

As for Akiki, we have no clue as to how much she knew of Asan's torment. What is clear is that, perhaps through the power of the mirrorglass artefact, she became immensely influential, eventually ruling over the Narayayans effectively and successfully for some years. She almost certainly married Asan, probably to ensure political stability, but his role in the power structure of the dynasty during this time remains unclear. As far as our researches can tell, the marriage was never consummated and Akiki lived an isolated and lonely life. Just prior to her death, she left instructions for her remains to be laid in a simple stone casket carved with the following words: *Remember me as a shooting star that blazes swiftly and then fades. People notice it at the time and remember it when it has gone . . .*

Two other extracts may be pertinent here to give the story of Asan and his love for Kaiagish some semblance of 'roundedness'; one is again taken from the Avalon stone, the other was gleaned from hieroglyphs discovered in the inverted subterranean pyramid of Delta Camaeleontis, many light-years distant from Omicron Canes Venatici VI, but perhaps just a rung away on the ladder of legend.

L. F.]

4 – After Akiki's death, Asan the Emperor of the Narayayans grieved publicly, but perhaps in his heart of hearts he remained aloof.

He ordered that his wife's stone coffin be placed on a granite plinth in the middle of a plain, far away from the cities and trade routes. He summoned his most gifted architects and craftsmen, and a small army of labourers, instructing them to build a great palace as an eternal memorial to Akiki and as a tribute to the love that they shared.

Asan's chief architect was Ynsu. He followed his lord's wishes to the letter and oversaw the work as the huge edifice took shape. The entire project would take many years to complete. During this time, Asan began to leave the site, and indeed the Empire itself, to venture out on long journeys that, it was rumoured, took him to the farthest corners of the planet and, perhaps, beyond. Upon his return, he invariably expressed his dissatisfaction with the tomb of Akiki, ordering yet more chambers, more lavish carvings and decorations, grander façades and porticoes, as well as numerous alterations to the icons of his dead wife which were scattered throughout the mausoleum.

And it was the issue of the icons that led Ynsu to wonder if Asan's orders represented more than just the huge grief of his loss . . . For it became clear, as Asan personally directed the work of the stonesmiths, that the altered features of the statue no longer seemed to resemble Akiki, but those of another woman entirely, who was rather younger, thinner of face, and even more beautiful than the Empress herself had been.

Ynsu felt tempted to mention these disparities to his master, but clearly Asan's thinking was becoming increasingly confused. So the building continued, until the sheer size and grandeur of the tomb held all onlookers spellbound. It had also, by the by, been such an expensive project that the Narayayan Empire had become effectively penniless. And, it was said at the time, where there is not the strength of wealth, there cannot be the strength of faith.

Civil unrest ensued, but this itself was an insignificant thing when set against the more terrifying invasions of barbarian hordes, flocking to the Narayayan empire like scavengers around the weak and dying body of a felled gazelle.

To Asan, it was as though none of it was happening. Even as news of the incursions and subsequent atrocities was brought to him, he was busy ordering his master mason to chisel just a fraction farther here, and to add a tiny detail here, on the face of the stranger that had taken the place of Akiki.

Finally, old Ynsu was compelled to speak up. He walked with Asan through the vast labyrinth of the tomb one evening, as the smell of ravaged and burning cities drifted in on the cooling air. They came at last to the central chamber, which now was dominated by a huge adamantine statue of the woman who was the focus of Asan's infinite passion.

'Can it be,' Ynsu enquired gently, 'that you have come to love this girl more than you ever did Akiki?'

Asan stared at him, puzzled. 'Why no, Ynsu my friend. I have graven this woman's face in stone because I hate her. Because of her, I and my people and all the world have come to this. These rooms and likenesses are here so that I may never forget what she has done to me. I keep her face in front of me so that the blade of my vengeance stays sharp . . .'

Ynsu was appalled, and might have said more. But just then, the entire structure was rocked. Dust sifted down from the high ceilings. One of Asan's cadre of elite bodyguards hurried into the chamber and urged both men to leave quickly, for the oppressors were only a short distance away.

But Asan was not listening: he seemed to be preoccupied with some other matter, with the simple stone casket before him, inscribed with its few humble words –

Remember me as a shooting star that blazes
swiftly and then fades.
People notice it at the time and remember it
when it has gone.

'What is this doing here?' Asan demanded to know.

Ynsu, devastated by the madness he recognized in his lord, could only shrug and shake his head, the tears coming hot into his eyes.

'Then take it out,' Asan said, his voice rising shrilly. 'Take it out and destroy it. That thing has no place here!'

* * *

5 – The tale is told of a time long ago when some children were playing at the edge of their village, close to the desert that separated the settlement from the mountains. It was a warm evening, for the land had absorbed the sun's heat through the day and was now giving it back to the sky at dusk.

As they played their simple games of dance and catch and chase, the children were distracted by a sound that appeared to come from high above them. Looking towards where the sun had set, they saw a bright light streak across the heavens, grow to a glowing jewel that hovered in the purple twilight, and then drop quickly down to the plain, where it settled in a storm of billowing sand.

Soon afterwards, a solitary figure emerged from the sky ship and strode towards the village. By this time, word of the stranger's arrival had spread and every single villager had gathered to greet him. Within minutes, the stranger had reached the settlement. All could see that he was tall and proud and powerful. And yet, despite these strengths, his face was twisted with a pain the children didn't understand, and his eyes were full of agony.

'I am Asan,' the warrior declared, 'last of the Narayayan people. I demand to speak with your village elder!'

For a few seconds no one moved, for all were frightened by the stranger's fierce and tortured demeanour. Then there came a rustling among the crowd and an old man stepped forward. This ancient fellow had wispy white hair and a beard as fine as cobweb. He was stooped with age and needed to walk with a stick made from river willow wood. His name was Tsancho.

When Asan caught sight of him, he laughed aloud, although very soon the laughter changed so that it sounded very like sobbing.

'Surely you are not the leader of these poor, doomed peasants? How can you possibly survive – how can you prevail against her?'

Asan's voice was cracked with madness. The children cowered back. Tsancho looked upon the stranger coolly, though with pity in his eyes.

'Great lord, you are right,' Tsancho said. 'I do not rule these people. We are all ruled equally by the seasons.'

Asan seemed not to hear. He gazed beyond the old man and upward as the sky began to darken and the first stars appeared. 'Only I can destroy the Shiga, who will one day sweep through space towards this world and wipe you out with her breath! Indeed, that is my purpose now, to destroy her and destroy her each time she pours her spirit into a living form. She no longer deserves life and flesh and beauty after what she did to me. So bow down before me, old man, for I am Asan, slayer of the Shiga, and your protector!'

Tsancho glanced back at his terrified people, then looked upon Asan and shrugged his shoulders in apology.

'Mighty lord, alas the years have made me bow down as far as I am able. And while you might easily conquer this village and indeed the whole world, time conquers all in the end.'

Asan laughed loudly, a booming discordant sound like a fractured bell.

'It's obvious you don't realize your danger. Look here!'

So saying, Asan drew a weapon that might have been a sword and used it to trace a circle in the dust of the village clearing. 'This is what you poor people understand . . .'

Then Asan drew a much greater circle to encompass the first. 'And this is what I understand, so you should beware!' He grinned insanely at Tsancho and his people, nodding as though the point had been proven.

Tsancho regarded the markings in the dust and stroked his beard thoughtfully.

'Yes, powerful Asan, you are quite correct. There is a great deal that I do not know.' And everyone watched as he used his crooked willow stick to draw a much larger circle around the other two. 'But this is what neither of us understands, so we should all beware.'

As Tsancho's words faded to silence the people looked fearfully upon the stranger Asan. Had the old one offended him? Enraged him? He was surely powerful enough to obliterate them all with a wave of his hand.

Now he was gazing at the nested circles, letting out a slow breath, like a deep sigh of release.

'Yes,' Asan said presently. 'Yes, old one, of course. Only by knowing more about the Shiga and her ways can I hope to defeat her finally.'

At this, Tsancho hobbled forward and rested his crabbed hand on Asan's forearm.

'Is your mission so very important, young man, that you should spend your lifetime driven by such anger?'

'She who was dear to me,' Asan replied, 'who is now the Shiga, cannot be allowed to rest easy in her betrayal of my love. In killing her finally, I will put an end to my pain.'

Now the night had come and the sky was heavy with stars. Asan was a vague silhouette, his form palely defined by moonlight.

He pointed his sword to the heavens.

'I cannot stay any longer to discuss this with you. I must go there, I must see for myself. I must learn all there is to know.'

So saying, he bade farewell to Tsancho and his people, and returned quickly to his craft. Moments later it bloomed a flower of blue fire and rose out of sight as swiftly as the eye could follow. Very soon it was lost amongst the constellations.

'So,' Tsancho muttered after a while, breaking the silence of the villagers. 'I cannot help but wonder how strange will be that time and place when, at long last, Asan reaches his final goal and finds that for which he is searching . . .'

He smiled, but then felt a tugging at his sleeve. Glancing down, he saw that a child with his friends had gathered round him in concern. 'Sumai, the stranger has gone now. What still troubles you?' he asked.

Sumai said, 'But what will happen when Asan does learn all there is to be learnt? Will he come to the edge of the greatest circle? Will he kill the Shiga? Will he return to destroy us?'

'Such big worries for so little a head.' Tsancho ruffled Sumai's hair. 'Well, there is something that Asan failed to realize and that I, being a forgetful old fool, did not think to explain . . .'

'What was that?' Sumai wondered, frowning.

'We drew our circles in the dust, but really they should have been written on water.'

'How is that possible?'

'Walk with me to the pool and I will show you.'

Tsancho led the way, followed by the children and, behind them, the rest of the villagers. It was only a short distance, and as they reached the drinking pool, Tsancho asked Sumai to pass him a pebble.

'Here are the things the mighty Asan needed to learn, to make his peace with himself –'

Tsancho pitched the pebble high into the air. It dropped into the pool with a splash, sending ripples circling away from the point where it had landed. The villagers watched the outer circle growing larger and larger, until finally it faded completely away. Then, with contented smiles on their faces, the children bowed low to Tsancho in respect and thanks, and returned with lighter hearts to their play.

Translator's note:

The discerning reader may guess that I have used a certain creative licence in my interpretation of several details of this legend, most notably using the name of

Asan when, in fact, the sky-stranger is never specifically identified; and my assumption of the Shiga's part in the story, having extrapolated this from various technical correspondences between source materials, and the interesting coincidence of 'Shiga' and 'Kaiagish'.

I hope, therefore, that the reader (and no less the academician) will forgive me for these liberties, which I have taken to highlight a point that, at any age and level of influence, remains pertinent to we who follow our own individual myths through life: wisely it is said that we obtain the thing we most fear.

L. F.

ALSO AVAILABLE
IN
THE NEW ADVENTURES

OH NO IT ISN'T!
by Paul Cornell
ISBN: 0 426 20507 3

Bernice Surprise Summerfield is just settling into her new job as Professor of Archaeology at St Oscar's University on the cosmopolitan planet of Dellah. She's using this prestigious centre of learning to put her past, especially her failed marriage, behind her. But when a routine exploration of the planet Perfecton goes awry, she needs all her old ingenuity and cunning as she faces a menace that can only be described as – panto.

DRAGONS' WRATH
by Justin Richards
ISBN: 0 426 20508 1

The Knights of Jeneve, a legendary chivalric order famed for their jewel-encrusted dragon emblem, were destroyed at the battle of Bocaro. But when a gifted forger is murdered on his way to meet her old friend Irving Braxiatel, and she comes into possession of a rather ornate dragon statue, Benny can't help thinking they're involved. So, suddenly embroiled in art fraud, murder and derring-do, she must discover the secret behind the dragon, and thwart the machinations of those seeking to control the sector.

BEYOND THE SUN
by Matthew Jones
ISBN: 0 426 20511 1

Benny has drawn the short straw – she's forced to take two overlooked freshers on their very first dig. Just when she thinks things can't get any worse, her no-good ex-husband Jason turns up and promptly gets himself kidnapped. As no one else is going to rescue him, Benny resigns herself to the task. But her only clue is a dusty artefact Jason implausibly claimed was part of an ancient and powerful weapon – a weapon rumoured to have powers beyond the sun.

SHIP OF FOOLS
by Dave Stone
ISBN: 0 426 20510 3

No hard-up archaeologist could resist the perks of working for the fabulously wealthy Krytell. Benny is given an unlimited expense account, an entire new wardrobe and all the jewels and pearls she could ever need. Also, her job, unofficial and shady though it is, requires her presence on the famed space cruise-liner, the *Titanian Queen*. But, as usual, there is a catch: those on board are being systematically bumped off, and the great detective, Emil Dupont, hasn't got a clue what's going on.

DOWN
by Lawrence Miles
ISBN: 0 426 20512 X

If the authorities on Tyler's Folly didn't expect to drag an off-world professor out of the ocean in a forbidden 'quake zone, they certainly weren't ready for her story. According to Benny the planet is hollow, its interior inhabited by warring tribes, rubber-clad Nazis and unconvincing prehistoric monsters. Has something stolen Benny's reason? Or is the planet the sole exception to the more mundane laws of physics? And what is the involvement of the utterly amoral alien known only as !X.

DEADFALL
by Gary Russell
ISBN: 0 426 20513 8

Jason Kane has stolen the location of the legendary planet of Ardethe from his ex-wife Bernice, and, as usual, it's all gone terribly wrong. In no time at all, he finds himself trapped on an isolated rock, pursued by brain-consuming aliens, and at the mercy of a shipload of female convicts. Unsurprisingly, he calls for help. However, when his old friend Christopher Cwej turns up, he can't even remember his own name.

GHOST DEVICES
by Simon Bucher-Jones
ISBN: 0 426 20514 6

Benny travels to Canopus IV, a world where the primitive locals worship the Spire – a massive structure that bends time – and talk of gods who saw the future. Unfortunately, she soon discovers the planet is on the brink of collapse, and that the whole sector is threatened by holy war. So, to prevent a jihad, Benny must journey to the dead world of Vol'ach Prime, and face a culture dedicated to the destruction of all life.

MEAN STREETS
by Terrance Dicks
ISBN: 0 426 20519 7

The Project: a criminal scheme so grand in its scale that it casts a shadow across a hundred worlds. Roz Forrester heard of this elaborate undertaking, and asked her squire to return with her to sprawling and violent Megacity – the scene of her discovery. Roz may be dead, but Chris Cwej is not a man to forget a promise, and Bernice is soon the other half of a noble crime-fighting duo.

TEMPEST
by Christopher Bulis
ISBN: 0 426 20523 5

On the wild and inhospitable planet of Tempest, a train is in trouble. And Bernice, returning home on the luxurious Polar Express, is right in the thick of it. Murder and an inexplicable theft mean that there's a criminal on board; the police are unable to reach them; and so the frightened staff and passengers turn to a hung-over, and rather bad-tempered, archaeologist for much-needed assistance.

WALKING TO BABYLON
by Kate Orman
ISBN: 0 426 20521 9

The People – the super-advanced inhabitants of a Dyson sphere – have a problem: to stop an illegal time-travel experiment they must destroy ancient Babylon and all its inhabitants. If they do not, war will break out with the dominant power of the Milky Way, and whole galaxies will be destroyed. Their only hope is that Bernice can travel back to the dawn of civilization, and find the culprits – or Earth history will never be the same again.

OBLIVION
by Dave Stone
ISBN: 0 426 20522 7

A man called Deed is threatening the fabric of the universe and tearing realities apart. At the heart of the disruption, three adventurers, Nathan li Shoa, Leetha and Kiru, are trapped. Their friend Sgloomi Po must save them before they are obliterated, and in his desperation he looks up some old friends. So Bernice joins her feckless ex-husband Jason and her old friend Chris on the rescue mission; but then Sgloomi picks up someone who should really be dead.

THE MEDUSA EFFECT
by Justin Richards
ISBN: 0 426 20524 3

Medusa, an experimental ship missing for twenty years, is coming home. When one of the investigation team dies mysteriously, Bernice is assigned to help discover what went wrong. But to do so she must solve a riddle. Somehow the original crew are linked to the team put on board – their ghosts still haunt the ship. And the past is catching up with them all in more ways than one.

DRY PILGRIMAGE
by Paul Leonard and Nick Walters
ISBN: 0 426 20525 1

Thinking she has been offered a blissful pleasure cruise on Dellah's southern ocean, Benny gladly accepts. After all, she has some time on her hands. But trapped on a yacht with an alien religious sect who forbid alcohol, she soon discovers that all is not well. And, as the ship heads toward a fateful rendezvous, she must unmask a traitor or risk the system being torn apart by war.

THE SWORD OF FOREVER
by Jim Mortimore
ISBN: 0 426 20526 X

Forced to leave her home on Dellah for Earth, Bernice finds work on an Antarctic dig. Once there she uncovers a link between an ancient reptile race, a secret society and a desperate megalomaniac – as well as the fabled the Ark of the Covenant. A desperate race has begun, and she soon realises her deadly knowledge affects not only her own life, but the destiny of the entire human race.

Should you wish to order any of these titles, or other Virgin books, please write to the address below for mail-order information:

**Fiction Department
Virgin Publishing Ltd
Thames Wharf Studios
Rainville Road
London W6 9HT**

COMING SOON

BEIGE PLANET MARS
by Lance Parkin and Mark Clapham
ISBN: 0 426 20529 4
15 October 1998

It's the 500th anniversary of Mars' colonization, and Bernice Summerfield, expert on the planet's archaeology, has been invited to speak at an academic conference. On arrival, however, she is immediately distracted by a murder and its links to an old betrayal that has never been forgotten. Her own life threatened, Bernice soon discovers that the events of the famous Siege of Mars are far from ancient history.

WHERE ANGELS FEAR
by Rebecca Levene and Simon Winstone
ISBN: 0 426 20530 8
17 December 1998

Something very odd is happening on Dellah. A long-ignored religion is rapidly gaining recruits, and arcane arts are practised with dangerously successful results. At the same time, the most powerful races in the universe are withdrawing to their strongholds, leaving the lesser peoples to their fate. Reality has been warped somehow, and Bernice and company soon discover they are at the heart of a terrible conflict.